MAD POWERS

By

Mark Wayne McGinnis

Edited by:

Lura Lee Genz, Mia Manns & Rachel Weaver

Avenstar Productions

ISBN-10   0990331458

ISBN-13   978-0-9903314-5-2

PART 1

TAPPED IN

CHAPTER 1

Apparently, I had fallen asleep at the wheel. I imagine it was only for an instant—a gentle respite against the endless monotony. It happens. Eyelids got too damn heavy after a thousand miles of sameness and double yellow lines—lines that stretched out towards a distant horizon—a horizon I never reached.

Just sitting there, I had more than enough time to contemplate my situation. Without a conscious driver at the wheel, my car meandered on down the highway, maybe even for a few hundred yards. Eventually, it found its way onto the soft-sandy shoulder. 80 mph went down to 75 mph or even 65 mph. Then, of course, the inevitable was bound to happen. My car would crash into something. What I didn't know at the time was there are a variety of wood telephone poles: poles made from southern yellow pine, Douglas fir, jack pine, and western red cedar; the latter is the most commonly used tree pole throughout the country. But, on that one particular late afternoon, driving along a desolate high-way somewhere in Arizona, my telephone pole of no-choice was a Douglas fir.

I awoke to darkness and pain. I tried to move. Nothing happened. So darkness and pain and, apparently, paralysis. Or worse, was I to spend the rest of my life like this? A floppy piece of meat—moved from location to location—akin to a carcass dollied from delivery truck to Vons' freezer section ... nothing more than a burden on society and my family? Did I have a family? I couldn't remember. Again, I tried to move. But I couldn't feel my arms, specifically my right one. The one I wanted to use to wipe the blood from my eyes. That's when I realized I couldn't possibly be par-alyzed—not with this much pain racking every inch of my body. I lost consciousness.

How long was I out? I wondered. *One hour? Two? More?* It did seem lighter outside, or perhaps I was just getting used to the darkness. Something was pressed tight against the back of my skull. I tried to move my head. No can do. My visibility was restricted to just how far I could move my eyes within their sockets. I looked around; I had no idea what model my wrecked car was prior to the crash. Nothing all that fancy—must have looked like any other mid-sized economy car on the road. The smell of tar and chemicals permeated the air. My guess, I was right up against a util-ity pole. Things strewn about: a soda can, junk food wrap-pers, a lone shoe, blood—lots of blood, and a cream-colored envelope with stylized letters spelling *"Rob,"* written in a feminine cursive style, with a little red heart added for em-phasis. My view to the outside world was limited to the pas-senger-side window, or what was left of the window—just an open, jagged gap that pointed back down the highway, presumably from the direction I had come. I needed to sleep again.

* * *

A scream—my own scream, pulled me back to consciousness. There was something coming. I heard the low rumble of a diesel engine and then it slowly appeared, perfectly centered in the open window gap—a large vehicle heading in my direction. The truck was moving along at a good clip. Perhaps the driver was making up for the time he'd lost spent over scrambled eggs and ham at a greasy spoon in Modesto or Indio or Blythe.

The big tractor-trailer rig disappeared, falling below the horizon line into one of the subtle contours of the road. Only its two big vertical exhaust pipes stayed visible. If I could move even one iota, this would be the time to start squirming in my seat. Would the rig driver notice my small import tightly wrapped around a telephone pole at the side of the highway?

As the truck got closer and its exhaust pipes rose above the horizon, the speed of the vehicle seemed to increase. As the rig broke above eye level, I could make out the driver— even from this distance. The truck was close. The inside dome light was on. Perhaps he'd been looking at a map. The driver was a big, meaty-looking fella. He met all the stereotypical checkpoints: brawler-type, wide-brimmed baseball cap, grizzly muttonchops. And he certainly wasn't looking in my direction as he cleared the rise. No, it looked like something else had grabbed his attention. His eyes, wide open enough for me to see the whites above and below, were looking at something in the middle of the road. Something substantial enough for him to put his entire weight down on the brake pedal. Tires instantly screeched; black smoke poured from vaporized rubber.

The tractor-trailer began to turn sideways, as if in slow motion, and in a frantic, sickening blur, the rig lost all contact with the highway. It spun in the air—like a child's weightless toy—before smashing down again onto unyielding pavement. Horrendous sounds cracked across the desert landscape. Tractor, now separated from trailer, continued to slide along the road in a wash of bright yellow sparks. Even after the tractor came to a complete stop, with the driver hanging half in and half out of the front windshield, the trailer continued on down the highway until it hit something. By the sound of it, metal crashing against metal, another car had been hit. Then I saw it. The vehicle had ricocheted off of the long metal trailer, not unlike an aluminum bat hitting a ball, a ball that would find the most vulnerable recipient ... me.

I didn't black out this time, but I wish I had. The impact was jarring and violent. A salty metallic taste—blood and something else—permeated the inside of my mouth. My wrecked car spun several feet and was now separate from the telephone pole. I could see the pole in my peripheral vision. Sounds came from above. The separation left just enough space for a high-voltage power line to drop into my car. The line swayed back and forth, like an inky black cobra ready to strike. The big cable finally came to rest mere inches from my forehead.

There was no mistaking that this line was live, and still connected to a substation somewhere. I strained my eyes in their sockets looking up at the cable. It hummed and vibrated. I tried to inch further away. If anything, I was more jammed into place than before. It didn't take long for the headaches to start. Blinding pain radiated down from the top of my head and into my eyes. Bile burned at the back of my throat from the nauseous smell of my own singed hair. *I'm being radiated! I'm being fucking radiated!*

* * *

It felt like hours but was probably closer to minutes since the truck crashed in front of me. My view of the accident, the carnage, was slightly different now. I could see more of the highway and even part of the other vehicle ... a bumper, a side-view mirror, and broken safety glass. I'd avoided looking in the direction of the truck and its driver, but now my eyes were drawn there.

With every glance a wave of guilt and dread passed through me. The high-powered cable continued to stare down at me: a Cyclops, its ionized breath, like tiny needles, caused searing pain to come and go in waves. My vision was now blue-tinted from the cable's constant humming energy field. Inexplicably, I was drawn to it. And there was—something else ... like something forgotten that needed to be remembered, or something that was right there, on the tip of my tongue, or like a familiar song that reconnected the dots to long lost memories or experiences.

Other sounds from outside encroached into my consciousness—w*hat the hell?* Like crying—no, more like wailing. That was it, like eerie sad sounds of women wailing. I'd heard these sounds before. Coyotes. A whole pack of them were out there. They were hungry. *How did I know that?* They were curious about the smells: fresh meat, blood, feces. Their cries took on a more rhythmic yipping aspect, more frenzied. The pack's leader was old, but still formidable. The other males feared the older coyote. At first he would investigate alone and get the lion's share before the others could abscond with the quarry. *How did I know that?*

Then I saw him: a scraggly, gray coyote. He took slow tentative steps, sniffing the air as his thin body weaved back and forth. He crouched below the driver's lifeless, outstretched arm. Carefully, the coyote rose up on its hind legs and sniffed again. I didn't want to watch this. *Just leave the poor bastard alone,* I thought to myself. Still up on his hind legs, the coyote froze—as if hearing my thoughts. I wondered, had he maybe sensed me here, deep in the dark recesses of this mangled clump of metal and plastic? Was that possible? Am I next on the menu?

The coyote's attention was back on the driver, where he nipped at the man's blood-drenched shirt, then pulled, tugged, and ripped it. The sleeve came away at the shoulder. The coyote whipped and flailed the sleeve like a puppy with a new toy, only to drop it and return to the driver's exposed arm. The coyote licked at the skin, almost lovingly. Teeth bit and pulled into flesh, which peeled away in long, bacon-like strips. A wave of nausea came over me. That, and anger too. No, not anger—pure unadulterated rage. My thoughts, first radiating fear of the ever-pulsating high-power line dangling in front of me, were now filled with white-hot rage. *Get away from him, you mangy piece of shit!* Immediately, the coyote jumped back, seemingly scared, and quickly ran off into the desert.

CHAPTER 2

The pain was less—in fact, I felt almost… good. Something alive, even intelligent, was emanating into the confines of the car. I felt snug and nurtured as I listened to its pulsing language—something that was more like music than actual speech, but a form of communication just the same. My memory was still a total blank but, truth be told, I really didn't care. It would be hard to imagine life without this connection: this new and strangely intimate relationship. Had I ever felt this close to my own mother, father—a brother or sister? Could I possibly have felt, ever, this same level of belonging—of oneness? Christ! I needed to snap out of this. What was happening to me?

I awoke to the distorted voice of an Arizona Highway Patrol dispatcher. Blue and red lights bouncing off the pavement flickered on the tractor, the dead trucker, and the hood of a shiny black and white Highway Patrol cruiser. I could hear the patrolman talking on the radio.

"Yeah, Louise, this is a total clusterfuck here. What

a mess. Looks like three vehicles, including an eighteen-wheeler, a minivan, and a small import, probably a Hyundai or a Kia—can't really tell what the hell it is. No survivors—three DOAs, so just send the wagon, OK? Oh, and let Burt know we'll need three tows. The tractor and trailer are overturned; it's going to take some work."

"Ten four, Garry ... Out."

I took a deep breath and yelled, "I'm in here." My voice was barely a squeak.

The cop, now off of his radio, walked around to the front of the cruiser. I could see his legs and shoes through the open gap. The beam of his flashlight played over the accident scene. A reflection. Something wet on the pavement. I could smell gasoline.

I cleared my throat. "Hello, I'm in here ... Christ, can't you hear me?" The problem was I had no saliva; my throat and vocal cords were dry as a bone. Nothing discernible was coming out of my mouth. More like a croak. I heard something else. Actually ... *thought* something else.

Just what I need—and at the end of a long shift, too. Shit. Now I'll be here all night. What I should do is have Burt pick me up something to eat. Maybe pizza. God, I could eat a horse right now. Wonder if Domino's delivers way the hell out here. That would be sweet.

Wait a minute. Those aren't my thoughts. What's going on in my head? I must have a serious concussion or something. Thoughts ... why am I picking up this guy's thoughts? It's like the coyote thing, again. It's probably my imagination. Maybe I've lost my mind. I don't care. At this point I'll try anything. *Need to concentrate ...*

Hey, you, policeman! I'm down here—I'm alive! In the Kia or Hyundai, just bend the hell down and look inside. I'm alive!

Through the open gap I could see the patrolman stop in

his tracks. He hesitated and slowly bent down.

That's right, you heard me ... down here!

He got all the way down on his hands and knees and used his flashlight to peer inside the car. Since I was pinned upside down, he seemed to have a hard time finding my face. Then the beam found my eyes—my open, blinking, alive eyes.

Startled, the cop fumbled his flashlight. "Holy shit, man, hold on ... just hold on, we'll get you out of there. I'm officer Garry Sullivan, and I'm not going anywhere." With that he stood up and disappeared from view. I could hear him back on the radio, excited and out of breath.

"Louise! One of our DOAs is actually alive; get EMT out here—hurry!"

How could I have missed that? Shit! Look at his car—he should be dead, that's why.

I could hear his thoughts—which had been kicked into overtime—a rapid-fire, machine gun spray of questions no one could answer.

He was back and looking at me again through the open gap. He was saying something to me. I answered him without actually talking.

Listen up. I'm wedged in here tight as a cork in a bottle and I can't move a muscle. I'm injured—not sure where exactly or how bad, and I have a hot 30,000 volt power line dangling inches from my head. Oh, and I think you're squatting in a pool of gasoline— probably from that truck right behind you.

Officer Sullivan's forced-smile dropped its pretense, now showing total alarm. For a large man, Garry could move quickly. He was up and back at his cruiser, rifling around in its trunk. He returned a few moments later with a small fire extinguisher. He pulled the pin on the nozzle and began spraying down the street with a layer of thick white foam.

Then he was back on the radio. "Hey, Louise?"

"Go ahead, Garry," the dispatcher replied, now with cool efficiency.

"Yeah, we need Edison out here pronto—we've got a live power line hanging off a utility pole. It's hanging right into the vic's car. We also have a major diesel leak." Garry's voice was filled with tension.

"OK, I'm on it, Garry. Sounds like you're having a real night. I'll see if I can light a fire and get people moving."

I could only see Garry's legs, but he was obviously moving with far more purpose and urgency. And why shouldn't he? The scene had gone from a three vehicle, three-fatality pileup—one where any rushing around would have little effect on the unfortunate victims—to something far more immediate. Not only was *someone* alive ... he was injured, with a live, high-voltage power line hanging just inches from his forehead. Oh, and just to complicate things, diesel fuel was leaking *all over* the fucking place. Yeah, without a doubt, Garry was having a night. I heard sirens blaring in the distance.

* * *

The feeling of loss was profound. It had only been ten minutes or so since the power had been shut off, but I *needed* them to turn it back on. Someone needed to turn it back on. Tears welled-up in my eyes as I saw the power line pulled and heaved upward and away, and disappear somewhere above and behind me—such a loss, such a shame. Wow, I really need to get a grip. Seriously, what the hell's wrong with me?

The next face I saw was a young fireman. His oversized

yellow helmet cast a deep shadow across his face, making his features hard to discern. As with Garry, clear as a bell, I could hear his thoughts even before he spoke.

You make it through this, man, and you're truly lucky. I've never seen this much blood. You should be stacked in the coroner's wagon with the other guy ...

They used the Jaws of Life to pry open my misshapen automobile. Three firefighters grabbed hold of the door and peeled and twisted it back, creating an opening large enough for an Hispanic-looking EMT worker to wiggle in next to me.

"How you doing, sir?" he inquired, while checking my pupils with a small pen light. I tried to talk but couldn't. "My name is Juan. I just need to do a quick assessment before we transport you. You're going to be fine," he said.

I need water ...

He nodded, but furrowed his brow, seemingly confused how I'd conveyed that information. He positioned the straw-end of a plastic water bottle between my lips and gently squeezed. A small amount of wonderfully cool water filled my mouth and burned its way down my throat. Desperate for more, I inhaled some into my lungs, which only made me gag and cough.

"Easy man, just sip it ... just a little at a time, okay?" he said, letting my coughing subside before offering me more. Looking down, he assessed the condition of my body.

Multiple lacerations to the lower extremities, some pretty deep. Severe trauma to right arm; that needs to come off. Top of head is red and blistered. Scarification above left eye ... I'll need to clean off some of this blood ...

Eventually we made eye contact again.

What the hell do you mean, "That needs to come off?"

Shocked, Juan looked at me with surprise. Just like the

coyote and Garry, Juan was startled having *someone else's thoughts* intrude on his consciousness. Watching him, only a foot away from my face, I could hear his thought processes.

Was this guy reading my mind? No. That's impossible. There has to be some other logical explanation. I must have spoken out loud ... or something. He shook his head and smiled. "No, man, the seatbelt, that's got to come off. You're lucky. Really lucky—it saved your life. You should be fine."

Juan got an I.V. going, cut the seatbelt away from my shoulder, and prepared to get me extricated from the car. I could feel the narcotics entering my bloodstream. Probably morphine, or something equally mind numbing—I started to slip in and out of consciousness. At some point, the back of the car was cut away, and light from above poured in. Multiple hands were being positioned, ready to lift me out. But something nagged at me, something important—what was it? I just wanted to sleep. My drug-induced thoughts pleaded for my eyes to open ... just one more time, and I peered around the mangled car interior. What is that? There, on the floor, or what was now the ceiling ... something caught my eye. Oh, yeah ... the little red heart on a cream-colored envelope. I needed that envelope. That just might be the one connection to who I am. Am I Rob? I put all my attention back on Juan again.

Juan, I need you to pick up that envelope. It's by your left knee. Yes, that one ... now put it in your top left pocket.

Juan did what I asked, as if I'd spoken the words aloud. The top of the envelope peeked out above the pocket flap, which was now unable to close. He looked at me, irritated. *You need to stay the hell out of my head, man ...*

In one fluid motion I was lifted from the car to a waiting gurney. Everything was moving much faster now. I only saw glimpses of things ... the accident scene, the truck driver now gone, crews busy spraying down the pavement, a bright blue tarp draped over the other vehicle. I looked back at what had been my car. It was a misshapen ball of crushed and torn metal. I can't believe I lived through that. But my full attention was really on the telephone pole behind it. My eyes traveled up the deep brown wood, up to its very top, where the pole tapered nearly to a point. Several large black cables, one hanging down several feet lower than the others, swayed back and forth, back and forth … And I felt a deep longing for that connection again. *I don't want to leave you.*

CHAPTER 3

Harland Platt had decided to stay, just in case, to make sure he was in fact dead. He'd been perched up high on a ledge about a half-mile from the accident scene for hours. Of course he was dead. Look at that car. He took one more look through his binoculars, readjusted the focus, and steadied his arms on the rocky surface beneath his elbows. Finally, they were extracting the body. Shit! Dead men don't require an I.V. Harland wasn't one to typically show his emotions. His training had been impeccable—the best in the world. But now he was angry. He inhaled, held the desert air deep in his lungs, and concentrated on calming himself as he slowly exhaled through pursed lips. He'd spent the better part of two days setting this up. Everything timed to the second. Everything calculated, using probability matrices that clearly showed Chandler should be dead.

Harland removed the binoculars from around his neck and stowed them in his pack. An early morning mist floated several inches above the ground, adding an almost mystical aspect to the rocky terrain. Red and blue lights continued to strobe from the emergency vehicles on the highway.

Being an independent player, a choice he'd made years ago when he'd left the CIA, was not for everyone. But Harland had come to realize he was different than others in covert ops. Those with a moral compass were best when aligned with an agency where they could, at least somewhat, justify their actions. Harland had no such restrictions. Feelings of guilt or remorse were as foreign to Harland as the emotions of love and compassion were. *Does that make me a sociopath?* he wondered as he headed off into the desert. *Undoubtedly, it does.*

Killing Chandler had been his sole mission for nearly two years. Even while Harland was still at the Agency working alongside Chandler, sometimes on a daily basis, his orders had been implicitly clear. Terminate Chandler; ensure the hit would not be tied back to them. This was his second attempt, an embarrassment. He either completed the assignment, or faced being terminated himself.

He found the stolen black 1990s vintage Ford Explorer with switched-out plates right where he'd left it. He wouldn't call it a road, more like a dirt path that paralleled the highway about a mile to the east. He opened the driver's side door, placed his pack on the seat and dug out a map and a small penlight. He held the light between his teeth and, moving his head around, surveyed the greater Kingman-area map. *Easy peasy,* he said out loud. Only one hospital. He refolded the map and pushed it into the pack, but dropped the flashlight in the process.

In the cool early morning dawn, the single best place

to find radiating heat had been underneath the slow-cooling engine of Harlan's Ford Explorer. Not one, but three Diamond Head rattlesnakes had quickly settled in there for the morning. Even before Harland opened the driver's side door, they'd become agitated, leery of his presence, coiled tight, ready to strike, if warranted.

The first of the strikes came when the flashlight dropped. Only when Harland reached for it did the other two snakes strike simultaneously. He pulled his hand back reflexively and saw the four puncture wounds. The pain wasn't instantaneous. But by the time Harland had the truck up and running and was headed back down the dirt path toward the city of Kingman, he was having a difficult time focusing and staying conscious.

Fortunately, he knew right where to go, and traffic at this time of the morning should be minimal, but he didn't think he could stay conscious the fifteen minutes needed to drive to the Kingman Regional Medical Center. The SUV shook as it traversed over uneven ground. Pain, like bolts of electricity, shot up his arm. Once the path turned to a dirt road, and finally into a paved street, Harland accelerated. He needed to cut minutes from his trip across town, so light signals and stop signs were ignored. Two cars were together up ahead, facing in opposite directions; the drivers pulled in close to converse. Harland didn't slow; if anything, he gunned it even more. Veering to the left of the two cars, the Explorer's right-side mirror swiped one of the vehicles, disintegrating into a hundred fragments onto the pavement. Harland briefly lost consciousness, and then sideswiped a pair of garbage cans left on the side of the road. Coming awake with a jolt, he saw a slow-moving trash truck lumbering along less than a block ahead. Darkness was pulling at him, engulfing him. His last thoughts, before totally blacking out, were of Chandler shooting his wife.

CHAPTER 4

Pippa Rosette, delayed by an extended overseas phone conversation with an envoy at the Turkish Embassy, had wanted off the phone ten minutes earlier. She had to pee and she crossed her legs, but it gave her little relief. She didn't like being rude, but she had to cut off the foreign diplomat mid-sentence.

"Well ... thank you, Adiguzel, again. Let me follow up with a few things here on my end and get back to you in a few days. How does that sound?"

Impatient, her foot had started to tap rhythmically against the leg of her desk.

"Good, good. Yes, I'll definitely do that, and say hi to Sevda for me."

Pippa could still hear Adiguzel's voice as she hung up the phone and darted toward the ladies' restroom. An obstruction. Halfway down the corridor, Agent Giles, in his too perfect-looking suit and too perfect-looking hair, was on his hands and knees looking up into the internal workings of the massive office printer. A ream of paper and a large paper tray sat on the floor at his side. The end of his nose was black, and she noticed ink stains covering his fingers.

"I've got to get by you, Giles ... Like, now!"

Giles looked up at her, not seeming to understand what she wanted.

"Oh, sorry, I've made a bit of a mess here. Just give me a minute or two—"

"Nope, can't do that." Pippa edged in behind him, her legs brushing against his not insignificant backside. Surprised, he looked back at her and then smiled. Pippa furrowed her brow in response. She felt his eyes on her ass as she ran down the corridor and disappeared into the restroom.

Sitting in the quiet solitude of the stall, she reviewed her morning to-do list on her iPhone. They'd loaded her up with more work than she could possibly handle. Still considered a *newbie* at the Department of Homeland Security, Office of Intelligence and Analysis in Washington, D.C., she huffed out loud. Hell, she actually had more field experience than most of the agents here put together. She'd transferred from a five-year stint with the CIA, but she knew the rules. She'd have to prove herself all over again. That was fine with her. It felt good to be back in the U.S.— she was ready to start her life again and get past waiting to hear from Chandler. She'd been staying with her mother in Georgetown for several weeks, but had recently found a flat with rent she could afford ... barely. She felt her phone vibrate and when she pulled it out, a text message displayed.

"Hey, Pippa! Just confirming—dinner tonight?"

She'd forgotten about the tentative date she'd made with Ted Williams, an old flame from college. How she'd changed since then, she thought. She knew she needed to get back out there. Start dating. And Ted was certainly no slouch: handsome, rich family and, if she remembered correctly, had the endurance of a racehorse. Pippa smiled to herself, letting her mind reflect back, then replied to his text.

"Sorry, Ted—crazy work schedule this week. Rain check?"

CHAPTER 5

My hospital room was clean and sparse. I was in a room with two beds, close to a window. My roommate was a middle-aged man who seemed to be sleeping. There was an older-model TV secured high up on the wall; bright colored cartoons silently jittered across the screen.

I took stock of my condition. I felt disoriented and still had no idea who the hell I was. Looking down I saw that I had both arms—one was bandaged. I had both legs—both bandaged. I had something wrapped around my head, which was throbbing, and there were numerous clear and white polyurethane tubes connected to medical equipment, off to my side and behind me. I could hear a soft, rhythmic beeping sound, which must be coming from a heart monitor. The door to my room was open and I saw pink and blue-clad nurses scurrying back and forth. Then a candy-striper *... is that what they're called?* carrying a bouquet of flowers walked by. Within several minutes a nurse, followed by a doctor right on her heels, walked into my room.

The nurse made a beeline for my I.V. After checking its fluid level, she looked at me. She was pretty, maybe thirty, with empathetic, caring eyes. She put her hand on my cheek, either out of kindness or to check the temperature of my skin, I wasn't sure. The doctor was at the foot of my bed, reading my chart. And then I realized something else: I couldn't read their thoughts. Had I imagined my ability to do that at the accident scene? Of course I'd imagined that! I had been traumatized, physically and mentally.

"Good morning, how are you feeling today?" the nurse asked, leaning in closer to me and checking my bandages.

She had small freckles, which she'd tried to conceal with makeup, and the glint of a tiny pierced diamond on a cute, upturned nose. Her face was inches from my own. Noticing me staring up at her, she pulled away with the beginnings of a smile.

"I'm okay, I guess ..." I said, in a hoarse but discernible voice.

"Well, you've been through a lot; your body will need time to recover, so don't push it—sleep as much as you can. My name is Jill. Use this to signal the nurse's station if you need anything." She placed a call button within reach at the side of the bed and hurried off. The doctor towered over me from the opposite side of the bed; a beaklike nose supported black-framed reading glasses, and his hair was meticulously combed to cover a balding head.

Looking up from my chart, he spoke in a gentle voice. "Hello, I'm Doctor Madison. I was on duty when they brought you in several days ago. Fortunately, with the exception of some bruising and deep lacerations, you're in pretty good shape. No broken bones, no internal injuries ..."

"How long have I been here? How long was I out?"

I asked, confused that he'd mentioned several days had elapsed.

"It's been three days. You have a pretty bad concussion, so that's not abnormal."

"I must have fallen asleep at the wheel ..." The memories from the accident were coming back to me.

The doctor gently shook his head. "Let's not think about that right now, OK? Do you remember who you are ... can you tell me your name?"

I drew a blank. "I don't know, doctor. I woke up in that car this way. I seriously have no idea who I am."

The doctor must have recognized the concern on my face, because he smiled and placed a reassuring hand on my shoulder. "It's quite common to have short-term memory lapses after major head traumas such as yours. It's commonly referred to as *Retrograde Amnesia*—where the patient has difficulty remembering things prior to receiving a severe blow to the head. I'm no expert in that field. We'll need to have a specialist check you out and run some tests ... but I wouldn't put too much into your memory loss right now. One day at a time." He started to walk away.

"Wait, there was an envelope—the paramedic had it." *What was his name ... Juan.* "His name was Juan."

The doctor nodded and gestured towards the nightstand. "Are you Rob? You had no wallet on you; they needed to cut away your clothes at the scene ... and, unfortunately, a little while later your vehicle, as well as the others involved, exploded—they say there was a fuel leak ... ignited by a spark or something."

"So ... anything left in that car which would help identify me is—"

"Pretty much gone," the doctor said, shaking his head.

I looked over and noticed the cream-colored envelope

sitting on the bedside table.

"We opened it and read the card inside, hoping to find out who you were—perhaps someone to contact." Doctor Madison pointed his nose toward the envelope and shook his head. "We really didn't get much from the card, but perhaps it will jog something for you. Take a look?"

He handed me the envelope, with *Rob* and the small, hand-drawn red heart on the front ... I opened it and pulled out a small rectangular card. Just five words written in that same feminine cursive ...

"Okay, I'll wait for you."

The doctor was watching me: "... so, are you Rob?"

I shrugged. "Sure, why not. Call me Rob." I had no idea if I was Rob or not, but I was tired of not having an identity, and the thought that somebody was waiting for me, anyone, was compelling.

* * *

Jill's afternoon shift had just started and she was back in my room—busy disconnecting me from various tubes and cords. "We need to get you up and moving around, Rob," she said with enthusiasm.

"Are you always this cheery?"

"No," she said, eyebrows raised and shaking her head at the question. "I'm just having a really good day. You have to take them when they come—right?"

"Yeah, I guess ..." I said. "So what are we doing here?" Jill was in the process of pulling down the covers and moving my legs over the side of the bed.

"We're going for a walk. Need to get the blood moving, your muscles active again."

"Don't you think it's a bit early for that?" I wasn't ready to face the world just yet. I still felt like I'd been run over by a truck, which I almost had been, and the weight of those other drivers' deaths clung to me like a black shroud. I looked down at the bed covers and wanted to bury my head beneath them.

"Yeah, well, it's time for a change of scene; it'll do you good ... up, up, come on!" she responded pleasantly.

Using my I.V. stand for balance, I was able to stand. Everything hurt, especially my head. Jill put her arm around my waist and we slowly walked out of my hospital room.

"So what's that symbol on your wrist? The tattoo?" I asked, gesturing towards her left hand.

"Oh ... that? It's a birdcage. And see, the little door is open." Jill released her arm from around my waist and put the tops of her two hands right next to each other. "See here, this is the little birdie that got out and is flying free."

Less than halfway around the corridor my legs started to throb. As we turned the next bend I asked if we could take a short breather. Leaning against the wall I took a couple of deep breaths. Across from me was a utility door with a sign that read:

MECHANICAL

WARNING: HIGH-VOLTAGE AREA

"What's in there?" I asked, nodding towards the utility room.

"What does it look like? It's an electrical room ... and that one down there is a broom closet, and that exciting room further down the hall is a bathroom. And if you're done stalling, maybe we can get back to a little more exercise?"

Once back in my room, all tucked in for the night, with Jill off tending to other patients, I tried to watch some TV, but nothing held my interest. The guy in the next bed hadn't said much. And from what I could tell, he was most likely Russian or from some other Slavic-speaking country. Even though he couldn't understand a word of what I'd said to him, from his chortles and giggles, he could understand old Seinfeld episodes just fine. I lay in bed and stared at the ceiling for several more hours. The floor was quiet; on-duty nurses and doctors had disappeared behind computer screens or into break rooms.

I quietly climbed out of bed, found my hospital-issued slippers hiding under a chair, and made for the hallway. The lights had been dimmed, and a feeling of calm and quiet permeated the floor. I retraced my steps from my walk with Jill and located the door marked Mechanical. I just stood there in front of the door, hoping it would be unlocked.

With a quick check of the knob, I found it was indeed locked. *How do I get in?* Then I remembered Jill had mentioned a broom closet. I shuffled down the corridor and found the door labeled Utility Closet. Luckily, this door was unlocked, so I let myself in, closed the door and, after searching in the dark for a few seconds, found the light switch. Just as I'd hoped—several rows of keys hung from little metal hooks screwed onto a plywood plank. Someone, presumably the maintenance person, had nicely handwritten the various names of rooms the keys belonged to. *Here we go* ... Second row, third one over—the MECH ROOM key ... I snatched it up and let myself back out to the corridor.

I made my way back to the room. Someone was coming. I could hear low murmurs of a distant conversation getting closer. I inserted the key. *Crap!* Upside-down. The voices were mere feet away now from just around the corner. I tried the key again and the knob turned. Two nurses came into sight before I had a chance to duck inside, but, fortunately, they made a right turn down the opposite hallway and didn't see me. Once inside I really didn't know what I was looking for. Earlier, when walking with Jill, I had felt the pull … the undeniable hunger to reconnect with *whatever* I had tapped into on that accident-scarred highway three days ago. Even now, standing several feet from the large metal breaker cabinets, I could feel the energy.

The song was there again, just faintly, but there just the same. The room was covered with wall-to-wall long gray metal breaker cabinets. One cabinet in particular was bigger, and the words High Voltage were stenciled above it. I found the release lever and pulled open the panel. My mind flooded, bonded, and merged with the energy. I needed more. I stepped in closer to the cabinet, letting my face come forward closer still. I rested my forehead against the cool metal surface and tapped in. The music filled my consciousness. It was like coming home, and then, just as quickly, I was spiraling up to new levels of consciousness; others were there with me—connecting to me at a personal, intimate level.

* * *

The police arrived in the morning. Two of them, both black and both all business. Like twins, they wore dark gray suits, white shirts, and thin, striped ties. One tie had blue and yellow stripes; the other one was blue and maroon. The only other discernible difference was that the cop closest to me, surprisingly, had light hazel eyes. They flashed me their badges and got right down to business. Hazel-eyes spoke first: "I'm Detective Whittier, and this is my partner, Detective Barns. Would it be all right if we asked you a few questions about the accident?"

"Sure, go for it," I replied without enthusiasm. I knew exactly what was on Whittier's mind. My late night visit to the High Voltage Mechanical room had reignited my mind-reading capabilities again. Whittier was convinced I not only fell asleep at the wheel, but had also been drinking. He was angry, at a personal level—for reasons I hadn't deciphered yet. He had every intention of bringing me to justice—at the minimum, for vehicular manslaughter. Meanwhile his partner Barns, on the other hand, was primarily thinking about a woman named Bambi. Apparently, when not swinging from a pole at Jerry's All Nude Girls, Bambi wasn't adverse to bumping and grinding in the back of his 2008 Chevy Malibu.

"What can you tell us about the accident that occurred on Arizona State Highway Route 60, near Kingman, three days ago?"

"Only that I woke up hugging a telephone pole and later witnessed a big rig careen into another car right in front of me. I really don't remember anything prior to the accident. Although, I think my name may be Rob, if that helps ..."

"Don't you think it's awfully convenient ... you suffering from some sort of amnesia ... not remembering what went down prior to the accident?" Whittier wasn't even trying to hide his distaste for me—or what I had done. And to be honest, I didn't blame him.

But there was something Whittier wasn't telling me. *Why?* Or something else ...

He's hiding the fact there weren't two fatalities at the scene, just the one—the truck driver.

"Detective, can you tell me about the other accident victim, the minivan driver?"

Whittier's face flashed irritation at my question.

"There's very little left at the scene. Soon after you were transported, the truck's fuel tank exploded, which in turn ignited the other two vehicles. It's a miracle you caused no one else to be injured or killed. With that said, there wasn't a body in the minivan. In all likelihood, it had been abandoned there on the highway."

Jill came in and handed Whittier a clipboard. His brow furrowed as he read. Jill and I watched him in silence. Eventually, Jill turned to leave, but not before giving me a little wink and a smile. I knew what Whittier was going to say before he said it.

"It seems your alcohol levels were well within legal driving parameters. Good news for you. Truth is, we were prepared to have you transported to lockup just as soon as you were released from here."

"The other car, the minivan. Can you tell which side of the road it was on?"

Detective Barns, who had been watching Road Runner cartoons on the TV, had his interest back on his partner. Visibly irritated, Whittier continued, "Our techs are still piecing things together."

Jill was back checking my I.V., smiling and not hiding the fact she had done her part to show I was innocent of drunk-driving charges. I had avoided reading her thoughts. Not sure why, perhaps the *gentlemanly* thing to do … not sure. An interesting aspect of my *mind reading* capability— it gave me the choice to peer into someone's thoughts or not. That and they needed to be fairly close. Once someone left the room, such as the stocky orderly who had delivered the two detectives to my room, their thoughts became harder to read. Whittier was looking at me, studying my face, and obviously saw my relief at knowing I hadn't been the cause of that trucker's death. In fact, I may have been as much a victim of circumstances as he'd been.

I said, "So, like the truck driver, when my car rose above that dip in the highway, I too had to swerve to avoid hitting the minivan?"

The detective shrugged. "It will take us some time to determine fault. We'll see." Whittier let the corners of his mouth turn up.

"By the way, any idea who I am? Was there anything in that car—"

It was Barns, this time, who cut me off. "No, man, that car's toast. Can't even get a valid VIN number from it."

Whittier took one more look around the room. The detectives were done here. Walking out the door, Whittier looked back over his shoulder.

"Listen, come on by the station when you get out of here. I'll take your prints; maybe you're in the database."

I nodded and they left. Whittier still wasn't convinced I was totally innocent, but I really didn't care what he thought. The middle-aged guy next to me was awake and seemed to be upset about something. With a quick look into his thoughts, I discovered the TV was on the wrong channel. He was missing the Road Runner marathon. I picked up my remote and changed the channel for him.

* * *

The rest of the day was primarily spent with brain trauma specialist Dr. Adams, who seemed to have no clue when my memories would return—if ever. Jill and I took another lap around the floor. By this point I didn't need her arm around me to hold me up, but I think she enjoyed the close physical contact as much as I did. As before, crossing in front of the high-voltage room prompted the same feeling of longing—an urgent need to connect to the raw power waiting just inside.

"What is it with you and that room, anyway?" Jill asked, seeing my attention on the door. "Maybe you were an electrician or something? Does that ring any bells, or bring back anything?"

I just smiled and shook my head. The last thing I wanted to do was talk about my fixation with high-voltage power lines, nor reveal to her my mind-reading capabilities. I'd be transferred to a mental ward before I knew it. One thing for sure, I'd be making another late-night visit back there later on. I'd come to rely on my new ability to read minds, and even to make mental suggestions. But the condition was temporary—fading as time passed. My guess was the effects lasted about twenty-four hours before I'd need to *tap in* again.

Jill and I stood off to the side, letting an orderly with a patient on a gurney move past. I looked down at the bald-headed patient, his face bruised black and blue and covered with a myriad of scrapes and deep lacerations. One heavily-bandaged hand lay across his chest. His eyes lazily opened as he turned his head in our direction. As if he was startled, his eyes widened. He moved to sit up, but then seemed to fall back into an unconscious state.

"You know him?" Jill asked.

"Not that I remember. I wasn't sure if he was looking at me or you," I answered.

Truth was, my pulse had doubled—I felt anxious, and I didn't know why. I felt his hatred. At some level, I knew this man. I also knew I needed to get far away from him as soon as possible. I continued to watch until he was gone, rolled down a perpendicular corridor. His thoughts had merged with those of hundreds of others.

Jill was talking again. "Listen, you'll be released soon. Physically, you're in pretty good shape. But I'm worried about you. What you'll do without your memory. I've been doing some research online, you know, on others who have gone through this sort of mental trauma. Truth is, you'll basically be homeless, with no job history and no recalled skills to fall back on."

"Are you just trying to cheer me up, or are you always this motivational?" I was making light of what she said, but I'd been thinking the same thing: *What would I do when I left here?*

"Rob, I don't know you all that well; in fact, you may have been a rapist or axe murderer, but I think you're OK—a good guy ... I hope you are. Anyway, you can stay with me for a while, if you want? You know—just until you get your memory back. I have a spare bedroom ..."

I was walking without her help now, thinking about what she was offering. I was unprepared for her kindness. In fact, I found it difficult to believe someone would be willing to do such a thing for someone who was, virtually, a near-total stranger. I also felt something else: a feeling that I needed to make it on my own—to do everything possible to figure out my identity. I could be involved with someone, even married ... and the note: *Okay, I'll wait for you* ... Who was waiting for me?

"You know," I said, smiling down at her, "I might just take you up on that offer, in time. But I think I need to try working things out on my own for a while." She nodded, but kept the same expression of concern on her face.

* * *

Still uneasy about the bald-headed man, I was anxious to get moving. But I had several parting gifts waiting for me in the morning—the first was an itemized bill for $32,589. Even without any legal identification, someone was responsible for the care and treatment I'd received over the last five days, and I was expected to be the person who'd make good on the debt—one way or another. Jill walked in while I was still looking over the bill. Smiling, she plopped several department store shopping bags onto my lap.

"I think I guessed your sizes right." She gestured towards the bathroom. "Go try them on."

I plucked up the bags and disappeared into the bathroom. Everything fit fine, although the shoes were a bit snug at the toes. All in all, not bad! I looked at myself in the mirror—still not recognizing the person's reflection. I was easily over six feet tall, blue eyes, longish dark hair. The bandage around my head had been replaced with a smaller band-aid and there were numerous scrapes, scratches and bruises on my face. I guess I wasn't a bad looking guy, considering, and ... whoever I was in my previous life, I'd taken good care of myself. Flat belly, toned muscles ... but more than a few older scars and what looked like two bullet wound scars on my chest. Clearly, I had a violent past. I quickly shaved and brushed my teeth. I was ready for the world. When I emerged from the bathroom, Jill was waiting for me. She crossed her arms beneath her breasts, tilted her head and gave me a once-over.

"So tell me, can I shop or what?" She smiled up at me and, as if she'd forgotten something, reached into her scrubs pocket and pulled out a small bundle of bills. "I want you to take this; it's not much but—" her voice trailed off and she shrugged.

"You've been very kind, Jill. I won't forget it. Well, I hope I won't, my memory being what it is."

At that moment, I let myself peer into her thoughts and discovered, surprisingly, her strong feelings towards me. I leaned down and kissed her. She closed her eyes and kissed me back, even more passionately. We were interrupted by a stocky nurse's aide positioning a wheelchair by the door. I took one last look around the room and noticed the little envelope still on the nightstand. Once I'd retrieved it, I eased myself down into the wheelchair. Jill walked with us part of the way, but was waylaid by a doctor in the corridor. I waved a silent goodbye as we rolled towards the exit.

CHAPTER 6

Once outside, the cool morning air felt good on my skin. I reached into my back pocket and pulled out the bills Jill had given me. $350. Somehow, I needed to survive on that—at least until I could remember who I was. On my way out, I'd removed a Xeroxed copy of a Kingman city map tacked to a bulletin board. Intended for waiting room inhabitants, it indicated the area's major locations of inter- est: hotels, restaurants, bus and train stations, city parks, and the police station. I was about eight blocks from the po- lice station—my legs, not used to this much walking, were already starting to stiffen up. I took another look at the map and spotted a bus stop just a block south. I headed off in that direction.

I got off the bus on Andy Devine Avenue in front of a Denny's. I was three blocks from the police station. I looked down the street and then back at the big yellow Denny's sign. My stomach was grumbling. Over the last five days

I hadn't eaten much of the bland, over-processed hospital food. I went inside and sat at the counter. There was a feeling of decrepitude about the place: cottage-cheese acoustic ceilings turned gray after years of greasy, smoke-filled air; vinyl booths patched by similar, but slightly-off colored tape. Well-worn carpeting led to the kitchen.

"What can I get you, hon?" An ample-bosomed, middle-aged waitress with a Lucille Ball hairstyle stood in front of me—pen poised—with a faded Brenda embossed on a well-worn name tag.

"What do you suggest?"

"I suggest you look at the menu, then let me know when I get back." She poured me a cup of coffee, slapped a syrup-spotted menu in front of me, and waddled off. Before I could pick it up, another hand plucked it from the counter. At the counter to my right, three guys were seated next to me. The one closest to me seemed to be the leader and the largest of the three. He easily had four inches on me and a hundred pounds. He liked being noticed. His sleeves were torn away to expose large tattooed biceps. A long ratty ponytail fell down his back, partially covering a circular diagram patch of a cigar-smoking bulldog riding a motorcycle. The monogram Silent Guardians was written above it. Definitely bikers—probably ex-cons.

A mixture of tobacco, engine oil and sour body odor permeated the air around him. His two friends were similarly dressed, just smaller versions of the same ... tattoos, bad smells, exceptionally low IQs. Each one a proud gang member. I wondered if they were the total extent of the gang or if they were part of some larger organization, such as the Hell's Angels. Brenda was back and handing out more menus and filling coffee cups. My stomach rumbled again and I let her know I wanted the three-egg omelet, toast and bacon. The big biker's head jerked in my direction.

"What are you doing?" he asked, scowling—opening and closing his fist for extra impact.

"Ordering my breakfast … three-egg omelet, toast and bacon …" I turned to the waitress: "Oh, and Brenda? Can you add a large OJ to that order?" I looked back at him— bored and unimpressed.

"You stepped on my order, man," he bellowed, ensuring everyone within earshot could hear him. "Unless you have some sort of death wish, I suggest you make this right."

The big biker turned and looked over at his two friends— both smiled back and nodded their heads in unison.

"So you'll be buying me and my two friends breakfast today."

They both leaned forward over the counter to watch my reaction. Denny's was hopping. I noticed there had been a morning rush; the restaurant's tables along the front window and the seats at the counter were nearly all filled.

Heads swung in our direction, the noisy patron chit-chat had turned quiet. Expressionless, I used my napkin to clean my knife and fork. I inspected them for more water spots, all the while peering into his mind. He was amped up on something. Lots of anger there—his thoughts a virtual powder keg ready to blow. He certainly didn't like me ignoring him. No one ignores me! He wanted me to know just how dangerous he was—I'm a very dangerous man. He stood, moved his imposing bulk in close. Close enough for me to smell his hot, foul breath.

"I'm going to hurt you," he said, just loud enough for the others at the counter to hear.

This was as good a time as any to see if I really did have powers of suggestion. Had that even been real? Probably not. But what the hell … As a test, maybe I could have him say something—something a bit more interesting.

"And … I wear pretty pink panties!" he blurted out, not realizing what he'd actually just said.

Everyone around us went quiet. Confused at what had just spilled from his mouth, he surveyed the restaurant with steely eyes—challenging anyone to make a joke. Louder this time, he tried again.

"I'm going to hurt you—and I wear pretty pink panties!"

Low murmurs erupted from the other patrons—which soon turned to giggles—and eventually to out-and-out laughter. Humiliated, he turned to see his two cohorts had joined in with the laughter. This earned the closest one a backhand to the mouth. The big biker stood up, confused. He was the center of attention all right, but also a laughing stock. He pulled the two by their collars right off their stools. With a shove to each, they hurried towards the exit. I read his thoughts as he passed outside the front window. Sure enough, he was convinced I had, somehow, caused this humiliation. He was right. My order arrived and I ate in relative quiet. I paid with several bills of Jill's money—leaving a little extra for Brenda.

* * *

The Kingman police station was more akin to the workings of a small-town library than a crime-stopping police station—although I couldn't remember ever being in another police station, or library, to make that comparison. Definitely no hustle and bustle here. The front desk officer watched me approach the counter. Tall and lanky, her uniform was overly snug, with sleeves that stopped an inch above her wrists.

"Can I help you?" she asked in a surprisingly deep voice, while inspecting my cuts and bruises much as Doctor Madison had done several days previously.

"Morning," I said. "I'm looking for Detective Whittier."

"All right, let me see if he's available." She dialed a number and spoke into an ancient-looking telephone. As she listened she nodded her head as if the person on the other end could see her.

"Okay, you can go through the double-doors, up the stairs and turn right at the corridor."

"Thanks."

A dozen or so desks were spread out in a large, mostly uninhabited, room. Detective Whittier and Detective Barns had their desks facing each other. While Barn's desk, with the exception of his computer monitor, was clear of anything else, Whittier's was the complete opposite, with virtual mountains of file folders and paper stacks covering the entire desktop surface. Whittier stood up as I approached; Barns stayed engrossed in something on his computer screen.

"Rob ... How are you doing?" he asked with a condescending smile, as if privy to an inside joke only he was aware of.

"Well, I'm hanging in there ... thanks. Listen, I'd like to take you up on your offer to run my prints through your database. Maybe figure out who I am."

"Sure, come with me and we'll get you printed and swabbed."

"Swabbed?" I queried.

"Yeah, it's painless—a quick Q-tip swab of the inside of your mouth. We'll run a DNA query along with your prints—it's pretty much standard procedure these days. No sense doing one without the other."

I knew what getting swabbed was, I just didn't know if having my DNA cross-matched was such a good idea. Alarms were going off in my head, and I didn't know why. There was something in Whittier's manner that was off-kilter, and I didn't trust him. Unfortunately, I couldn't read his thoughts. How long had it been since I'd tapped in? Twenty-four hours? Twenty-five? My head was throbbing again. In just a few short days I'd come to rely more and more on that extra sense; while losing any of my five senses would seem almost catastrophic, the loss of my new, heightened sixth sense seemed no less important. I followed Whittier back downstairs to Bookings, and he ran me through what must be the same scenario those arrested would go through—even talking me into getting my picture taken.

"Listen, you may want to check out the Cornerstone Mission; it's a men's shelter two blocks northeast of here on Sycamore Avenue. It's not much, but it's a roof over your head until you get your life back. Give me a day or two to see what comes up on the database." Whittier handed me a paper towel to wipe the fingerprint ink from my fingers. He then went quiet, as if considering some inner dialogue.

"Come back upstairs for a minute; I want to show you something."

I followed him back to his desk and sat in an open chair. Barns' chair was now empty. Looking for something, Whittier rifled through several folders and grunted approval when he found what he was looking for. He took out six 8" x 10" color photographs. He looked at the clutter on his own desk and decided to lay them out on Barns' clean desktop instead.

"Take a look at these—your accident scene, prior to everything going up in a fireball. What do you see?" He was watching my face, measuring my response. I looked down at the two rows of photographs. Several of them were taken from higher up, perhaps someone standing on the roof of a patrol car. The others were at various angles—showing the car I was in, the overturned truck and its disconnected trailer, and the minivan, now pushed up against my car near the utility pole. I looked at each of the photos, going back and forth, rechecking …

"This was no accident," I said, no doubt in my voice. Whittier's condescending smile disappeared for an instant; I'd obviously stolen some of his thunder.

"Tell me why."

I found a Sharpie on Whittier's desk and held it up, questioning. He nodded his approval. On the widest-angle shot, I drew three oblong spheres—one around the truck, one around my car, and one around the minivan. I numbered these 1A, 2A, and 3A. Then I drew three more circles approximately the same size—these were positioned in the best-guess locations of where the vehicles had been just prior to the accident. I numbered these 1B, 2B, and 3B. Then I drew an interconnecting line between the A and B spheres. "This shows the beginning and ending locations of each of the vehicles, all starting with my car here. This here is the dip in the highway." Whittier's brow furrowed. Based on these lines, it would have been virtually impossible for the disconnected trailer-rig to strike the minivan and have it end up next to my car at the utility pole. "The geometry doesn't work. I assume you do see that." I said, glancing over at Whittier. I continued by drawing one more sphere indicating a new beginning location for the minivan—this one having the van parked on the wrong side of the road, pointing towards oncoming traffic.

Whittier's condescending smile was back. Before he

could say anything, I changed the orientation of the original minivan sphere. "The minivan wasn't only on the wrong side of the road, it was parked perpendicularly, blocking the road entirely. And because of the dip in the highway, here, it should be a forgone conclusion a driver would have to swerve off the road to avoid it. To the left you've got this solid rock wall, to the right the utility pole. It's really quite ingenious."

"I'm glad you have such an appreciation for what could only be described as an attempted murder. Yours. Whoever they were, they knew you would be on that highway at that particular time. And if that's right, this was a well-thought-out, even strategic, bit of planning." I agreed with him. It was a hit—someone wanted me dead—which made figuring out my identity even more important.

I moved to head on out, but Whittier put a hand on my arm. "Just hang on. Although I have no intention of holding you right now, I'm uneasy—this whole thing stinks. Until I have more information, you're free to go. Don't leave the greater Kingman area. Is that understood?" Whittier walked around Barns' desk and crossed the room to one of the open desks by the far wall and small grimy windows. After rifling through several drawers, he returned with something in his hand.

"Normally, we'd simply call you. But you don't have a phone. So take this and keep it with you at all times." Whittier placed a small black pager on the desk. "If you get paged, I expect you to call me right back within several minutes. As soon as I have anything, I'll page you."

I picked up the pager and looked at it. "I assure you, Detective, I have no idea who I am or what I'm involved with. I'm hoping you'll be able to help me with that," I said, looking up from the pager and returning his stare.

His blue eyes didn't blink for some time. "Something about you makes me nervous. I want to trust you, take you at your word. For the time being I will." Whittier sat down at his desk. "Answer the page when it comes. Don't leave town," he repeated.

"Thanks, I look forward to your continued assistance." I headed for the exit.

CHAPTER 7

Harland was sitting up in bed. A plastic bedpan lay on his lap. He looked down at the remnants of his lunch—bits of peas and carrots floated in a pool of vomit. He retched again, producing several waves of dry heaves.

Earlier he'd tried to leave, looking for his clothes after he'd seen Chandler. The effects of the snakebite, or perhaps the anti-venom stuff, had made him dizzy. He'd awakened on the floor of his room, his cheek against the cold linoleum. As they lifted him back into bed, he'd noticed the same nurse, Chandler's nurse. Then he'd lost consciousness.

Killing Chandler would have to wait. In his current state, he would be in no condition to go up against him, or anyone for that matter. Best to give it a few more hours. Maybe learn what he could from that nurse. Even in that brief moment he'd seen them together, it was obvious they had something between them. Where the hell was she? Harland looked out the window. It was nighttime. How long had he been out?

In the distance he saw a highway. Red taillights of evening commuters moved in a procession, eventually disappearing into the city. His mind wandered to where it always wandered: that last night with Veronica. Chandler was turning. His gun raised and then the gunshots. But what had stayed with him the longest was the smell. The GSR, or gunshot residue. A mixture of burnt and unburnt particles from the explosive primer, the actual propellant, as well as the various components from the bullet, the cartridge case and even the firearm used. In this case, a Beretta 92.

Harland noticed her reflection in the window as she entered his room. Always so fucking happy.

"How you feeling, Mr. Shinn?" Jill asked, taking his bedpan into the bathroom. He'd used the alias Peter Shinn when they'd filled out the basics on his chart. They'd come back several times for more information, but he'd been able to put that off.

"It's good to see you're sitting up. Back amongst the living."

"I'm feeling a little better."

"Well, give yourself a few more days. One bite is enough to kill you. Two? I'm surprised you're alive. You've got quite the constitution ... Strong like bull," she said jokingly, in a Russian accent.

Harland simply smiled and shrugged. He watched her move around his bed and check his I.V. Pretty little thing, he thought, feeling movement between his legs. His face flushed. Irritated at himself, his weakness, he cleared his mind of stray thoughts.

CHAPTER 8

Cornerstone Mission was a large, one-story, corrugated steel-sided building in the industrial section of town. As I approached, I could see a group of men huddled up and waiting at the entrance. Whittier had mentioned something about it being open only in the evenings.

I sat down in the shade, with my back against the building. As usual, my eyes were drawn to the high-power lines overhead. I needed to tap in, and I had no idea where I'd be able to do so.

My head was throbbing; the headaches were back in full force. I let my eyes track the cables, from down the street to directly above my head. These power cables were connected to a utility pole at the back of the building. They carried high-voltage power, anywhere from 2,400 to 35,000 volts of electricity, and I could see they were connected to a large transformer, which, in turn, split off to a smaller feeder cable that swayed down to the roof of the mission. I'd come to know that higher voltages were what I needed—I also knew that most small businesses and homes were fed stepped-down power of only 220 volts. Maybe I had been an electrician.

A middle-aged Hispanic man, in a plaid shirt and dirty jeans, sat down next to me. He put a small backpack down and started rifling through it. He eventually came up with a couple of granola bars. He offered me one.

"Thanks," I said, surprised by the offering.

He smiled and pointed to himself. "Me llamo Marco—¿habla usted español?"

I nodded, "Buenas tardes ... Sí, me llamo Rob." I didn't know I could speak Spanish, and apparently I was fairly fluent. "¿Habla usted inglés?"

"Sólo un poco, sí," he said with a smile. We ate in silence for a while until I tested his English.

"You've stayed here before?"

"Yes, three days now. I leave for San Joaquin Valley in several days. My wife and child wait for me." He gathered up his pack and stood up. "It will be a while before the mission opens." He smiled, gestured toward the park across the street and headed off in that direction.

I didn't like the idea of just sitting around here for another hour or more. I got to my feet and followed after Marco. My guess was many of the same men who spent their evenings at the mission spent their days in the park among others with similar reasons for living at a mission.

At the entrance I passed a large wood-carved sign that read Firefighter's Park of Kingman. Like a lone oasis, lush trees and open grassy areas made this a welcoming respite from the miles and miles of bleached concrete, and from the intense Arizona desert sun. Street vendors sold snow cones and churros, while families huddled in shady areas to picnic. A mariachi band played somewhere in the park, adding a light-hearted carnival atmosphere to the place. I followed the sidewalk to a line of tables where men and women played chess. I stopped and watched with several other onlookers. Then I realized that lone chess players sat at each table—contemplating their own in-process match. A scruffy, bearded man, wearing contrasting plaid shirt and shorts, moved from table to table. He would sit for a few moments, make a quick, decisive move, then move on to the next seated opponent. I knew this game.

Marco stood alongside the other onlookers. "That is Drako; he's here some Saturdays. He never loses," said Marco, admiration in his voice. "I've tried several times—he shows no mercy." Marco smiled and pointed to one of the players getting up from a quick defeat. "You play?"

I shrugged, "I think so." But I was curious to see how I'd stand up against this guy. Maybe the game would unlock more of my past. I sat down at the small table and quickly set up the pieces. Drako was two tables down, making quick work of his latest opponent. He was breathtakingly fast, dispatching one player after another without any hesitation. Oh, what the hell. I couldn't resist looking into his mind. Drako was now seated at the next table down. They had opened with a standard Sicilian move: white pawn to e4, and pawn to c5, which led to white pawn d2 to d4. Drako glanced up and caught my eye. He was evaluating me even before our match started.

He made quick work of his opponent; after each move, Drako commented with explicatory comments such as "What, are you stupid?" or "You embarrass yourself, you disgust me." I detected an eastern-bloc accent, maybe Czech, or perhaps Slovakian … how did I know that? Drako's opponent was getting frustrated. His black hair was

wet with perspiration from the hot afternoon sun. He wore
a red T-shirt and dirty jeans. I also took a quick peek into
his thoughts and immediately read, and felt, his annoyance
at Drako's bad manners and intolerable arrogance. The man
in the red T-shirt was soon defeated and left the table without a word. Another conquest for Drako. If nothing else,
this guy needed to be taught a lesson, I thought to myself.
Truth is, I had no idea if I was the one who could give it
to him. I definitely had an advantage over his previous op-
ponents—I could read Drako's thoughts. The other six tables were now empty; apparently, no more combatants were
willing to face humiliation.

As Drako moved over to my table and sat down, I pointed
down the line. "I'll play all those tables as well, if you're still
up to it?" Drako looked surprised and somewhat amused.
We stood and reconfigured the pieces on all the boards.
Marco and several others from the mission were among the
growing crowd of onlookers. I had the white pieces at table
one, so I would move first. I peered into Drako's mind. He
not only was deciding his opening move for this game, but
for each of the others as well. I found it interesting that he
was giving himself additional mental challenges—not similar opening moves. Each game its own strategic challenge.
He expected to finish me off quickly and looked forward to
my inevitable embarrassment.

"We play five moves at each table before moving on to
next, yes? We start now," he said. His guttural, eastern-bloc
accent had a menacing tone to it.

Play started out fast, never a hesitation from either side.
One table started a play from Drako with a standard Sicilian
Defense move; the next, a Zukertort Opening; Symmetrical
Variation from me, followed by Drako with a Trompowsky
Attack ... The irony wasn't lost on me: how I knew, in ridic-

ulous detail, what each of these chess maneuvers were, and how to implement each one precisely, yet remained clueless in remembering my own last name.

We made several runs up and down the line of tables. I wondered if I could play at this level without the advantage of reading his thoughts. Probably not. Drako was nothing short of genius-level, a savant. The crowd had grown too. Over a hundred onlookers, virtually all cheering for the new guy: me ... someone who could avenge their lost honor.

As each of the matches came to a close, fewer and fewer chess pieces were left on each board. The level of concentration became almost overwhelming. It seemed the amount of time between Drako selecting his next move, and then implementing that move, was in mere fractions of a second. In the end, Drako won two games to my five. I tipped over his last standing king; checkmated. The crowd rushed in with a chorus of hoots, cheers and pats on the back and men wanting to shake my hand. Drako, his face expressionless, picked up his chess pieces and chessboard and placed them in a canvas satchel. As the crowd dissipated, he walked back over to me.

"My name is Drako Cervenka." He put his hand out to shake, which I accepted. He continued, "I can't remember the last time I was defeated. Thousands and thousands of matches. Then, I lose five matches in one day. So, I wonder, who is this man—one who can beat me like no one else ever has?"

"My name's Rob," I said, "and I think luck played a big part in that ... you play extraordinarily well."

"No, Rob, luck had nothing to do with it. Do not act stupid. I do not need to be coddled. You must acknowledge this win with pride. As I would have done," he said with conviction. "This is great day. We must play again, very soon." Drako hesitated, as if considering something—then continued: "You come again tomorrow and we play here at park," his broken English becoming more pronounced.

"Um ... Well, thanks for the offer, Mr. Cervenka, but I'm not sure where I'll be ..."

"You call me Drako. What's wrong with you? Why you here with these people?"

Annoyed at his these people comment, I was more than ready to get away from the guy.

"Look, Drako, I was recently in a car accident—just left the hospital yesterday and I'm having some difficulty with my memory. Truth is, I'm not really sure who the hell I am ... I'm living at the homeless shelter till things ..." I realized this was more information than I wanted to provide, especially to this abrupt stranger. "I have to go ... perhaps I'll bump into you again here sometime." I headed back toward the mission; my head was pounding. Drako was fast on my heels—I could hear him running to catch up with me.

"I help you," he said eagerly. "Yes?"

I stopped and looked at him, ready to tell him to just back off. Peering into his mind, I found something unexpected. Was it kindness? Yes, but something else too: concern.

It seemed as though I had made another new friend. I walked with Drako out of the park, briefly explaining my predicament and the events of the last few days. He turned to look at me.

"An interesting puzzle, huh? You tell me what you do remember and maybe I help put pieces together, yes?"

Drako's convertible was parked beneath a large oak tree at the side of the road. "It's my baby. A 1957 Porsche 356. One of my favorite automobiles. What do you think?"

"Nice." I noticed there was a laptop computer laying on

the passenger seat and a wad of cash on the center console. Drako saw where I was looking.

"I am a wealthy man, Rob. But people here know I am not one to steal from. I will think about your problem, find out who you are, Rob. Then we play chess again."

As Drako got in his car and drove off, I headed across the street.

CHAPTER 9

People had started to file into the mission. Marco was there and we joined the line. An elderly husband and wife team were greeting people at the door. The wife, Malinda, was all smiles and welcoming warmth, while the husband, Ken, wearing a Vietnam veteran's cap, took a much closer look as we came through the door. First at Marco ahead of me, and then at me, as he explained the simple rules of the house: "No weapons; no drugs; no smoking in the hall; dinner at six; lights out at nine; breakfast at seven; and everyone gone by eight-thirty—no exceptions." Ken shook my hand and held it. "Where you from, friend?" he asked, his piercing blue eyes unwavering from my own.

I shrugged. "That's what I'm trying to figure out," I said, matching his stare.

"Well, my name's Ken—let me know if you need anything."

"Name's Rob, and thanks ..."

He nodded, smiled, and released my hand. I followed after Marco into the main hall of the mission. There were close to one hundred cots set up, and by their precision, barracks-like in straight rows and blankets symmetrically-placed, I was betting it was the meticulous work of the Vietnam vet, Ken. There was some part of me that was comfortable with this level of organization and order. There were twenty or so other men, who mostly appeared to be migrant workers, spread throughout the room. I moved to the back of the mission and selected a cot close to a wall.

Privacy was not an option in a homeless shelter, but my cot location was about as close as I could get. I didn't have anything to lay dibs with on this particular cot, so I unfolded the blanket and laid it out. Then I pulled off my belt and laid that across the pillow. Marco had chosen a cot several rows over, and I wondered if he always chose the same one or liked to mix things up a little every night. The cafeteria was open and a line was forming. Then I spotted three familiar faces—Russell and his two idiot friends, whom I'd met earlier at Denny's. They were making a beeline towards the cafeteria. No one stopped them when they cut to the front of the line, grabbed two trays each, and proceeded to intimidate the young volunteer server into piling mountains of mashed potatoes, gravy, extra slices of turkey and multiple pudding cups onto their trays. Ken made his way across the cafeteria and headed toward them as they commandeered an open table.

"Hello, boys, I see you've got yourselves quite a spread there. We make it a policy to provide a well-rounded meal to those in need—but I feel you're taking advantage of our offerings." Russell was seated now and had tucked his paper napkin into the top of his shirt. Without acknowledging Ken in the slightest, Russell took his plates and pudding cups from his two trays and set them on the table. Then, with casual disregard, tossed the trays onto the floor at Ken's feet. The loud clatter brought startled stares from the other tables. Ken stepped around the trays and stepped up closer to Russell.

"I'm going to have to ask you to leave ... all three of you. Get up and get out—don't come back here." For the first time Russell looked up at Ken. Although he was trying to stand tall, Ken must have been pushing seventy, maybe seventy-five. Age spots covered his hands and he walked with a slight limp, perhaps a souvenir from the Vietnam conflict years earlier. Heads down and quietly eating, those around the three men were minding their own business. Ken was on his own. With eyebrows raised, Russell smiled at his two friends and looked down at the food on the table.

"As you can see, we've just sat down for this beautiful feast. Me and my two associates, Wriggly and Jordan, would like a little peace and quiet while we enjoy our supper. If you would be so kind as to fuck off, I'd be most appreciative." Wriggly and Jordan, mouths full of mashed potatoes and gravy, chuckled and looked up to see how Ken would respond. Moving fast for an older guy, Ken reached for Russell's arm, obviously intending to forcibly drag him out if necessary. Russell stood up to meet Ken's advance and slapped him, open-handed, across his face. The loud crack reverberated throughout the now silent room.

This was the second time these three had acted inappropriately in my presence. The first time, I'd pretty much let it go. But not now. Even before Ken grabbed for Russell, I was well on my way to their table. I stepped in between Ken and Russell and turned my back on the larger biker. I faced Ken and smiled. "Let me talk to them. I might be able to convince them to leave." Few things are as humiliating as being slapped in the face, especially by another man. Ken didn't say anything, but took a tentative step backward. Russell was ready for me when I turned to face him. Knife in hand, he would not have been happier to see his own mother's face.

"If it isn't my friend from Denny's. You know, I've been looking for you. Seems like destiny, don't ya think?" His mistake was taking his eyes off me, even for the quick second it took him to look over at his two friends. I'd moved just slightly to his right. When his head jerked back, catching my movement, I was in a better position to grab his wrist with my left hand and then, using both hands now, I twisted his knife in and towards his own body. Even after he'd been forced to release his knife, there was an audible crack as his carpal bones snapped like dry kindling. Russell yelped in pain, bending over to protect his ruined wrist. Wriggly and Jordan had lost their smiles and were up out of their seats. Wriggly, the taller, fatter of the two, moved to my left, while Jordan, the more muscular and seemingly more intelligent of the pair, was attempting to flank me around the right. I waited for them, expending no more energy than necessary. Almost simultaneously, both pulled knives from their boots. I had the distinct feeling they had rehearsed this maneuver before. Even with my memory a total wash, I instinctively knew that how an opponent holds their edged weapon speaks volumes. While untrained combatants hold a knife skyward, as if waving a flag, pros typically hold a knife downward, in line with their wrists, keeping it moving. Both Jordan and Wriggly had opted for the flag-waving technique.

I had just enough time to pluck Wriggly's tray off the table. Plates with half-eaten mashed potatoes, turkey and gravy scattered to the floor. With eyes on Wriggly, I spun

180 degrees around backwards and caught Jordan by surprise with the edge of the tray, hitting him in the temple. He went down like a bag of rocks. Then I turned to face Wriggly. "Your two friends are on the floor, do you want to join them?" Apparently, Wriggly did not. He took several steps backward, looked down at his two friends and rushed for the door. Ken was still standing where I'd left him. Malinda, at the far end of the cafeteria, was on her cell phone—it wouldn't be long before the police were dispatched.

"Thank you for ..." Ken paused and looked around the room. "Listen, we're not unaccustomed to trouble. It comes with the territory. It follows people like them—and it follows people like you. I saw the way you moved; you're military or ex-military. What you're doing here, I don't know—or particularly want to know. But I don't want any more trouble. You got that?"

I knelt down to clean up the mess we'd made. Marco was at my side and stacking plates onto a tray. Ken slowly walked out of the cafeteria without saying another word. As I thought about what had just happened, what I had reflexively done, it occurred to me that my past was quickly catching up to my present.

By nine o'clock, everyone was hunkered down on their cots for the night. The other men had given me a wide berth, with the exception of Marco, who brought out a deck of cards and schooled me on the intricacies of Conquian, a Mexican card game he'd played since he was a child. It seemed to be more a game of chance than of skill, such as poker or even black jack. We ended up about even when Malinda made her rounds, letting us know it was lights out in five minutes.

The large room was dark; someone was snoring several rows over. I stared up at the ceiling above me, in thought. I made two mental columns for positives and negatives. On the negative side, I still had virtually no memory of my life prior to the accident. I also discovered someone, or even some organization, might be trying to kill me. I was hampered by continual headaches and quickly moving toward a strange addiction to getting tapped-in to high-voltage power lines. On the positive side, I had a new ability that was nothing short of incredible, if not unbelievable. An ability to look into people's minds and influence their decision-making processes.

As I lay there, I thought about future implications. How others could manipulate circumstances with this same ability, my ability. I needed to be careful. And what about me? I obviously had ties to a military background, perhaps a special forces unit—martial arts seemed second nature to me. Also, I was educated, apparently, and had a good range of diverse knowledge at my disposal. Speaking one, perhaps several foreign languages, electrical engineering know-how, and analytically-inclined enough to break down the factors that had contributed to a major traffic accident. But none of it brought me any closer to my identity. I rubbed my eyes. My head throbbed—it had been too long since I last tapped in. So I got up, found my shoes and headed off towards the bathroom. I'd done a quick check earlier and discovered there was a sliding window high up on a wall in the ladies' bathroom. Since this seemed to be a men-only shelter, with the exception of Malinda and a few younger volunteers, I felt fairly confident I'd be able to get in and out without being noticed.

Now, looking up at the window, I wondered if I could even squeeze through it. It would be a tight fit. I took several running steps, jumped up and caught the edge of the window sill. Precariously perched there, I reached over and slid open the window—then, with a bit of squirming, I was able to crawl through and jump down to the parking lot behind the mission. I could see several cars, probably Ken's and Malinda's, or perhaps those of the volunteers. My first impulse was to simply climb up one of the utility poles I'd spotted earlier, but, upon closer scrutiny, rungs for hand-climbing the pole, if they were there at all, rarely went above the lower hanging cables provided for basic telephone company maintenance.

Reaching the top of a pole for the more dangerous high-voltage cables typically required a special cherry picker-type utility truck. But an idea was forming in my head. I headed east, crossed over Sycamore Avenue, and thirty yards later was in the back parking lot of a Motel 6. The good thing about motels is that they're always open. The other good thing is they need ample electricity to power hundreds of TV sets, coffee makers, industrial-sized water heaters, and high-capacity kitchen equipment. No light industrial or residential connection for this building. No, they'd need a full 30,000-volt utility hook up.

I barely made it to the motel's back entrance. Halfway across the parking lot, more intense withdrawal symptoms descended on me—headache, nausea, and a case of the shakes so bad walking became problematic. I needed to tap in, and quickly. What was it now, 28 hours? Other than being unconscious in the hospital, I hadn't gone this long without tapping in since the accident. Even my vision was beginning to fail. Somewhat relieved, I made it to the back door. It was locked. Crap! Walking away, I heard it open behind me.

A short Hispanic woman, wearing a gray and black uniform, peered out at me. "You lock yourself out?"

"Yeah, came out here for a quick smoke; didn't realize

the door would lock behind me," I replied, with as sincere a smile as I could muster. She opened the door wide and I scrambled by her and a cart filled with large bath towels, toilet paper rolls, shampoo bottles and bed linens. I had no idea where the electric utility room would be, so I set out to do some exploring.

The motel had two floors with two separate wings. It made sense the room would be on the bottom floor some-where. I found it in the other wing, around the corner of the front lobby. As expected, it was locked. I didn't think I'd have the same good fortune of finding the key in a nearby broom closet as I had at the hospital. I backtracked to a room I'd noticed holding several vending machines and a big ice-maker. I hadn't really thought what I'd do next … First of all, I needed some change. I checked under both vending machines and found a dime and two quarters to-wards the back of the second machine. I had to lie down on my stomach and reach with my fingertips.

"Can I help you?" It was the same maid standing behind me, and by her furrowed brow she was tiring of me—obvi-ously, I was one of those troublesome guests who made life miserable for everyone. "You drop monies on floor?"

"Yeah, I wanted to buy a Coke." The creases in her brow deepened. She pulled her pocket open at the front of her skirt, inspected the contents, and pulled out three quarters. Before I had a chance to remove my arm from beneath the vending machine, she had placed the coins next to me on the floor—with a huff she was gone. "Thank you!" I yelled after her. I wasn't completely confident that the next as-pect of my plan would even work. I did a quick check of both directions down the hall—all clear. I popped the tab on the Coke, cupped one hand beneath an open wall outlet and carefully poured in half the liquid. Nothing. Half the Coke remained. I tried again ... Bingo. With an audible clunk, the little room went dark, the fan on the ice-machine went quiet, and the vending machines clicked off. I'd tripped the breaker.

Using my hand, I did my best to wipe away the messy coke remnants from the wall and floor. I told myself it wasn't all that noticeable. A quick trip back down the hall and around the corner, and I was in front of the reception counter. An ample-bellied man, wearing a white button-down shirt, a gray and black vest, and a large bundle of keys hanging from the right side of his belt, greeted me with a smile. "Good evening, sir, my name is Benny. How can I be of help?"

"Evening, Benny," I said, not looking all that happy. "I know this is probably the last thing you want to hear this time of night, but the vending machines down the hall are not working. Matter of fact, the lights are out in there as well."

"Let's take a look," he said with good humor. Perhaps it was the most exciting thing to happen all day. I followed Benny back to the little room where he scrutinized the vending machines and the ice-maker. He flicked the switch on and off several times. The overhead lights didn't flicker on. "Well, you're right. Electricity is out in this room. Why don't you go back to your room and we'll get this fixed by morning." Benny must have seen the disappointment on my face.

"Hankering for a Coke, huh? Well, maybe it's a simple fix—let's see if I can just flip the breaker."

Back down the hall, Benny used one of his many keys to open the utility door. I was close on his heels, but fortunately he didn't seem to mind. Inside the utility room, Benny went right to the center cabinet. I stayed back and felt for the door handle behind me, releasing the button so the door wouldn't auto-lock again. At the same time, Benny, with a "Yep, that's the problem ..." flipped the appropriate breaker. I held the door open and then followed him back down the hall where we did a quick check of the vending machines. "Here you go, sir. Everything is up and running. Enjoy your cold refreshment."

I thanked him and turned my attention to the variety of soft drinks behind the glass—not wanting him to see my quickly worsening physical condition. In fact, I was ready to black out. A minute later, I made it back to the unlocked utility room. Dizzy, I nearly lost my balance. Bent over with my hands on my knees, I took several deep breaths. I had to get better at this tapping in process ... and not wait so damn long next time.

The high-voltage cables were encased in large, four-inch pipes coming up from the concrete floor. I instinctively knew which pipe to go to. I sat down on the floor, Indian-yoga style, leaned forward and unceremoniously placed my throbbing head against the cool metal pipe. I tapped in almost immediately. The warmth and familiar music filled my consciousness. My body shuddered with relief as waves of blue energy pulsed and flowed through my skull and into my mind. As grateful as I felt for the pain relief, the inflowing energy too seemed to welcome me to stay, to merge with its infinite intelligence—to become one with it. I was lost in the moment—oblivious to anything but the energy coursing through my mind and body. Oblivious that Benny was back and standing behind me.

CHAPTER 10

Harland kept his eyes on the hospital's main entrance. He didn't recognize the young nurse at first. She had changed out of her scrubs into dark leggings and a long sweater-shirt. She looked a bit tired, but still wore a smile on that small, pretty face. Harland could see why Chandler would be attracted to her.

He caught his own reflection from the car window he was hiding behind. The expression death warmed over came to mind. His skin looked sallow and yellow under the dim parking lot fluorescents. His hand, and halfway up his arm, was a color combination of black, blue and some green. He curled his fingers into a fist and immediately regretted it as spikes of pain shot all the way up his arm and into his shoulder. Hours earlier he had found his clothes, stolen another patient's shoes, and made his way out of the hospital. It was ill-advised to leave at this early stage of recovery, but in his business, staying hot on someone's trail was often the difference between success and failure. Chandler had been close enough to touch—so close. The thought of killing him, seeing him struggle to stay alive, made this next course of business necessary. Unpleasant, yes, but necessary.

He watched as she made her way across the parking lot to her car. Only then did she stop and dig through her purse for her keys. If women only knew how this one act could impact their lives, or subsequent deaths.

Jill had retrieved her keys and was slinging her purse strap back over her shoulder. Harland was upon her from behind. His lips were at her ear.

"Do not scream—do not try to run. I will kill you if you do not do exactly as I ask."

"Oh my God, oh my God, please, please, please, don't hurt me," she cried, her voice barely audible. She pulled her crossed arms in tight to her chest.

"Ouch!"

"What you're feeling in the small of your back is a knife. By now you are also feeling the warmth of your own blood flowing down your legs."

"Oh no. Please. You don't need to hurt me. Just tell me what you want. I have some cash. Take my credit cards." Tears streamed down her cheeks. Her eyes searched frantically for someone else in the parking lot—someone who could help.

"Open the door, Jill."

Harland saw her hand shake as she pressed the unlock button on her key fob. With his left hand he took hold of her wrist and got in the car—pulling her in behind him as he positioned himself onto the passenger seat.

"Start the car."

She did what Harland commanded and, with a quick glance, saw his face.

"Why are you doing this? You don't have to—"

"Listen to me carefully. Stay calm and answer a few simple questions, and you won't be hurt."

"But why do this? I would have—"

"Stop talking. You are a chatty little thing, aren't you? That was a rhetorical question. Just drive, I'll guide you."

"Oh my god, I'm bleeding. I'm sitting in a pool of my own blood. I need to stop the bleeding."

"We'll attend to that soon, just drive for now. If you want to live, drive now!"

Jill's eyes were drawn toward the metallic object in Harland's hand, which shone dimly. A scalpel. She started the car, put it in reverse, and backed out.

"Good girl. Now, pull forward and make a left at the stop sign."

Jill's rapid breathing had fogged the windshield. She used her hand to wipe the glass.

"Please let me go. It's Peter, right?"

"My name is not important. I want to talk to you about your friend Rob."

Harland watched Jill. He needed to see her reaction. And there it was. Harland wouldn't have thought it possible, but she was now even more frightened than she had been.

"Where was Rob going? When he left the hospital, where did he say he was going?"

Jill was driving on the main road now. Harland realized he had misjudged her fright. He studied her face in the dim light. Her expression was no longer one of panic and desperation. No … now it was one of resolve.

He directed her to turn right at the next stop sign.

"Where are you taking me?"

"I'm taking you to a place we can be alone. One where we won't be disturbed. Someplace dark. And, frankly, where your screams will go unheard."

Good, he thought, the panic in her eyes had returned. He couldn't work with her if she wasn't terrified. She needed to be desperate. She swiped the mist from the glass again. Then, uncontrollably, started to cry again.

They drove in silence for a while. Harland stared out the side window. They'd driven into a more industrial part of town, which was run down, graffiti covering the sides of buildings and on the sidewalks. Several empty lots, home to abandoned cars and piles of rubbish, added to the feeling of desolation. The streets were empty, and what few street lamps worked were so sporadically placed as to be rendered useless.

"Pull over, Jill. I think this will be just fine, right here." Off to their left was a chain-linked fence—beyond that, a concrete culvert.

She did as he asked. With her hands up to her face, she continued to weep. Harland noticed the small tattoos. He saw the little bird in flight, free at last. How apropos, he thought.

"Now you will tell me everything. You will leave out no detail, no matter how insignificant."

CHAPTER 11

I was just about to disconnect when I detected Benny standing several feet behind me. Immediately, I was in his head—observing his thoughts. He wasn't sure what I was doing there, but he was leaning toward my having some kind of mental instability issues. *Interesting*—my abilities were far more powerful *while* tapped in. Everything was sharper, more vivid.

My access to Benny's mind was nothing short of profound. Not only was I seeing exactly what he was seeing, I was feeling and reading his thoughts to a much deeper degree than I thought possible.

Benny was now looking around. *Well, nothing seems to have been disturbed. But what the hell's he doing? Looks like the same man I helped at the vending machines. Seems to be in some sort of a trance ...*

I looked into his mind and was surprised by its simplicity. *This guy is by no means an Einstein.* I interjected into his

thoughts: *Benny, the man on the floor is perfectly harmless. It's best if you don't disturb him. In fact, you want to help him in any way possible. Do you understand that, Benny?*
Confused, Benny was questioning his own internal dialogue. *Why would I want to help this guy?*
I fought to stay patient and not lose the connection. *It's not for you to question, Benny. This man needs your help. You want to help him.*
Benny seemed to be bouncing this around in his head. He seemed to have come to some sort of conclusion. *I do want to help this man.*
I felt relieved and continued communicating with Benny: *Very good. He'll need full access to Motel 6. Do you know what that means, Benny?*
Benny's thoughts didn't hesitate. *Yes, he should have a full set of master keys.*

* * *

I didn't return to the mission. Instead, I had taken advantage of Benny's generosity and slept at Motel 6. With a set of keys, including a credit card type master key-card in hand, I found not only an empty guest room, but a nearly uninhabited upper floor, on the south wing of the motel. I took a quick shower. Standing with a towel wrapped around me, I turned on the TV and muted the volume. I opened the plastic bag of toiletries and the plastic razor I'd collected from the hotel's supply closet. Someone was walking past the door in the hallway. I stopped moving and listened until the footfalls moved on down the corridor. I wasn't sure how long the mental constraints I'd placed on Benny would last. One day? A week? Forever? But like any good experiment,

I'd need to test it and verify the results. I also needed to come to terms with the moral and ethical issues of reading other people's inner thoughts and manipulating their actions. The truth was, I hadn't asked for this ability, but it was a part of me now. How I used it, and with whom, well, that needed to be held to some sort of measurable standard. I thought about that as I shaved and brushed my teeth. I assessed myself in the mirror. I looked almost human again. Then I noticed something on television reflected in the mirror. It was a news bulletin describing a local homicide. I sat on the edge of the bed and turned up the volume. The camera was pointed downward into a cement culvert that was strewn with trash and weeds. The camera angle then zoomed outward to focus on a bright blue tarp on the ground and several uniformed cops standing near. The feed changed to a solemn-looking reporter standing close by, holding a mic. A red banner at the bottom of the screen scrolled the words: *Young Nurse Dies In Brutal Homicide.*

They showed stock footage of the Kingman Regional Medical Center, and then a small, outlined picture of Jill appeared on the screen. The reporter said the victim's name was Jill Connolly—my heart stopped beating—time collapsed around me. *No... Oh my God...* The correspondent continued, obviously emotionally affected by what he was reporting:

"... and was killed sometime between midnight and three this morning. Apparently, the young nurse was found partially clothed with multiple stab wounds to her upper and lower torso. Although actual cause of death is pending via the coroner's report, an officer at the scene, who has asked not to be identified, told me that beyond doubt she'd died from significant blood loss—in his words, she'd completely bled out."

Someone had brutally murdered Jill—her body indifferently tossed into a drainage ditch. I thought of Jill and her little tattoo: the bird free from its cage. *I'm so sorry, Jill.* The only person in my life I cared about, at least that I could remember, had been killed. I'd find out who was responsible and I'd end him—of that, I had no doubt.

I cleared out of my motel room, doing my best to leave it as undisturbed as possible. I needed to get to the hospital.

CHAPTER 12

The largest conference room in the building held six-teen occupied chairs at the mammoth-sized table, and another eight chairs along the glass wall. Pippa slipped in, trying to be quiet and not disrupt Assistant Director Hayes' presentation. She took the last remaining seat by the door. As she settled in—digging out a pen in her breast pocket and opening her notepad—Pippa realized the room had gone quiet. Looking up, she saw everyone staring at her.

Embarrassed, Pippa smiled and said, "Sorry, didn't mean to disturb—" Then she saw Rob's face looking back at her on the sixty-inch TV monitor behind Assistant Director Hayes' shoulder.

"As I was saying, Agent Rosette, after eighteen months we've had our first solid indication that Chandler is still alive."

He is alive! Pippa's mind raced. Looking at Chandler's image, her heart nearly leapt into her throat. She had to physically check herself from jumping to her feet.

Giles lifted a pen into the air.

"Agent Giles?"

"Yes, I was just wondering if he's still in custody?"

"No, he was never in custody. Local Kingman PD ran his prints and DNA early this morning. Apparently, it was voluntarily given following an automobile accident—one that involved one or more fatalities. He was hospitalized, then released. That same day, he walked into the Kingman police department. They didn't hold him."

Pippa listened intently, ignoring the occasional glances in her direction. It was no secret she and Chandler were partners. For three years they worked together at the CIA as field agents assigned to the U.S. Embassy in Berlin. They also worked out of Lebanon and Ankara, Turkey. Eighteen months ago her partner, her friend, disappeared and was assumed to have gone rogue. Reports of possible sightings, usually unsubstantiated, cropped up from time to time, but no one, until now, knew for certain if he was actually alive or not.

Other hands went up, some just blurting out questions, but the assistant director was quick to take control of the meeting again.

"Listen, it's too early to give any particulars. Agents will be dispatched within the hour. We'll know more within the next twenty-four hours. Needless to say, none of this leaves the room." Hayes changed the subject and continued on with the typical day-to-day information-gathering minutia she was in no mood to listen to. Pippa was impatient for the meeting to end. Forty-five minutes later, the room started to clear out. Hayes, collecting the remainder of his notes from the table, didn't bother to look up as Pippa approached.

"As I said, it's too early to know anything, Agent Rosette."

"You and I both know that every international agency in the world is now aware Rob, Agent Chandler, is still alive. Some will wait and see what turns up; others, undoubtedly, have already dispatched teams. I'm sure you're aware Chandler's made his share of enemies over the years."

Assistant Director Hayes looked up, irritated. "You work for the DHS now, Rosette, not the CIA—if you haven't forgotten. The Agency has its own agents investigating."

"The CIA thinks in terms of black and white. They'd just as soon terminate a possible threat as—"

"This, Agent Rosette, is not a conversation to have standing in an open conference room." He'd raised his voice and continued to gaze down at the younger agent. He spoke again, but in a lower, hushed voice. "What is it you would have me do?"

"Let me go to Kingman. Let me join the team you're sending. I can evaluate the situation. I know how he thinks. I'll be able to anticipate his moves. I'll find him."

"You had plenty of time after he'd gone to ground. Why's now any different?"

"Something's obviously changed, unless he's purposely trying to attract worldwide attention. No, something's happened to him. And if I do find him, I'll be able to evaluate him far better than agents who never knew him." Pippa was aware desperation had crept into her voice.

"Listen, I knew you would request to be part of the Kingman team. But I need to know you haven't lost your objectivity. If Chandler can be brought in, fine. If he's been turned, which is the likely assumption, then you'll be expected to act accordingly. Can you do that?"

* * *

Pippa wondered if Assistant Director Hayes had deliberately paired her up with Giles just to spite her. *Who wears aftershave like that, anymore?* She'd scrambled for the window seat, hoping he'd opt for the aisle seat and not take the cramped middle one. But he'd plopped himself next to her, releasing another waft of his sickeningly sweet cologne. *Why was he even here?*

By the time Pippa and Giles had checked their bags, and then their weapons, Pippa felt she needed a shower after his fawning closeness. There was nothing about the way she was dressed—a plain navy suit, white shirt, and sensible flat-heeled shoes—that should evoke such attention. At five feet, nine inches, she was on the tall side. But it was her Scandinavian features—blue eyes, blonde hair and delicate bone structure—that inevitably got men's attention. Not a positive in her line of business. Looking unremarkable, forgettable, would be an advantage. Subsequently, she'd had to work harder to prove herself.

"All right, let's get down to business, Pippa. You up for a little business talk?"

Pippa just looked at him. *What other kind of talk would there be?* "I imagine we'll head on over to the Kingman PD. Until we know any more details, what's happened so far, it's senseless to start planning too far ahead, don't you think?" Pippa asked back, her eyebrows slightly raised, letting him know the obvious scenario.

"Oh, of course. I just meant our overall strategy: you know, the thirty thousand foot perspective," Giles responded, back peddling. He turned back forward and retrieved a comb from his shirt pocket. He gave his thick black hair a quick couple of strokes and then, eyes closed, hunkered down for a nap.

Pippa had had little time to think about Chandler since the morning's briefing. For several years she and Rob had often been paired together—playing well off each other's strengths and compensating for each other's weaknesses. Not that Chandler had many of those. She'd heard all the rumors about the two of them. How they'd been intimate for years, undercover lovers. It wasn't true. They'd never gotten intimate. But that had been about to change that just days prior to Chandler's disappearance. She had decided to leave the Agency and see if it was possible to start a new life. He was an idiot if he didn't know her feelings. Then he was gone. After several months he was presumed dead, but Pippa didn't buy it. She also didn't buy into the whispered speculation he had turned. She noticed her palms were wet. She was nervous at the prospect of seeing him again ... even more nervous of the possibility that she wouldn't be able to bring him in. The assistant director had been perfectly clear: Chandler could not be allowed to disappear again.

CHAPTER 13

First feelings of loss, and now raging anger, filled my thoughts. My only concern: could I show enough restraint to hold back and question the bald-headed man, or would I just kill him on sight.

I crossed over to Sycamore Avenue and passed the Cornerstone Mission off to my right and Firefighter's Park off to my left. It was still early, but the buses were running, making frequent stops, off in the distance. I felt their presence even before I looked up and saw them. A gang of bikers. The rumble of their Harleys filled the air. Black leather, long hair, an assortment of tattoos, and the distinctive emblem—a cigar-smoking bull dog riding a motorcycle—left little doubt that Russell's gang had arrived on the scene.

And there was Russell himself—middle of the pack; he'd come to a stop ten feet in front of me. He had a cast on his wrist on which someone had scrawled something, though from this distance I couldn't quite tell what. He and his friends, obviously, had been scouring the streets for me. All told, there were ten motorcycles holding eleven bikers. They'd encircled me, some coming at me from the park. I only noticed the woman after a silver-haired biker killed his engine and stepped away from his Hog. Without a doubt this guy was their leader. His woman, smiling, stayed seated and seemed to be enjoying herself. He was about sixty, easily six-five, and I estimated he weighed upward of two hundred and fifty pounds. Both he and the woman wore jeans, boots, and black leather chaps ... their black leather vests hung open enough to display the sizeable chests on both bikers.

I'd been lost in thought with Jill on my mind. Their presence was juvenile and an unwelcome distraction from what I needed to do.

"Well, if it isn't my friend from Denny's," Russell said, back to his cocky bravado.

"What do you want, Russell? Brought your pals to fight your battles for you?" I kept my eyes on the older guy, though, now standing several feet in front of me.

Russell moved to get off his bike, but the older biker held up a hand and shook his head.

"My name is Tag. You've already met Russell, Jordan and Wriggly. You've probably also noticed that they're idiots. There's nothing I can do about that. But I do value their loyalty. What's a gang of bikers without loyal dependability?"

"Was that a rhetorical question or do you actually want me to answer?" I asked, straight-faced.

Tag was not amused, and he looked tired. He looked like a man no longer inclined to do the types of things expected of him from the gang's less-bright members. I almost felt sorry for him. He stood tall and puffed out his chest.

"I'm not going to kill you … What's your name?"

"I appreciate that. You can call me Rob."

"Rob, you will need medical attention after this. Hopefully, you have health insurance." His last comment evoked several chuckles from the bikers.

Tag's mind was definitely on something else. I'd been peering into his thoughts. He had killed a lot of men—more than he wanted to remember. He feared an accounting was coming due. Not karmic, nothing so esoteric. But he was realistic enough to know every leader, such as himself, eventually faced his own reckoning.

"Listen, Tag. I don't think you want to fight me. As you said, those three are idiots and you certainly must know they got exactly what was coming to them. I have no beef with you. How about we just—"

Tag was moving before I finished my sentence. He leapt forward, thrusting a hand out for my throat.

I blocked it and countered with a left punch to his lower lip, then a follow-up right to his temple. He staggered, caught himself, and stood with his fists raised.

"Do you really want this to be that day, Tag? The one you've been worried about?"

He looked at me as if I'd uncovered his deepest, darkest secret. Maybe I had. I continued: "When I put you down, right here in front of your gang, your woman—it will be too late. You'll never regain their respect … it will be the beginning of the end."

He lashed out with a wide haymaker to my head, missing me by a mile. He came at me again—eyes full of spite and teeth clenched and bared, like a crazed animal. He threw two more punches, one connecting with my cheek. I stepped back and let him follow after me. He'd regained some confidence, but had dropped his guard. He'd let his fists fall too low, instead of keeping them up, where he could block a punch. Or in this case, a crescent kick to the side of his face. His head jerked violently to the left, which caused his whole body to spin. With his back partially exposed and totally unprotected, I kicked out again, hitting him behind the knees. As Tag fell backward, I sent him to the ground with an uppercut to the chin. He was down for the count. On his back he looked up at me. I saw fear in his eyes. His thoughts were crying out for help. *Don't let this be the day.* His eyes stayed on mine for a long minute, then drifted to the crowd of onlookers. He took in their uncomfortable expressions. Some looked back, beckoning him to get up and fight the fight. Others looked away, embarrassed by his defeat.

Russell was the first to come at me. He'd pulled his knife from his boot and was quickly moving in my direction. Surprisingly, it was the woman who stopped him. With the palm of her hand held to his chest, she simply shook her head. Russell stopped, but kept his eyes firmly on mine. The woman biker dismounted, walked over to Tag's outstretched body, and stared down at her man. They looked at each other for what seemed an extended period. Then she smiled and started to laugh. Tag, anger subsiding, began to laugh too. She held out her hand and helped the big biker to his feet. They climbed on their bike—first her, then him. When he finally looked at me again, he simply nodded. He started his bike, and the others followed suit. They left. Russell was the last to leave and, by his expression, I'd be seeing him again.

I had just enough time to cross over Andy Devine Avenue and catch the bus. It would take about thirty minutes before the bus would reach the Kingman Regional Medical Center.

CHAPTER 14

By the time Pippa and Giles landed, showed their creds to retrieve their stowed weapons and had made their way over to the Hertz desk to rent a sedan, it was already close to noon. Giles was signing the auto rental form when Pippa's phone vibrated in her pocket.

"Rosette," she said, turning away from the counter.

Giles took the paperwork and the car key from the agent. He watched Pippa, who was listening intently, her expression serious.

"I understand. No, we were going to grab a quick bite, but we'll head on over there now. Yes, sir."

Pippa put away her cell phone and looked up at Giles. "One of the nurses who'd attended to Chandler has been killed. We're to meet up with the Kingman PD. A Detective Whittier will debrief us, and we can move forward from there."

Pippa had opted to drive. She needed to think, and driving always helped her work things out in her mind. With a three-hour trek ahead, from Phoenix International to the city of Kingman, she'd have plenty of time to mull things over. In light of the latest developments, catching up to Chandler had become even more pressing. She briefly wondered if Chandler was really capable of cold-blooded murder. Could she have been that wrong about him?

"Huh, look at that," Giles said, pointing at an all-you-can-eat advertisement on a billboard now disappearing behind them.

She'd realized early on that once Giles started talking he rarely came up for air.

"What kind of name is Pippa, anyway? Hey, you're a single girl, aren't you? You have roommates? You dating anyone right now?"

"That's all a bit personal, Giles. Yes, I'm single. Yes, I live by myself, but no, I won't talk about my relationships."

"That's fine. Hey, just making small talk here. We haven't really worked together—you know, in the field before."

Pippa nodded, but found it best not to say anything in response. Giles would take any comment she made and turn it into more questions, more talking.

Giles flipped down the sun visor and looked at himself in the mirror. He retrieved his comb and gave his hair a few quick swipes. He turned his head from side to side. Apparently pleased with his looks, he flipped the visor back into place. Pippa watched him in her peripheral vision. Surprised how obsessed he was with his hair yet he allowed more than a few inches to hang over his belt.

Pippa's mind was back on Chandler. The last time they'd seen each other was eighteen months earlier. They both were returning from completed assignments in the field, first Pippa and then Rob. He said it would take no more than a month to tie up some loose ends, and then he'd join her back in the States.

She smiled to herself, thinking how insecure he had been around her. For someone who was second-to-none in undercover ops, he had an almost childlike innocence when it came to forming a personal relationship. Their last week together at the embassy in Kabul, he'd asked her if she would see him exclusively, when he got back to Washington. She hadn't answered right away—wanting to make him wait for some stupid reason. She'd fallen in love with him long before he'd begun to take their burgeoning relationship seriously. They'd kissed a few times, but she had never let it progress very far. And now she regretted that decision, too.

Now she contemplated whether what she thought they'd once had was even real. She'd written him a note, letting him know that yes, she'd wait for him. *Of course she would.* But then he was gone without a trace. Thought to be dead, and after all this time she had come to terms with the loss. But now, knowing he'd been alive this whole time, she felt humiliated. Had she been played as easily as some characters he'd played while undercover? She drove in questioning silence for three hours.

Giles had dozed off. A large sign welcomed them to Kingman, Arizona.

"Giles, wake up. We're almost there."

* * *

Never staying in one place more than a day or two, Harland looked around his seedy hotel room. He pulled the thick inner curtains tightly together to keep any sunlight from streaming in. Even worse than the pain in his hand, he found bright light excruciating. He turned off the television set, pleased to see that each of the local networks had reported the murder. *Big news around here.*

Harland had gotten quite a bit of information from the nurse before she finally bled out. He'd dumped her limp body in the culvert and had made an anonymous phone call to the Kingman PD on her body's whereabouts. He needed her murder to make the morning news, news he was sure Chandler would see.

The discovery that Chandler had some kind of amnesia meant that finding him would be that much easier. Chandler had already made more mistakes than Harland thought possible. Stupid, amateurish mistakes.

Sweating, Harland wiped his brow. He'd definitely left the hospital earlier than he should have. He still had a fever, his hand hurt like a bitch, and his left knee wasn't working quite right either. "Fucking snakes!" he yelled out. *I tried to do too much yesterday,* he thought to himself. After the time spent with Jill, *exhausting,* he'd had to hide her car and find another one. Fortunately, he'd overheard an old man talking to his son in the hospital. He was dying, being fast-tracked to hospice. Harland had little trouble tracking down the old guy's address and absconding with his rarely-used Buick that had been tucked away in his garage for close to a year.

His phone was vibrating on the bureau across the room. Dizzy, he got to his feet, took a few steps and almost passed out. "Fucking-fucking-fucking SNAKES!"

Caller ID said the number was blocked, but Harland knew who it was. No one else had this number.

"I'm here."

"I take it that was your handiwork, last night?" the baritone voice questioned on the other end of the line.

"Collateral damage. It's not like I enjoyed it or anything."

"Uh huh. And Chandler?"

"I have every expectation that part of the contract will be fulfilled today," Harland replied.

"Well, there's something else I'm sure you'll be interested in."

"What?"

"Rosette. She was wheels down in Phoenix this afternoon—she's probably there in Kingman now."

Harland let that sink in for a beat. "Here?"

"Apparently Chandler voluntarily gave up his prints and DNA to the local PD. So you're going to have a whole lot of company in that hell-hole of a town in the next few hours."

Harland was having a hard time believing Chandler was the same man he'd known. "So what do you want me to do?"

"We want both of them. Alive."

"No. That was not our deal. You know what this is about for me, Dwight!"

"Don't say that name again; I won't warn you again."

"Let me take care of the two of them. Same contract, same price. Think of it as my way of making up for voicing your name."

There was silence on the other end of the line. Eventually, the man spoke again. "We want them apprehended and confined. Keep them alive until we question them. After that, you can do with them whatever you want."

Harland let it play out in his mind. He'd take Rosette right in front of Chandler—make him watch. Chandler would beg him to stop. Then Harland would kill her ever so slowly. Chandler's death would come only when he'd been beaten and humiliated. It wouldn't make up for Harland's own loss, but it sure would go a long way.

"Okay, I can live with that. I'll be in contact."

He lay down on the bed and tried to find a comfortable

position for his pounding, aching head.

Harland continued to stare up at the ceiling. "I really need to get up," he said out loud. He let his mind wander back to familiar territory and its inevitable replay of the same images, like a filmstrip run in slow motion: Chandler, hearing a sound, spins to his left. He raises his weapon and shoots. Two quick pulls of the trigger and Veronica's chest erupts in a wash of dark red. She looks surprised, confused. She then begins to drop; her hands rise up, but then fall limply to her side. She falls to the ground. Her eyes are open, but then slowly close. She's gone. Harland's wife is dead.

Harland sat up and swung his feet to the carpeted floor. *I'm certainly not accomplishing anything lying around here. Chandler will be making his way over to the hospital, and I'll be there waiting for him.*

PART 2

REMEMBERED

CHAPTER 15

I continued to listen to the drone of the big diesel engine. Practically empty, the bus to the Kingman Regional Medical Center allowed me several minutes to think. The problem was, the dots just didn't connect. What was I missing? I started from the beginning, with the well-planned highway hit on my life. Why go to so much trouble? Seemed overly elaborate, when a bullet to my head would have sufficed just as well. No ... whoever did this wanted it to look like an accident. I let that sit for now and moved on to ponder again who and what I'd been in my past life: highly capable in close-combat situations; riddled with bodily scars and bullet holes; bearing an affinity to orderliness and the military. Definitely a soldier at one time, but not recently. So what did that leave? I was some kind of policeman? No, that didn't feel right, either. The obvious conclusion was agency: FBI, CIA, DHS? Yes, that did feel right and it fit. Okay, so I am—or was—an agent. I let my mind wander to the bald-headed man. Another agent? An agent assigned to kill me—to rig the ridiculously elaborate highway accident?

I sat up straight in my seat. *Shit!* Had the bald guy, agent, whatever, somehow killed Jill? Killed her to get to me? He definitely had recognized me—he knew who I was.

I leaned forward, elbows on my knees, massaging my temples. *Where the fuck are my memories? How long will this amnesia last?* Frustrated, I kicked the back of the bench seat in front of me. I saw the bus driver's head tilt up and his eyes lock on mine from his elevated rearview mirror.

The bus pulled to the curb. This was my stop.

* * *

Middle-aged and wearing a floral blouse with hues of light pink and blue, the woman sitting at the reception counter was reading. I peeked into her mind:

As his passion grew—so had hers. She was instantly lost in his musky scent, his raw masculinity. Strong, rough hands enveloped her small hips and pulled her in close. She resisted, feigned objection, but they both knew she wanted him to continue, to dominate her ...

I cleared my throat, startling her. She folded and creased the top corner of the page and placed the paperback book down on the desk in front of her. She smiled and raised her eyebrows. Cheeks flushed and breathy, she said, "Hi, I'm Connie. How can I direct you?" in a friendly, albeit business-like manner.

"I'm actually not sure. I was recently a patient here. Released yesterday."

The woman nodded.

"While I was here I had made friends with another patient. I'd like to visit him, check in on him."

"That's nice; I'm sure he'll appreciate the gesture." She brought her eyes over to a computer monitor off to her right, her fingers poised over a keyboard. "What's his name? I'll give you his room number."

"Well, that's the thing. I can't remember ... But I can describe him. Would that help?"

Connie pursed her lips and continued to look at the monitor. "No, not really. Sorry, physical descriptions aren't listed," she said with a shrug and looked back up at me.

"He had an injured hand. Bald head?"

She was still shaking her head, then abruptly stopped. I knew what she was going to say before she said it.

"Wait. I know exactly who you're talking about. Snakebite victim. Snakebites, multiple, actually." Her fingers were tapping at her keyboard, her lips pursed again. "Yeah, I remember, he bolted in the middle of the night. He'd given the hospital a phony name. Skipped out on paying his not-insignificant bill."

I presented an astonished expression and looked speechless. "He seemed, I don't know, like a good guy. I guess you never know ... you know, who someone really is?"

"I guess not," she replied.

"I'll let you get back to your book. Thanks anyway."

As I turned to leave, something in my pocket vibrated. The pager Whittier had given me so he could stay in touch. I retrieved the small device, and saw the illuminated phone number. I turned back to Connie. "I need to find a phone for a local call."

"Right over there in reception; pick it up and I'll patch you to a local line," she said and smiled.

"Thanks." I sat down on a brown leatherette couch and when the phone rang, I snatched up the receiver. I mouthed a 'thank you' to Connie and dialed the phone number on the pager.

On the third ring, Whittier answered. "Rob?"

"Yeah. You paged me?"

"Yes, I did. I wanted to let you know your results came back quicker than I'd expected. I have your identity."

"Excellent. So who am I?"

"Your full name's Robert Michael Chandler. But listen, I'm in a meeting right now. There's quite a bit to go over here. You have an interesting past, Rob. Nothing to worry about, but I want to go through all this in person—if that's all right?"

I tried to read Whittier's thoughts through the phone. Nothing.

"Are you close? Where exactly are you right now?"

"I'm on the other side of town, taking care of some business. How about I come by in the morning? I can be there first thing—how's that sound?"

"Uhh, actually today's better. Tomorrow's pretty packed. Will be in and out all day. Why don't you finish up your business and come on over when you can, later this afternoon? I can stay late if necessary."

I heard nervousness in his voice. Sure, he was trying to sound nonchalant, but there was an almost desperate undertone. Pleading. Something was askew.

"Well, I certainly am excited to discover more about my identity. How about I see where I'm at in an hour and ring you back?"

"Sure. I'll be here," he replied.

I replaced the receiver onto its cradle and continued to look at the phone. There was something wrong ... Whittier was putting up a cool act. Feigned indifference. One thing was for certain: there was no way I was going to stroll into the Kingman Police Station without having more information first.

* * *

Pippa and Giles had arrived at the Kingman Police Station fifteen minutes earlier. They'd been rushed into the small, cramped conference room where they'd been introduced to the light-eyed black detective. They traded information, neither providing full disclosure. Now, looking at the center of the metal table, Pippa realized she'd been holding her breath. As she heard Rob's familiar voice amplified on the speakerphone, memories flooded back into her consciousness. She wanted to call out to him. *Why, Rob? Why no contact for all these months? Tell me—had it all been some kind of ruse?* But she said nothing, maintaining an expression of indifference.

Whittier tapped the disconnect button on the speakerphone.

Giles was the first to speak. "So that's it. Chandler will show up in a few hours and we'll take custody. Be out of your hair."

Before Whittier could answer, Barns entered the small conference room and handed Whittier several pieces of paper. He scanned them and placed them facedown on the table. Barns pulled out a chair and sat next to his partner.

"Sorry, that's not going to happen," Wittier said, matter-of-factly. "As of right now, Chandler has become our number one suspect in the death of Jill Wrigley—the nurse from Kingman Regional Med."

"That's ridiculous! I know Chandler. He'd never do anything like that!" Pippa blurted out her objection, with stronger indignation than she'd intended.

Whittier crossed his arms over his chest and leaned back in his chair. He stared back at Pippa for several beats before speaking. "From what I've read about Chandler—hell, from what you've told me yourselves—he's a trained killer. Possibly even a rogue agent? And add to that, he's been in a horrendous car accident where he's sustained head trauma—has amnesia. Hell ... he may think he's on some kind of mission. Who knows what's going on inside his head?"

"Chandler's not a murderer—"

"Hold on, just hear me out," Whittier said, casually lifting a palm in her direction. "Detective Barns conducted some interviews at the hospital. Apparently Chandler and the nurse had become close. She was observed by an orderly giving Rob both clothes and money. They exchanged a kiss."

Pippa's heart sank. Realization was sinking in. Had she been played? Been made a fool of?

Giles' voice brought her back to the present. "You know as well as I do that our government warrant trumps any local jurisdiction, Detective Whittier. Let's just get our hands on him and worry later about who'll be bringing him to justice."

CHAPTER 16

The midday Arizona sun was bright and relentless as I exited the medical center's front lobby. I'd interrupted the receptionist one more time, pulling her away from a particularly steamy passage midway into her romance novel. She'd told me the closest Internet Café where I could get online was several blocks up. I needed to pass under the U.S. 93 interchange and a mini-mall would be on my left. The café would be next door to the Kingman Co. Steak House.

I headed east along the sidewalk that paralleled Stockton Hill Road. Now, equipped with my full name, I'd be able to run a search. How many Robert Michael Chandlers could there possibly be? I'd also be able to query social media sites, such as Facebook and LinkedIn. Feeling hopeful, I stepped beneath the freeway overpass. *Ah—shade at last.* I looked up and listened to the *swoosh swoosh swoosh* of cars and trucks speeding along one hundred feet over my head.

A blue Nissan Murano SUV, traveling in my same direction, passed me, slowed, and made a U-turn. It pulled to the curb across the street, some twenty feet away. Thinking it was someone lost, perhaps someone needing directions, I watched as the driver opened his door and stepped out of the vehicle. Two things converged into my thoughts simultaneously. One, I was looking into the muzzle of a Glock 19, currently the most popular handgun sold in the United States. How I knew that, I had no idea. The second thing to intrude into my thoughts was the smiling face behind the Glock 19. The bald-headed man. The same man who had tortured and later killed a pretty young nurse named Jill. In the time it took me to access his mind, make sense of all its firing synapses, and process the subsequent imagery that was spewing forth, I knew I no longer needed to visit the Internet Café.

In a flash, in a mind-bending rush that could best be compared to falling off a cliff, wind buffeting my face, my eyes watering as adrenalin elevates my pounding heart rate into the stratosphere, the pieces come together. And then, as I plummet faster and faster toward my inevitable fate, and the ever-approaching solid ground below, I remember. I remember the man who's standing before me. I remember everything. I hesitated and watched a line of blurry shadows, moving in rhythm to the sounds of the highway above; countless indecipherable black shapes, dancing across the concrete. As if a shroud had been lifted, sight granted to a blind man, I welcomed home the lost memories of my lifetime.

"You look like shit, Harland," I said.

"Thank you. Get in the car. You're driving." He raised the Glock to underscore his demand. "Slowly. No quick movements."

I slowly walked in his direction, crossing the street. He moved away from the open driver- side door—his weapon now at his side, pointed at my chest. I needed to take as much time as possible—I still had some mental catching up to do.

I ground my teeth as more memories surfaced. Yes, I had killed his Veronica in Moscow—done so without any hesitation. Harland was there to witness her death, first hand.

As he cradled her lifeless body in his arms, I did my best to get him away, but he was lost in misery—frenzied, and vowing to kill me. As approaching sirens blared, I took flight—needing to go to ground. He had been well aware of my suspicions that day: she was a double agent. He was just as adamant that I was mistaken. Abruptly, she had pulled a weapon—she knew the jig was up and she had every intention of taking me out—right then and there.

Espionage is often a tangled web of half-truths, if not outright deceit. Moles are commonplace. At any given time, the CIA has an infestation of many. The rank-and-file agent-asset is often unaware of who is, and who is not, suspected of being a double agent. But Veronica, an eight-year CIA operative, had fooled everyone. She was that good. In an almost freakish chain of events, I had discovered her true allegiance. She was actually an agent for the SVR, the CIA's Russian counterpart. If I lived, her cover would be blown, would fall apart like a house of cards, and her corpse found floating dead in the Volga.

Mere hours before her death, Veronica had already blown Harland's and my cover. The SVR was everywhere. Safe houses had been compromised—I had little in the way of viable options to evade capture and certain death. I had one slim hope. I had made a friend, of sorts. Ladislav Skykora, another agent, was a Slovakian national and no friend to Russia. I made it to his small flat. Reluctantly, he kept me out of sight. Since his phones were tapped and he was soon put on the watch list, communications with the Agency would have to wait. Two weeks later, Skykora informed me that I had been Agency disavowed: determined to be a rogue agent. Putting the pieces together now, it was evident that Harland did make it safely out of Russia. He'd also lied, saying I killed Veronica and that I, not she, was the traitor.

It would be many months before I could get out of Russia. There was also a heavy price exacted for my yearlong refuge there. If and when I got out of Russia, I had a job to do for Ladislav Skykora: a mission, of sorts, that would take place in Kingman, Arizona. After that, Skykora, and the people he worked for, would validate my innocence. Do what they could to clear my name with the Agency.

Harland took another step back as I approached. He gestured with his gun for me to get in behind the wheel.

I paused in front of him, looked into his eyes. "Veronica was SVR. I was doing my job. You were blinded, Harland, from seeing the truth."

Harland's smile remained. It was his eyes that conveyed the true hatred he was feeling. I was in his thoughts—thoughts that were reeling, spinning in circles, always returning to a singular driving hub—getting revenge. He was replaying the events of the previous night. It was Jill's face, tears streaming down her cheeks, her lips quivering—then gasping for breath—her final—last—desperate—breath.

As I had done so easily with Russell, in our run-in at Denny's, and with Benny, at Motel 6, I tried to transmit my own thoughts into his: *I will enjoy snapping your neck, asshole.* But my emotions, my hatred for Harland was so all encompassing I was unable to synchronize to his mind. I needed to get my raging hatred under control—but that seemed unlikely at this point. I was definitely at a disadvantage until I brought some measure of detachment into my thoughts.

I sat down in the driver's seat and watched him move around the front of the vehicle, gun still pointed at my head. He opened the passenger-side door and climbed in.

Now, sitting close to Harland, I noticed his breath was foul. The pallor of his skin was pasty and perspiration was beaded on his brow. He looked like death warmed-over. His left hand was bandaged, with a yellow and green discharge seeping through the gauze.

Harland, seeing my interest in his hand, smiled. "Fucking snakes."

I nodded. "What have you been doing with yourself, Harland?"

"You mean after you shot my wife in the heart? Well … I left the Agency. Went independent. Which has given me time to look for you. So I could make you suffer. Destroy your life, as you have destroyed mine. But you want to know the best part?"

"Sure, what's the best part?"

"There are others who want you. Others, who are just as hell-bent on finding you as I am; people willing to pay me handsomely for apprehending you. Imagine my delight at the prospect of being paid to nab you."

"I'm glad things have worked out for you. So now what? Kill me? Finally get revenge?"

Harland smiled as if he was in on some kind of inside joke. I've learned over the last few days in observing other people's thoughts, *mind reading*, that it isn't a complete brain dump. Their older cognitive memories aren't mine to peruse, like files saved on a computer hard drive. I am able to read someone's thoughts, but usually only when those thoughts first screen across his mind. Sometimes I also pickup on stray, or errant, images—those evoking strong emotions, which may relate to something else entirely. Such insights, collectively, allow me to piece together a better understanding. So, when Harland's mind flashed to his current employer, someone named Dwight, I realized Harland had mixed feelings, more than a little fear, when it came to the guy. And there was something else. I wasn't the only one he'd been contracted to apprehend. Memories were continuing to seep into my consciousness.

Pippa walks away from me. I hear the sound of her laughing at something, and then she looks back over her shoulder at me. A strand of hair catches at the corner of her perfect mouth. She turns and continues to walk backward, away from me, still laughing. Playful. I take all of her in at once: her long legs—legs that have stopped traffic. She's saying something to me and, just like that, her expression changes—what is that expression? That face she's making? It's a wonderful mixture of competing emotions ... innocence and sultriness ... confidence and insecurity. She's beckoning me now; gesturing me to follow her into the bedroom.

When Harland speaks, the sudden vision, my own memory of Pippa, fades like wisps of a cloud. And with the sound of his voice I know Harland will stop at nothing to kill her—he'll kill her as I'm forced to watch.

Harland gestured to the street ahead. "Drive, fuckface."

CHAPTER 17

"You know, this is really an interesting city," Harland said.

I focused on a rocky plateau ahead in the distance then looked out the side window toward another rocky plateau. Everything was the color of dirt. Just a lot of sameness.

"I'll take your word for it," I replied. I needed to quell my emotions, but just hearing him speak only ratcheted up my need for revenge—my anger.

"The city of Kingman has two sections: the newer, more substantial, industrialized and commercial areas where the Regional Medical Center is located, and then there's the historic Route 66 section, along the southwestern side of the city. That's where we're headed. Turn left here."

I made the turn as instructed, while monitoring Harland's thoughts. Not that I was an expert on the workings of the human mind, but I had several days' experience of life-in-the-trenches mind-meddling. There was a similarity—a spectrum of thoughts, emotions, desires, and a whole range of cognitive thought patterns that, for the most part, were not so different from person A to person B. But Harland's mind wasn't functioning within that spectrum. Not even close. Manic and paranoid, his thoughts came in rapid-fire bursts. Often, nonsensical conversations would play over and over again, then abruptly cease and he would be functional, almost normal. I felt Harland's eyes on me and then saw what he was mentally conjuring: Pippa, her head pulled back—her chin forced forward—Harland's fingers entwined in her long blonde hair. He's pulling harder now, forcing her neck forward. His eyes never leave mine. He's smiling. He brings the knife, no ... the scalpel up and slowly, almost delicately, draws the razor-sharp edge across the mid-point on her neck.

I slammed on the brakes. Wheels locked and the SUV fishtailed in the middle of the street. Harland careened forward and his bandaged hand thumped against the dashboard in front of him. Cars behind honked.

"What the hell!" Harland barked, cradling his injured hand. He jammed the Glock deep into my ribs. "Another move like that, and I'll end you. You understand?"

His face was close—putrid breath hot on my cheek. I nodded my head. Several cars from behind us passed and, once clear, I accelerated into traffic again. The pain in my side wasn't subsiding. I might have had a broken rib.

"As I was saying, a lot of history here, Chandler. Two hundred years ago this was nothing but old trails laid out by early explorers. Soon it became a well-worn wagon route that helped establish Kingman as a trade and transportation center."

"Fascinating," I said.

"Uh huh, and in 1857, I think, or maybe it was 1858—

anyway, a Lt. Edward Fitzgerald Beale ambled across the present site of Kingman. A surveyor by trade, the once-old wagon road along the 35th parallel later became the infamous Route 66."

We were entering a section of town where the architecture was late nineteenth century, early twentieth century. Brick and slump-stone buildings, topped with ornate crown cornices, populated both sides of the street. Some looked to have been caringly restored to their original splendor, while other properties were nothing more than long-abandoned, dilapidated hulks—no visual similarity to their past glory evident.

"Now listen, Chandler. I don't want you to judge this place by its somewhat seedy exterior. I've gone to a lot of trouble procuring this hideaway. There's a certain charm about the place. I've been making some modifications to your accommodations, you know, to ensure your stay here will be fruitful. For all concerned."

We were approaching 4th Street and I brought the Murano to a stop at the intersection. Across the street, on the adjacent corner and taking up a full street block, was a faded pink building. High above, supported by a collection of steel support struts, was a massive discolored sign:

BEALE HOTEL
AIR-COOLED

As was common back when a room with a view wasn't so important, the hotel had several rows of dark and narrow windows. It was evident that plywood sheets, now dark and rotting, obscured every opening—every doorway.

Harland instructed me to turn right and then make the

next left. Halfway down what was more of an alleyway than an actual road, Harland indicated where I should park. He opened the passenger-side door. "Hold on till I come around and fetch you," he said.

I needed to make my move soon. I had a pretty good idea what Harland wanted—and it wasn't something I had any intention of allowing to happen.

Harland came around the front of the Murano with his gun steady, pointing in my direction. Once he stood directly outside the driver-side door, about eight feet away, he gestured for me to get out.

"Slowly, Chandler," Harland said, from the middle of the alley.

I had my emotions somewhat reeled in. Had stopped thinking about Jill and had settled down my accelerated heart rate. A plan had formulated in my head. Within the next few moments I'd give him a mental suggestion—something abrupt and frightening, perhaps that a car was coming, about to run him over. He'd be startled and turn. That's when I'd make my move.

I stepped from the SUV and swung the door closed. The alleyway was deserted—nothing for seventy-five yards in either direction. Harland hadn't bothered to look at anything but me. This just might work. I took a step and then another. He was letting me come closer. Perfect. I wanted to look defeated. Apprehensive. I slowed, reluctantly walking to what would most assuredly be my final resting place.

"Move it, Chandler!" He stepped in and grabbed for my arm. But it wasn't my mental suggestion, a goliath, Peterbilt tractor-trailer barreling down on him that caught his attention. No. It was the sound of a pager. The pager vibrating in my front right pocket. My mental suggestion, poised to enter into Harland's consciousness, evaporated …

and with it so went my opportunity.

"What is that?" Harland asked.

I shrugged. "I don't know, I thought it was you." The vibrating had stopped. His eyes continued to stare at my front pocket.

"Slowly, take it out."

I did as I was told. I looked at the last incoming phone number. It was Whittier.

"Who even uses a pager these days?" Harland asked, irritated. "Show me the number."

I showed him the end of the pager with the displayed phone number.

"Who is that? Who called you?"

"Your mother. We have a thing."

Harland brought the Glock up to my face.

"The police. I'm a suspect in the murder of a young nurse."

Harland's demeanor once again changed. Thinking that funny, his smile was back and apparently all was well with the world. "Okay, this way. Let's go." He gestured down the alleyway with his chin, toward the back of the Beale Hotel. Again, my hatred for him was all consuming.

I continued on down the alleyway with Harland, gun in hand, several paces behind me. The back of the faded-pink building stood there, fifty yards in front of us. Ominous, it seemed to be beckoning—*come closer*. Dark, blood-colored rust stains streamed from a hundred blackened window openings. Electrical and telephone cables converged, like tendrils, at strategic locations midway down the hotel's exterior rear wall.

As we approached the hotel's rear parking lot, Harland surveyed the area—ensuring we hadn't been observed. "There."

From what I could see, thick wood planks were nailed across two rear-entry doorways; the hotel was sealed up tighter than a drum. With another flick of the Glock I saw where I was supposed to go. On a secondary wall, maybe eight feet high, and out some ten feet from the back of the hotel, there was a cubbyhole. Must have been used to obscure several large, industrial-sized dumpsters. As I came around the corner all I saw was debris. Broken bottles, several sets of twisted pink venetian blinds, a large gray couch—its yellowed foam rubber, like a gutted whale, spewing from center cushions. A large rat scurried across the concrete and disappeared into the back wall of the hotel.

"Home sweet home," Harland said, eyebrows raised. "Move the couch out of the way."

I shuffled through the garbage, kicked a broken toilet seat out of my way, and positioned myself behind the couch. I shoved it over to the far wall. There, on the concrete, was a square metal grate approximately three feet wide by four feet long.

"Okay, back up against the wall. Don't move." Not taking his eyes from me, he knelt down, laid the Glock at his feet and pulled a set of keys from his jacket pocket. He unlocked two ancient-looking padlocks and pocketed both. He retrieved his Glock and stood. "Okay, in we go."

"What do you mean, in we go?"

"Pull open the grate and get in there," Harland commanded.

I bent down and reached over and grabbed the metal bars with two hands. Pain shot through my right side, where Harland had cracked one of my ribs with the muzzle of his gun. I shifted my position and used more of my left arm and pulled the grate straight up. I stared down at the deep, dark, blackness below.

"It looks worse than it really is. Here, take this." Harland took out a small Maglight from his pocket and passed it over to me.

I looked at the ridiculously small flashlight and turned the top portion to illuminate the light's radius. "You have to be kidding."

"Just get in there. I'll be right behind you," Harland said, his annoyance rising.

CHAPTER 18

I had to put the flashlight between my teeth to use both hands. I lowered myself into the darkness. A smell wafted up that was beyond disgusting. I found the top of a metal-runged ladder and eased myself down. Ten feet below, my feet were on solid ground. I heard Harland above me coming down the ladder, then stopping. Light from above reflected off his gun, which was pointed at my head.

"Keep going. You're in a drainpipe. You may be thinking this is your opportunity to strike. To make your move. It's not. I've thought this through. I won't hesitate to shoot you, Chandler. Ten more paces and you'll come to another vertical rise. Once there, use your flashlight to tap on the bottom metal rung. Then I'll follow."

Harland was right. I was about to make my move. I walked forward, flashlight in hand. The beam of the light was shaking. My hand was shaking. The telltale signs that I needed to tap in. With a quick check, I discovered I could no longer read Harland's thoughts. I came to a juncture where the drain split off in two directions, up or straight down. I gave the bottom rung of the ladder going up a couple of taps.

"Up you go," Harland said, from the darkness behind me.

Flashlight in teeth again, I climbed. *Shit!* Ten feet up my head careened into something metal.

"Oh, forgot to mention, there's another metal grate up there ... did that too, my first time here," came Harland's voice from the intersecting pipes below.

With one hand secured on the top rung, I used the other to lift up on the heavy iron grate. I moved it aside and out of the way. I climbed out and stood in what looked to be a large supply closet.

"Step away. Move over to the door," Harland said, his voice echoing from below.

I looked for something that could be used as a weapon. Perhaps a pipe or piece of lumber. There was nothing.

Harland's bald head suddenly appeared from the open drain, shortly followed by his gun. "This is going quite smoothly, Rob. I'm glad you've been smart enough not to try anything. It would be a shame to have to kill you."

So now he was using my first name. Like best buddies.

Harland was out of the drain and gesturing toward the door. "It's unlocked."

I opened the door and stepped into a large room. Streams of sunlight filtered in from three boarded up windows, allowing just enough light for me to make out what must have been the hotel's main dining area. Several tables, each upturned onto their sides, sat in the middle of the room. Multi-colored graffiti filled the walls and several stained mattresses had been laid, side-by-side, to the left. At my feet lay a used condom and three hypodermic needles. I heard the sound of a rodent skittering around between the floors above.

"Before she was boarded up, this had become a refuge for the homeless. We don't need to worry about that now. No one comes here anymore. We have the place all to ourselves." Harland looked at me with his ever-present smile. Then his brow creased. "You're not looking so good, my friend."

"Must have had some bad moo goo gai pan last night. I'm fine," I said.

He directed me toward a large swinging door to my left that I assumed would lead into the kitchen.

"Stop. I go first."

Harland passed to one side and, facing me, backed into the door. Sure enough, it swung open into a kitchen area that I could barely make out behind him. "Follow me in; stay close, Rob."

Seeing Harland standing with his back to the opened door, half in and half out of the kitchen, I thought this would be my best, and perhaps only opportunity to make a move. Harland knew this as well.

"Don't even think about it," he said.

I stepped in closer, while he moved back, until the swinging door was held open with the toe of his shoe. Harland, like myself, was a trained operative. So it was a surprise to me when he decided to go through the doorway first. This put him in a precarious position. A mistake. When I heard the sound of my pager go off again, I knew my luck had changed for the better. It was only a fraction of a second that Harland's attention was diverted. Eyes again went to my pants pocket. And in that instant I kicked out. Catching him in the wrist, the Glock flew sideways, somewhere into the kitchen—which, at this point, was still mostly obscured from my view. Harland dove to his left as I rolled forward through the doorway. There was a loud clattering of metal hitting metal—a tower of rusted catering pans fell and became a jumbled mess on the floor. Harland thrashed about, frantically looking for his gun. I dove again, this time directly toward Harland. He lashed out, and the edge of a serving pan connected hard against my chin. My momentum carried me into him and together we rolled further into the kitchen. He'd lost the pan and was repeatedly punching me in the face. I found his left arm, felt the wrappings of his bandage. I slid my hand up his wrist until I found his hand and gripped harder. Harland screamed. I used all my strength until I heard one, if not more, of his already swollen hands' carpal bones crack.

Harland shrieked. His face, inches from my own, had turned red and tears flowed freely from his tightly squeezed eyes. I maintained the pressure on his hand as I moved onto my knees.

"Get up," I said.

The clanging continued as Harland tried to get his balance. Keeping him in close, I pulled him up until we were both standing. It was only then that I felt the muzzle of the gun pressed tightly against my left temple. Apparently he had found the Glock.

"Turn around. Very slowly."

I turned around. I felt something hit the back of my head and everything went black.

* * *

When I came to, I was lying on a concrete floor, cold

and gritty against my cheek. I watched as a cockroach tentatively approached me from several feet away. The pain at the back of my head came alive and throbbed. The slightest movement, even breathing, shot hot spikes through my head and into my eyes. I continued to watch the cockroach. It stopped and seemed to be investigating a small pool of liquid: my drool. How long had I been out? I tried to move my arms. They weren't bound—neither were my legs. I saw a light, a single low-wattage bulb in my peripheral vision. I turned my head and saw that a light bulb hung by a wire from a high ceiling rafter. Hot bile burned at the back of my throat. Slowly, I turned over onto my back. I was in the basement. Pipes of all sizes crisscrossed on the ceiling above and down the walls. Like ancient sentries, two black hot water boilers towered over me, as if keeping guard over this hellish, underground domain. I turned my head and saw that there was some kind of electrical generator. Rust beneath peeling green paint and a fountain of frayed copper wires were obvious signs that it was inoperable.

A creaking sound from above brought my still somewhat blurry vision over to a wooden platform against the slump stone wall on my left. No less than twelve feet off the ground there, next to a long, retractable extension ladder, sat Harland.

"Welcome back to the land of the living, Rob."

"Where am I?"

"Still at Kingman's beautiful Beale Hotel. We're in the basement, if you hadn't guessed that already."

I tried to sit up, and failed.

"You may want to take it slow, my friend. That's quite a conk you've got at the back of your head."

I managed another attempt and this time was able to stay up in a seated position. Harland was watching me, his legs swinging back and forth, hanging down from his high perch above.

"Make yourself comfortable. You're not going anywhere for a while. The only way into this cellar is through that opening above me. You see, I've removed the stairway. No small feat with only one working hand," he said, holding up his yellowy-green bandaged hand. "Understand, without this ladder, there's absolutely no way out for you."

"So why don't you just shoot me?"

"Come on. What fun would that be? No. I have other plans for you two."

"Two?"

"You and Pippa."

"What are you talking about? Pippa has nothing to do with this."

"Oh, but you're wrong about that. But all that will become more evident in time. Perhaps you two can figure it out together," Harland said. Watching, and seeing my confusion, he added, "You didn't know, did you?"

I stared back at him.

"She's here. I mean right here in Kingman."

"What the hell are you talking about?"

Harland stood, leaned down and came up with a thin square box. He threw it down onto the concrete floor in front of me. The box lid flew open revealing its pizza contents. He then tossed down a six-pack of plastic water bottles.

"I'd love to stay and chat, catch up and all that, but I've got a few errands to run. Enjoy the pizza."

CHAPTER 19

Pippa listened to the ringtone emanating from the speakerphone and then the follow up series of beeps. For three hours she'd been there, in the same claustrophobic conference room, along with Whittier, Barns and Giles. Each time they expected Chandler to respond to his pager beep and call back. Each time he hadn't.

"Look, it's late," Whittier finally said. "What do you say we give this a rest for the evening—try again first thing in the morning? You two must be tired and want to freshen up at your hotel."

Pippa ran her fingers through her hair and let out a long breath. She hadn't planned on staying overnight. Yes, she'd packed an overnight bag, but that had only been for the remote off- chance she'd need to stay here, which now, evidently, she would. She nodded and pulled her chair away from the table.

Whittier said, "I've put out an APB on Chandler. Kingman isn't that big of a town. I've put two additional teams on overtime so we're actively out there looking for him."

Pippa nodded. "Thank you, Detective Whittier; we appreciate that."

"No problem. Why don't you call me Bruce?"

"Okay, Bruce. So where's a good place to crash tonight that will fit within the government's per diem?"

"There's the Ramblin' Rose Motel a few miles up the road. Kinda nice, especially if you're into the whole Route 66 nostalgia thing. Next door to that you'll find a Quality Inn."

"Yeah, I think Quality Inn will be fine. Thanks," she said.

Giles shook both Whittier's and Barns' hands. "Let's talk food. I bet you have outrageous Mexican here, am I right?" Excited, he rubbed both palms together in anticipation of their response.

Barns and Whittier looked at each other, then Barns pointed a finger at Giles. "I bet you'd like El Charro."

Giles repeated the name slowly, then again with more of an ethnic flavor to "El Chaaaa-rrr-ooo. Yes, I think I need some of that."

"Good. It's right across from the Quality Inn. Can't miss it; right next to the Kingman Club, with the two neon martini glasses sign," Barns said.

Giles slightly turned his head and gave Barns a sly look. "Martini Club. What a combination. Have ourselves a little Mexican feast and stroll on over to the Martini Club for a nightcap."

"All right, that's enough, Giles," Pippa said, feeling her patience stretched to the breaking point.

* * *

In the police station's rear parking lot, Pippa resumed her position behind the wheel of their rental car. Once Giles had strapped himself in, she pulled the car around the building and eased onto North Main Street.

They drove in silence for several minutes before Giles turned in his seat. "Say half-hour to clean up, wash the day off ourselves, and then hit the town?"

Pippa gave Giles a weary smile and shook her head. "You know, I think I'm just going to hang out in my room tonight. You go. Enjoy yourself."

Giles nodded and let the car become quiet as they drove down Main Street. "I know this is tough on you, Pippa. It was no secret that you and Chandler had a thing. I can see you're hurting, and I'm sorry."

Pippa was startled by Giles' unexpected words of compassion. Although annoyed her personal life was once again brought up for discussion, when she looked over at him she saw he was sincere—meant what he'd said.

"Thank you, Giles. I appreciate that. I'll be fine."

"Good. Half-hour; be ready to go ... we're going to El Chaaaa-rrr-ooo!"

They pulled into the Quality Inn's parking lot. Pippa was smiling. "Why not? El Chaaaa-rrr-ooo, it is."

* * *

Giles knocked on Pippa's door twenty minutes later. She'd barely had a chance to shower and brush her teeth when she heard him knocking. "Hold on," she yelled. "You're ten minutes early, for God's sake."

She finished getting dressed. Jeans, T-shirt, and sneakers

were all she had packed—it would have to be good enough. She opened the door several inches and walked back toward the bathroom, toweling her hair dry.

Giles let himself in and plunked himself down on her bed. Pippa applied a fresh coat of lipstick and pinched her cheeks, hoping she could put a little color back into her pale Scandinavian complexion. She looked around the corner at Giles. Although wearing the same dress slacks he'd worn earlier, he was now wearing a soft pastel pink shirt. She could smell his sickening cologne.

"You! In here—now," she said sternly, pointing at Giles.

He looked up surprised and pointed his own finger back at himself. "Me?"

Giles got off the bed and nervously joined Pippa in front of the bathroom mirror.

"You want to have dinner with me?"

He nodded.

"Maybe get a quick drink at the Kingman Club afterword?"

He nodded again.

"Okay, then. You need to get that cologne off your body. Every bit of it. Stay in here until it's gone and never ever wear that shit around me again. Got it?"

Giles nodded. Looking somewhat hurt, but not putting up any resistance, he started to remove his shirt.

"Better yet, go back to your own room. I'll come by and get you in ten minutes."

Ten minutes later, Pippa was at Giles' door. At a quarter past seven, it was still relatively light outside. Before she could knock, the door opened and Giles came out, wearing a new light green shirt and smelling much better. He passed her by and headed for the stairs. She followed after him, hurrying down the stairs, and together they crossed over Main Street toward the row of 1950s-era shops and restaurants.

What looked like a sleepy little hole-in-the-wall joint from the outside was anything but sleepy on the inside, they discovered. Mariachi music filled the space. At the far side of the restaurant, on a small stage, there was a five-man band playing: two trumpets, two guitars—one was ginormous—and a violin. Giles was feeling it—moving his feet in what, Pippa guessed, was some kind of Salsa step. The truth was, he was pretty good. Pippa couldn't help herself from laughing out loud. When he grabbed her hand and spun her around, she tried to push him away. He'd have none of that and soon she was doing her best to keep up. She knew how to salsa ... and cha-cha and mamba. Others were getting to their feet and soon most everyone was dancing.

By the time they sat down for dinner they were both spent.

"You've got some moves there, Giles," Pippa said, grabbing for a menu. She had found her appetite. Giles flagged down a waitress and ordered two margaritas—yes, of course, with salt.

Pippa had decided early in the evening to let the situation with Chandler wait until morning. Although Giles was a buffoon, he was a well-intentioned one. When their meals arrived they both ate with gusto. Two more drinks arrived and, with a bit more coaxing from Giles, more dancing ensued as well. Yes, she thought to herself, tomorrow it's back to business.

CHAPTER 20

Harland indeed had errands to run. Step one was to obtain a boatload of both Co-trimoxazole antibiotics and Demerol—his painkillers of choice. Not as difficult to find as one might think. Harland was well aware that virtually every city had an underground means to obtain pharmaceuticals. Pricy, but what else could one do with an infected hand from multiple snakebites? Add to that the recent fractures to his thumb ... He needed the meds at any price.

Harland sat in his car, having just finished cleaning his infected hand. The black market pharmaceutical punk had thrown in a bottle of Isopropyl rubbing alcohol and several rolls of hospital-grade gauze and medical tape. He'd already downed the antibiotics and enough Demerol to keep a horse off its feet for a week. Three more wraps of the gauze around his wrist and he was done. He placed two strips of tape around the gauze to secure it in place. He turned his hand over several times to inspect his work. *Not too bad.*

Harland's second errand was to locate Pippa Rosette. With little effort he had earlier found where she and her fellow agent, someone named Giles, were staying the night. Two hours on the phone talking to a myriad of hotel reception-desk bimbos had paid off. It's amazing what a little friendly chatter can produce. And when they discover he's a high-ranking government official with the FBI or CIA or DHS ... whatever, they bend over backward to help. Pippa—Quality Inn, single occupancy, second floor, room number 256; she'd requested a queen-sized bed ...

Harland listened to the tic tic tic of the Murano's engine as it cooled. He watched the outside stairway that led to the second floor of the inn. He already knew she currently wasn't in her room, but there, parked out front, was her rental car.

Harland's attention shifted to a group of tourists casually walking the sidewalk in front of restaurants, bars and closed antique shops. His gaze settled on two couples; maybe they were friends, or even family—perhaps brothers and sisters? Their faces became blurred-out circles, like how TV shows sometimes hide people's identities. Now, other people's faces took their place. This had happened to him before. People he'd killed, or people he wanted to kill, or sometimes even his own face would appear on someone else's body. He was well aware his mind was caught in a frenetic loop that was becoming more and more an issue. It was one thing to be crazy but oblivious to it; it was quite another thing to know—to slowly lose grip on your own mind, your sanity—and to be cognizant of it all. Unfortunately, it was getting increasingly worse. He wondered, *could grief really make a person go crazy?* He thought of his Veronica. No, not grief, but maybe hatred could. And oh how he hated him ... Chandler needed to suffer, just as he had suffered. Harland felt his anger building, erupting from deep within him, and realized, as if watching from outside himself, that this particular psychotic episode—where negative emotions were feeding on one another, spiraling upward into a virtual tornado of hatred—he was about to lose it. Harland's vision had turned red. Now, with a steady, determined effort, he reined in his oh so crazy mind.

Harland reached for the cellphone sitting on the passenger seat. A cheap burner phone, he was getting his money's worth out of it. He was fairly certain Pippa's phone number hadn't changed. He placed the phone on his thigh and brought up his text-messaging app.

Pippa… it's Rob. I need to talk to you… to see you. Back parking lot.

Harland pocketed the phone and climbed from the Nissan Murano. Just as the group of tourists had done, he walked along the row of shops and restaurants. He smiled at an elderly lady walking with a cane. He turned left on the sidewalk that led to the rear of the buildings, where there were overflow parking slots.

* * *

Giles was paying the bill when Pippa felt her phone vibrate with two quick bursts. She pulled it from her back pocket and read and then reread the message.

"We need to go. Now!" Pippa held up her phone to Giles and let him read the message for himself.

His eyes went from the phone to hers and he nodded. "We'll split up."

She felt adrenalin pumping into her bloodstream but knew she wouldn't be at her best. Too much alcohol. *Damn!*

Pippa made her way to the back of the restaurant where a narrow hallway led to men's and women's restrooms and an exit door beyond that. She stopped at the exit door and breathed in. Consciously, she slowed her heart rate and cleared her mind—a simple practice she had perfected over the years as an agent. But the thought of seeing Chandler again was too much for her mini-meditation exercise, and excitement eclipsed her every thought.

She pushed open the door and stepped into the night. When the text had come in, she noticed it was 10:45 p.m. It was not a large parking lot and not very well lit. Three light poles for an area as long as a football field. Her phone vibrated in her hand.

I see you. Go north. Back row of cars. Look for a yellow minivan.

Pippa was well aware it could be someone else. A ruse to get her alone—isolated. She texted back:

Not getting any closer until you show yourself. If you are who you say you are, prove it.

Pippa sent the message and saw that it had been delivered. Immediately, three dots appeared. He was texting her back. As she waited for the reply, she heard a sound off in the distance. A quick cough and then a rustling—like feet on pavement. Pippa ran. She shoved her phone into her back pocket, then pulled open her purse and retrieved her Glock 22. Right arm and hand stretched out holding her weapon, left one held out and cradling—supporting the Glock from beneath. She moved north down the center row of cars. She slowed her stride and fell into cautionary alertness, what years of training had taught her. She checked behind and all around—lowered, and widened her search. She'd passed the last of the three light poles thirty yards back and was coming to the end of the lot. Something yellow in the distance caught her attention. *Was that a minivan?* She slowed and listened, before moving in closer. She felt two quick vibrations in her pocket. An incoming text. Pippa moved in between two cars. Another quick look around and she pulled her phone from her pocket. But it wasn't Chandler this time, it was from Giles' phone.

Got him! North end of the lot - Hew yah!

Pippa pocketed her phone and cautiously continued down the last row of parked cars. Definitely a minivan, and it was definitely yellow. With two cars in front of her, she was coming up on the right side of the van. There was no one there. Then a sound came from the van's other side. Pippa brought her weapon up higher. One step and then another, she slowly moved around the front of the vehicle. Outstretched legs came into view. One leg moved. Pippa spun and surveyed the terrain around her. No one was there. She continued moving until the figure on the ground was in full view. He coughed and blood sputtered from his mouth onto his light green shirt.

Pippa ran to Giles' side. His throat had been cut. A gaping trench stretched evenly from one ear to the other. His eyes were locked on hers—pleading—desperately wanting to be saved. She felt his hand grip her wrist. Only then was she aware that blood was all around her—she was kneeling in it. As blood spilled from his open wound, his eyes lost focus. A final sputter and his breathing ceased. Giles was dead. Her mind raced. *I'm going to kill you, Chandler ... So help me God.*

It was then that she was aware that someone was standing right behind her.

CHAPTER 21

I must have slept for several hours. The cockroach on the floor was gone, and Harland was gone from the perch above. I sat up slowly and felt dizzy. My head was pounding and the telltale signs of withdrawal had increased. *I really need to tap in.* I crawled to where the bottled waters lay next to the open pizza box. I drank two bottles straight away. My roach friend was feasting on the pizza and he'd brought along a friend. I flicked them away and proceeded to eat one piece and then another. Even cold, they tasted good.

I needed to do something. Come up with a plan while Harland was still away. I surveyed my surroundings. The basement looked to be about sixty feet wide by one hundred and fifty feet long. Walls were gray slump stone about the same color as the concrete floor. Black and rusted pipes entered the space from above, as well as from the sides and from below. The two boilers, each twelve feet high, cast long dark shadows in front of me.

On what I guessed was the south wall there was a wooden bench—what must have been the hotel maintenance guy's fixit area. Several tools were lying about, as well as a small toolbox. I'd be surprised if Harland hadn't already checked it for sharp objects that could be used as a weapon. At the far end of the bench was a twenty-year-old coffee maker, which was still plugged into an electrical outlet.

On the other side of the basement were all the wall-mounted, ancient-looking electrical panels. But what captured most of my attention was big and rusted, with patches of pea-green paint. It was the hotel's electrical backup generator—about the size of a large industrial-sized washing machine.

With the exception of the one hundred and ten volts powering the single light bulb overhead, my options were limited for tapping in. What I needed was high-voltage—220 volts would be good. Looking at the obviously inoperable generator, with parts of it disconnected and wires hanging free, I wondered if it could be repaired.

My father, Bill Chandler, was an electrician of sorts—as well as a plumber and a carpenter. He was the guy you'd go to who'd fix or build virtually anything. In the small town of Moulton, Texas, population around 900, trust and reputation trumped everything, including those who had acquired appropriate tradesman licenses. I smiled as memories flooded back into my mind—memories that just yesterday I had no recollection of. I wondered if my parents were still alive, still living in the Midwest on the same small four-acre farm I grew up on? It was a simple life, and I realized right then how much I missed them both.

As a teenager, I was my father's helper. Sometimes paid, usually not. After school there was always something needing to be done: be it building a barn, pulling out wires or old conduit, rewiring a neighbor's furnace, or the starter motor on Mom's old Ford Taurus. I learned how things worked—I learned how to repair things when replacement parts were no longer available or the cost of a new part was out of reach financially.

But even with all that experience, I'd never repaired an electrical generator this old, or one this size. *How hard can it be?* They basically all do the same thing, don't they? They convert mechanical energy into electrical energy. The mechanical aspect of this thing was a four-stroke diesel engine.

I mustered enough energy to stand and shuffle over to the generator. I paused---dizzy, and feeling nauseous, I wondered how long before I was incapable of performing even the most rudimentary functions?

Kneeling down, I wiped grime off a small metal information tag. It was an Onan Electrical Plant generator. It listed the various technical specs. Made back in 1957, this thing was a brute at 15 kilowatts and 110/220 AC volts. That made sense, considering it would have to power the entire hotel when city power went out. Something, I imagine, that was far more common fifty years or so ago. I opened the fuel cap and looked inside the tank—it was empty. That would definitely be a problem. The other problem would be the batteries used to start the engine. There were two six-volt batteries strapped to the side that were nothing more than corroded remnants of what they once were. These were two fairly big problems but I could address them later. The most important thing right now was determining if the generator was seized up—rusted stuck. I looked around for a crowbar or something long and solid.

I wandered the cellar looking for anything that could work. I kicked at the debris on the floor, moved the folding wooden table, checked out the workbench, and noticed something else. There, sitting next to the coffeemaker, was an old twelve-volt car battery charger. I may not have batteries, but I had twelve volts of DC power. That is, if the charger still worked. I plugged it into the outlet and nothing happened. It made sense. The power to the building had been off for many years. Harland must have hijacked power from somewhere for the hanging light bulb, via an extension cord plugged into, maybe, the building next door.

Back to the folding wooden table. It too must have been fifty years old. What was left of the wood was turning to dust from my slightest touch. I grabbed up one of the table's metal supporting struts. This would work fine.

Back at the generator, I wedged one end of the metal strut, the smaller thinner end, into a slot behind the main drive pulley. I gave my makeshift-fulcrum a push and the pulley assembly, along with the main drive shaft, moved freely. Progress! But I was also aware that time was not on my side. I needed to find a way to tap in before Harland returned. I needed to have an advantage or my prospects for the future looked dim. It was then that I heard him coming.

I took a seat against the far wall and waited. Something was different. Murmurs and other noises were coming from the ceiling opening above the perch. Multiple footsteps were getting closer. I heard Harland's voice and then a woman's. There was something familiar about her voice.

Pippa stepped down to the wooden perch from the opening above. Harland, gun in hand, followed. "Back away from the opening," he said, looking down from above. Harland had a difficult time holding on to the gun, while easing himself down onto the perch, without the use of his other, bandaged, hand.

But all my attention was on Pippa. She still had not noticed me sitting below. Her hair was tied back and she was wearing a T-shirt and jeans. Jeans covered from the knees down with what looked like blood. My heart was racing and I couldn't take my eyes off her. How would she react to seeing me? Would she understand why I hadn't contacted her? That I couldn't contact her? Would she still feel the same about me?

Harland was pointing his gun at Pippa. "Slide the ladder over the edge and use it to climb down."

Pippa didn't move for several seconds, then said, "What do you hope to accomplish keeping me hostage? What does that buy you?"

"It buys me plenty keeping you both around just a bit longer. Don't worry about it—all will become clear shortly. Now do as I said."

Pippa's brow furrowed; she didn't understand what he meant by *both*. She turned and looked down into the cellar—her eyes eventually found me sitting against the wall. Our eyes met but she said nothing, her face expressionless.

The moment, any connection, was gone when Harland fired a round into the ceiling above. Pippa crouched and I was on my feet.

"Move it!" Harland barked.

Pippa slid the long extension ladder over the edge of the perch and let its weight carry the end down to the floor. I moved to the ladder and held it as she turned backwards and climbed down. She stepped onto the floor and immediately took several steps backwards, away from me.

Harland pulled the ladder back up and slid it away from the edge. He stood and smiled down at us. "Do I detect a chill in the air?"

Neither of us replied.

"Enjoy your last hours together," he said, moving toward the opening above. "What lies ahead for both of you will not be pleasant." With that, he was gone. I thought I heard him whistling in the distance. Pippa moved in closer and, without giving any warning, punched me in the face.

CHAPTER 22

I lost my balance and went down on one knee. I tasted blood in my mouth and licked at the crack in my lip. Pippa looked down at me, hand still raised and clenched in a fist. Her eyes conveyed everything she was feeling. Anger ... hurt ... and something else. As she took in the rest of me, her expression changed. Her eyes went to my trembling hands, and the band-aid on my forehead.

I stood, gave her a half-hearted shrug, and walked over to the generator. It would need fuel. Nothing would happen without fuel. I turned and surveyed the basement. There was a good chance the two boilers burned oil, or maybe even diesel. I followed the myriad of small pipes coming in and out of the boiler on the left and determined which one was most likely the fuel line. Yes, there was the fuel reservoir. Pippa silently watched me cross over to the boilers. I tapped on the reservoir. It sounded hollow—not a good sign. I unscrewed the large cap at the top and looked inside.

It was faint, but I saw a reflection of liquid at the bottom.

I stood back and looked at the bottom of the tank. There was a small bleeder valve but I'd need a wrench to get it open.

"What are you doing?" she asked.

"I'm attempting to drain off some diesel fuel from the boiler's reservoir."

"Do you think that's the best use of our time? You know, under the circumstances?"

I was back at the workbench looking through the contents of the toolbox. I found a small crescent wrench and headed back to the boilers. I then turned back and grabbed the toolbox, too.

"If I told you what I was doing and why, you'd think I was insane."

"Yeah, well, you really don't want to know what I'm thinking about you as it is."

"Probably not."

I looked over at her. "You could help me, you know," I said.

She stood in the middle of the basement, her arms crossed.

"*Pfft*, help you? Like that's going to happen," she replied angrily.

"On that workbench. See if there are some coffee filters to go with the coffee maker," I said.

She stood immobile for several moments with an impassive expression. Then, as if coming to some kind of decision, walked over to the bench.

I adjusted the wrench to fit the bleeder nut and turned it counter-clockwise until fuel started to drip. I emptied out the top of the toolbox, wiped at the dust there with the palm of my hand, and placed it on the floor.

Pippa was crouched down rifling through items on the shelf beneath the bench. She turned and looked over her shoulder at me, scowled, and returned to what she was doing. A moment later she stood up, holding a faded box of Mr. Coffee filters.

"Perfect. I'll need the brew basket from the coffee maker as well."

She hesitated, then turned to fiddle with the coffee maker. Facing me again, she held up the small brew basket. "This thing?"

"Yep."

She tossed the items over to my feet. "There you go, your coffee filters and that other thing."

There were about ten filters in the box. The first seven were unusable. The bottom three were in better shape. I used my foot to position the toolbox beneath the bleeder valve. Holding the filter basket with one of the filters in place, I opened the bleeder valve the rest of the way. A stream of thick, gummy, black fuel poured into the filter. Eventually, a stream of less congealed fuel was dripping into the toolbox. It took fifteen minutes and all three of the filters to fill the toolbox.

I walked to Pippa's left, giving her a wide berth in case she took another swing at me. Dropping the diesel fuel would be tantamount to game over. She followed me over to the generator. I gestured with my chin, "Can you open that cap?"

She opened it and placed the cap on the floor. Slowly, I poured the diesel fuel into the generator's gas tank.

"You might want to get some of that in the tank instead of all over the floor," she observed.

"I see you still have your sense of humor."

She didn't reply.

I set the now-empty toolbox down on the floor and re-placed the cap on the tank.

"The sweating ... jittery movements ... coloring not good—you're going through withdrawal," Pippa said—a statement, not a question.

"Yeah, I am. But I'm working on that."

"By fucking with this old machine?" she asked.

I pointed to the light bulb hanging eight feet over her head. "I need that extension cord."

She looked up at the light and then around the cellar. "It's too high up. No way to reach it."

"There's a way. If you'll let me."

"Let you what?" she asked.

"Let me hold you up by your legs," I said.

She walked around, looking up at the light. "I don't understand."

"There may be some play in the cord. If you pull on it, we may be able to bring it down here, over to the generator."

"I guess we can try. You'll get blood on yourself," she said, pointing to the dark, rust-looking stains on her pants.

"Not yours?"

She shook her head, but didn't elaborate. She positioned herself so she was directly beneath the light bulb. As I moved closer, almost touching her, her eyes stayed on mine. I lowered myself to her knees, grabbed hold of her legs and slowly stood, bringing her up higher into the air. I felt one of her hands on my shoulder. With the other she reached up. Her fingers were an inch away from the light.

"It's too high."

I brought her back down. "Let's try it again. This time I'll grab you lower on your legs."

"You're not looking so good. Sure?"

"I'm fine."

She nodded and we repeated the same steps. Now, several inches higher in the air, she was able to reach past the light bulb and wrap her fingers around the cord.

"I've got it. Bring me down," she said.

Slowly, I brought her legs back down while keeping my eyes on the cord above. It was pulling free. I saw where the light bulb cord was knotted and plugged into an orange extension cord. It was coming free from a hole in the ceiling. Once Pippa was standing on the floor she continued to pull on the cable until she handed it over to me.

She took a step backward and crossed her arms again. "I still don't understand what you're doing."

I headed back to the workbench and found needle-nose pliers and a role of sticky electrical tape. I put them in my pocket. I unplugged the battery charger and carried it back to the generator. "I'm trying to get this generator working."

"Yeah, I figured that part out. Why?"

"I'll have to show you. I already told you, you wouldn't believe me."

She rolled her eyes.

I needed more wire to splice things together. My hands were shaking almost uncontrollably now. Walking was becoming difficult. At the electrical panels on the wall were several conduits. I used the pliers to pull one of them away from the wall. I yanked it free from the panel and then tore it away from a junction box that was six feet away. I sat down on the floor and spent the next few minutes pulling each of the wires free from the conduit.

Pippa watched and shook her head. "Why don't you let me do that? You're barely able to hold on to the pliers, let alone strip those wires."

"Okay," I said. "Strip an inch from both ends of each wire."

She sat down next to me and took over from where I left off. She pursed her lips and glanced in my direction. "Are we going to talk? Are you going to tell me why you turned—went rogue?"

"I never turned. Never went rogue—"

The anger was back in Pippa's face. "How can you even say that?"

I held up a hand. "I promise, I'll explain everything. First, the generator. Then I can tell you and show you what you need to know."

Pippa let out a long breath and continued to strip an inch of insulating coating from the wires. When she was done, she handed the bundle of wires over to me. The next step was going to be the trickiest. Especially with my hands not working well.

"Just tell me what you want to do. I'll do it for you," she said.

"We need to strip back the insulation from the two wires connected to the light bulb, and do so without cutting all the way through them."

"Seriously? It's plugged in. Won't I get shocked?"

"Not if you do them one at a time. But if you cut the wire we'll be in the dark. We won't be able to get the generator running."

"I'll do the best I can. It's not like I'm an electrician or anything."

We moved closer to the generator and Pippa brought the light bulb cord onto her lap. She separated the wires of the cord away from each other and slowly started to strip back the plastic insulation. Her long fingers moved with a dexterity that surprised me. Once she had an inch of copper wire exposed I told her to cut the plug off the battery charger cord, splice in one wire, and wrap it secure with electrical tape. We did the same thing on the other side of the cable. Within minutes we had the battery charger up and running, as well as keeping the light bulb lit.

Next, we needed to repair the wire bundle on the generator itself. With little direction, Pippa used the spliced wires she'd previously cut and stripped and, one by one, connected them as I instructed.

I made a few more connections on my own, including the attachment to the twelve-volt cables, now taking the place of the old battery cables. I stood up uneasily and walked around the generator. *Had I forgotten something?*

Pippa's eyes were on me. When I looked at her, she raised her eyebrows. "Well? What now?"

The truth was, I had little faith that this would work. A hundred things could go wrong. A fuse could blow ... the engine's starter motor, or alternator, or any combination of things, could be defective.

I checked the battery charger and saw that it was constantly putting out twelve volts. I flipped the generator's power on/off switch to the ON position. The engine immediately cranked and sputtered, then died.

Pippa looked up from the generator. "That sounded promising, didn't it?"

I nodded. I flipped the power switch again and this time the engine roared to life. The noise was loud and the generator shook like it wanted to fly into the air, but it was running.

Pippa was smiling and looked triumphant. Within seconds, I felt the effects of the power coming off the generator. Earlier, I had attached a bundle of insulated high-voltage wires to the 220-volt output of the generator. I sat down on the floor and pulled them close to me—cradled my head right onto them.

I tapped in. The familiar song was there, waiting for me—welcoming me. It filled my consciousness as blue light surrounded me, bathed me in its nurturing grace. I felt the familiarity of the presence there. It was alive and once again I was becoming one with it. As the moments passed, my strength returned. My mind became clear and I was able to reach out beyond myself—I found Pippa. In a flash I was in her mind—experiencing the depth of her own inner-beingness. I sat up and looked into her eyes.

How about I start from the beginning?

CHAPTER 23

Pippa was up on her feet, looking infuriated. "What the hell was that!?"

I had only been in her mind for a few seconds. I communicated directly with her via my mind to hers. In those few moments I understood her, felt her anger toward me. I grasped how her life had been turned upside down and why she had decided to follow through with her orders to apprehend me and escort me back to Washington.

I jumped to my feet and let her come toward me, her face full of fury. She spoke quietly now: "I asked you a question. Answer me."

I reached over and turned off the generator. "I can read minds. I can influence thoughts."

I watched her. She stared back.

"Several days ago I was in a car wreck," I told her. "I'd careened into a telephone pole. Sustained head trauma and what's called retrograde amnesia. That's another story

... Anyway, a high-power line was severed and for several hours dangled inches above my head. Something happened in that time period, something physiological, to my body, to my mind. Sitting trapped in what was left of my car, I started to hear the thoughts of animals, the EMT workers around me, everyone. At first, I chalked it up to having a serious concussion; maybe I was having delusions. Later, at the hospital, I found a way to what I call *tap in* to high-voltage sources and the ability returned. Again, I was able to communicate directly into minds, if I desired to. Later, I discovered I could influence people's actions as well. I've also discovered a limitation to this new sixth sense. I need to tap into a power source within twenty-four hours or I go into withdrawal. You've seen those symptoms first hand. And you've felt my consciousness intrude in your mind."

She was shaking her head. "You know how utterly ridiculous this sounds, don't you?"

"Of course I do. If I hadn't experienced it myself, I'd say I was definitely delusional—that I was seriously over the edge ... crazy. So test me. Prove me wrong."

She smirked—more shaking of her head. She shrugged. "Fine, what number am—"

I cut her off: "Sixty-two."

Her expression changed; now serious, she no longer shook her head. "Lucky guess. Very lucky. I'm thinking of a place—"

"The top of the Washington Monument, where we kissed," I said.

The beginnings of a smile pulled at the corners of her lips. "Whoa! How did you do that? Okay, one more. Talk to me without talking. Like directly—"

Again, I cut her off, not by talking, but with my thoughts speaking directly into her mind. *Pippa, I am so sorry ... so very sorry. I was trapped in Russia for months. Please forgive me.*

Her eyes never left my lips, as if she was trying to uncover some kind of trickery, some magic trick. "This is real. Oh my God, you really can do this. This is so freaky." Her expression changed again. "I don't want you in my mind, Rob. Promise me you won't do that again—promise me right now."

"I promise. Your thoughts are safe. Although I already saw your memory of us kissing in the Washington Monument."

"Well, don't read too much into that. You still have a lot to answer for. There's not a U.S. Intelligence agency not looking for you, not to mention most international ones."

"Listen. Veronica was a double agent. Pippa, I'd discovered she was working for the SVR; her cover was blown. She pulled her weapon, was going to shoot both Harland and myself. I shot her first."

"That's not how Harland reported events went down when he got back. As far as he was concerned, you shot his wife in cold blood, then went to ground. He was so devastated he eventually had to leave the agency."

"The only reason I went to ground was because Veronica had the SVR already coming for us. How Harland got out still has me baffled."

"So where did you go?"

"Remember Ladislav Skykora, the Slovakian national? You met him in Moscow several years back. Anyway, he was a friend and I knew he was no ally of the Russians. He agreed to keep me hidden, but he extracted a price from me for doing so that I still need to pay. Over that next year I couldn't leave his flat. He was being watched ... his phones were tapped; twenty-four hour surveillance on his flat. Several times, I had to hide in a crawlspace between the walls.

I owe him my life."

"Why didn't you come in once you got back to the U.S.?" she asked.

"I was planning to. But I needed to keep my promise to Skykora first. It was only going to take me a day, two at most. That's why I'm here in Kingman. I had to keep my promise."

I watched Pippa's face. She still looked skeptical.

"What was it you had to do for Skykora—what was your promise?"

"I had to kill a man. Another Slovakian national. I've actually already met him, but at the time, with my amnesia, I had no idea who he was."

"Who is he?" she asked.

"A man named Drako. Drako Cervenka."

Chapter 24

Y ou just can't kill a man in cold blood. It's not like an agency sanction, it would be murder," Pippa said incredulously.

"Drako's a pretty bad dude. I'm not going to lose sleep over taking him out. I've taken out worse—so have you. He's been getting rich off human trafficking, mostly Slovakian women and children, for years. A master strategist, he's always one or two, or even three steps ahead of the authorities. My friend, Skykora, lost his sister and niece to Drako's trafficking enterprises. They were abducted from their small eastern bloc village, smuggled into an oceanic shipping container with thirty or forty others. Skykora was able to alert the authorities, and the freighter was boarded and searched. Unfortunately, they'd gotten to the container too late. Everyone inside was dead. His sister, niece, everyone, had run out of water halfway across the Atlantic. Died of thirst."

Pippa was quiet for a while. I wasn't sure if she had come to some kind of acceptance of my predicament. "If we get out of this, Rob, I need to bring you in. I believe what you've told me. And after what you've shown me, what you could show them—"

"No! No one can ever know about these abilities, Pippa. Can you imagine the potential for misuse? How I'd never have a life again?"

"You won't last long on your own. There's too many looking for you," she said.

"I'll think of something. But my days working for the government are over. If you think about it, you'd realize too what I've come to know. In a profession where everyone lies to everyone else, I'd quickly become a liability."

She seemed to accept that. She continued to stare at me. The unspoken words were written in her expression. *What about us? What about what we had?*

Noises were coming from above. Harland was returning.

"Get directly under the perch—stay out of sight," I said. I fetched up the same long piece of metal I'd used as a fulcrum and waited for Pippa to get across the room. I licked my fingers and unscrewed the light bulb until the basement went black. Carefully, I moved forward in the darkness to where I remembered Pippa was standing. I walked right into her. Her arms instinctively came up, her hands resting on my chest. We stayed like that as the noises from above got louder. I felt her breath on my neck, could smell her light perfume. Then we heard Harland's footfalls right above us.

A beam of light shone as his flashlight moved in slow, wide arcs around the basement.

"What are you up to, Chandler? I know you're down there." The beam of his flashlight had settled on the light bulb and extra coils of extension cord lying on the floor, then on the generator and the spliced-in wires. "Someone's been busy here. What are you two up to, Rob?"

I heard him rack the slide of his handgun to chamber a round. Not so easy with only one working hand.

What Harland didn't know was that I was already in his mind, tracking his erratic thoughts, feeling his ever-increasing apprehension that we, somehow, had actually found a way out. I interjected a suggestion into his mind:

They're sly. They may be right below—below the perch. I'd be able to see them if I got down on my hands and knees and looked over the edge …

As I wondered if he had accepted these thoughts for his own, I heard the shuffling of his feet above as he lowered himself to his knees and squatted down on all fours onto the plywood perch. I was seeing through his eyes in real time. I knew exactly where he was—where he would be looking. My fingers tightened around the metal in my hand. I gently pushed Pippa to the side and stepped backwards until my back was up against the slump-stone wall. I waited. I could see what he saw as he positioned himself onto his belly. He placed the gun close by his side. Slowly he inched his body forward, out over the edge of the perch, right up against his hipbone. He held his bandaged hand behind him to steady himself, while his free hand held the flashlight. He lowered his upper body over the edge almost enough to see if anyone was hiding below. I pushed myself off the wall and took one, then two running steps, and leapt. I brought the piece of metal up over my head, gripped firmly in my hands. First, I saw the beam of the flashlight, then his head silhouetted behind it. I also saw my own face through his eyes. There, in midair, I aimed my metal spear high up toward his left eye.

I missed. Harland must have jerked to the right just as the metal shaft came near. It hit him in the temple instead. I saw the shaft's edge dig into his flesh, and then break free, glancing off the side of his head. He yelped, and in a series of rapid movements, recoiled, grabbed for his head, and dropped the flashlight. For a moment he held steady there, but with his center of balance too far over the edge of the platform, he fell to the basement floor at my feet.

He'd landed on his back and the fall knocked the wind out of him. I fetched up the flashlight and walked over to the generator and the nearby light bulb. With several twists it was back on and the basement was again illuminated.

Harland had a hand up to his temple and his eyes were following my movements. Then he saw Pippa beneath the perch.

"Not sure how you two did that, but I have to give you credit. I'd say clever, but now you must realize all three of us are trapped down here, right?" He laughed abruptly and his eyes darted back and forth between us—he looked somewhat manic.

Pippa stood over Harland. She'd picked up my piece of metal and was holding it in two hands, like a bat. "You killed my partner. You slit his throat, Harland ... let him lay there in that parking lot while he bled out."

Harland kept his eyes on Pippa but spoke to me: "I can clear you, Chandler. But if you let her kill me, well, then the truth dies with me."

"She doesn't answer to me, Harland. Personally, I'm inclined to let her bash your head in. You're a worthless piece of shit."

"No! I can help you," he said, with a distorted, forced smile. "Tell me what I have to do."

"Well, a good start would be telling us who you're work-

149

ing for, and why you've taken us hostage."

Harland didn't answer fast enough. Pippa swung the bat down on Harland's bandaged appendage. He screamed out in agony. As he pulled his arm in to cradle his hand, fresh blood started to seep through the gauze wrappings.

This time it was Pippa asking the question: "Who are you working for?"

I knew the answer before he said the words—saw Dwight Calloway's face in his mind. The Deputy Executive Director (D/EXDIR) with the CIA. Four levels down from the top, the head of the CIA.

Harland reluctantly muttered his name aloud. "I work as a private contractor for Dwight Calloway."

Pippa and I looked at each other. Neither of us had ever had much direct contact with the man. He was significantly above our pay-grade.

"What's he want with us?" Pippa asked.

Harland was sitting up now, his hand still tucked into his stomach. "It was Calloway, his team, that got me out of Russia."

"What do you mean his team? We were all his team."

"No, I'm talking about his black-ops team. He runs a separate covert group; one that's outside government channels. No one knows about it."

"How did he drag you into that?" I asked.

"I've worked for Calloway for years. The price for my service, doing his special projects, was allowing Veronica to stay alive."

"So you knew she was a double?" I asked.

"You're ridiculously naïve, Chandler. Even you must realize the lines between treachery and heroism are often blurred. People like Calloway take in the big spectrum of things. He's not blinded by single-minded patriotism."

"What the hell does that mean?" Pippa asked.

"It means that it's not the world's various governments making the crucial decisions. It's the financial consortiums. Economics span across borders. Interests must be protected, even if that means one's country, or origin, takes a slight hit."

"And what part does Calloway play in this organization?"

"As far as I'm concerned, and soon for you both as well, he's God."

"What's the name of this consortium?"

Harland hesitated. His eyes leveled on me and I could see the hatred rising in him again. He was unstable—even crazed. I saw in his mind that he was poised to make a charge at me. His hatred for me trumped everything... his mission... even his own survival.

Pippa brought the bat back, ready for another swing.

"SIFTR!" he replied.

I was getting impatient with Harland and he knew it.

"It stands for Services of International Financial and Tactical Resources."

I was back, probing into his mind, trying to get as much detail as I possibly could from him. It was then I heard a concussive explosion from above, while simultaneously seeing a dark red hole appear between Harland's eyes. I spun toward Pippa, wanting to protect her from whatever was above us.

CHAPTER 25

Standing above us was a man in an impeccably tailored light-gray suit. He was flanked by four men: two on either side. Soldiers, they were dressed in black combat fatigues and each held an M4 carbine semi-automatic rifle, with both laser and night vision sights; their weapons also had the RIS vertical forestock handgrip and a suppressor.

The man had short-cropped gray hair and striking blue eyes. He was holding a Glock in his left hand and still had it pointed at Harland's head. He nodded, as if satisfied with what he'd just accomplished. Handing the weapon to a soldier on his left, he brought his full attention down to us.

"Mr. Chandler, Agent Rosette. First off, I'd like to apologize for the way you both have been treated. Agent Rosette, I especially would like to convey my condolences on the loss of Agent Giles."

Pippa said nothing, only stared up at the man standing on the perch above. I was already in his mind, monitoring his thoughts. What grabbed my attention, above anything else, was his total lack of emotion. Where Harland was an emotional powder keg, this man was ice. His mind was organized and his motivations were clear. He didn't want to kill us—just the opposite. He wanted ... no, needed our help. Harland had been right; Calloway was certainly the top player in the organization, this *SIFTR*. He was the one pulling the strings. It was Calloway's ability to make decisions without the encumbrance of emotional conflicts that made him so effective. I wouldn't have gone so far as to label him a sociopath, because in his reality he seemed to be concerned with taking the noblest course of action. From what I determined, in the brief few seconds I had to scan his thoughts as I stood below him on the basement floor, was that he was prepared to do anything, eliminate anyone, as necessary, to accomplish his directives.

The sound of the retractable ladder being lowered from above brought me out of his mind. I wondered, was he aware at some level that I'd been intruding there? That something was amiss among the incalculable order of things? I'd need to be ultra careful the next time I peered into his thoughts.

Two soldiers made their way down the ladder, while the other two standing above had their weapons trained down on us. I hadn't noticed Calloway had left.

Arbitrarily, I picked one of the soldiers, the first one down the ladder, and peered into his mind. I arrived into a rush of frenetic thoughts and spiking emotions—images of a pretty young wife and two small children. Was he fearing for their lives? Was this man being coerced somehow into helping Calloway and this *SIFTR* organization? No, I soon realized, it was just the opposite. This man had been saved from a desperate situation. His loyalty to Calloway, and the SIFTR organization, was absolute. He would do anything, including killing Pippa and myself, if it came down to it.

At gunpoint we were ushered up the ladder to the plywood perch and then up into the opening at the ceiling. We followed the forward two combatants into the gloomy darkness of the hotel, back to what had become the deteriorating dining area. All trash and overturned furniture had been cleared from the room. Not a scrap of paper or an errant dust ball remained. Three chairs were positioned in the center of the room. Calloway sat primly in the one facing us as we entered.

"I know you must be uncomfortable and would like the opportunity to get freshened up. Please allow me to explain things first."

He gestured toward the two empty chairs facing him and smiled. We both sat and said nothing. Calloway's eyes lingered on Pippa's bloodstained jeans and his smile faded for a brief moment.

He turned to me. "Miraculously, you survived a momentous automobile accident. One Mr. Harland had planned and executed down to the smallest detail. Your death needed to look like an accident. A fluke. The converging of events no one would question—most notably myself, and the organization I work for. His hatred for you was all encompassing. That was my mistake; I misjudged Harland in that regard. I apologize." His eyes moved over to Pippa. "And I apologize to you as well, Agent Rosette. Again, Mr. Harland acted inappropriately."

"Inappropriately? That's what you call it?" Pippa was leaning forward in her chair. She looked as if she was on the verge of springing onto Calloway. Rifle muzzles came up from Calloway's assault team.

He waved them down and sat forward in his own chair, meeting her stare head on. "This is a messy business. Espionage. You've chosen a career path that by its sheer nature is at odds with itself. Layers of lies and deceit, motivated by greed for personal advancement, from virtually all parties involved, has put this country in jeopardy. What you think you know, what you have based your ideals on, is incorrect. The flag of patriotism being waved before your eyes is often nothing more than a deceptive lie."

"Let me guess. You're going to be the one to enlighten us," I said. I'd already infiltrated his mind, while taking extra care this time to remain unobtrusive.

Calloway smiled. His tan, handsome face, with those penetrating blue eyes, regarded me for a moment before he spoke. "I assure you, Mr. Chandler, when presented with an unbiased accounting of the workings of the world order, including that of the United States, you'll be far less skeptical of what we're trying to accomplish."

Calloway certainly believed in what he was saying. Righteous and arrogant in his rhetoric, he had a mind like a machine. Nothing was going to get in his way. But there was only so much I was able to decipher from the streams of thought in his focused, uncluttered mind. Without all the typical errant images or emotional sidetracks most of us produce, I wasn't getting much out of him.

Calloway sat back in his chair. "I would like for both of you to work for me." He held up one palm as he saw Pippa poised to rebuff his overture. "Let me continue for one moment, Agent Rosette. The simple fact that you both survived and were in the process of escaping Mr. Harland's prison cell below speaks to your ingenuity and resourcefulness. Your deaths as well as that of Agent Giles was never our intention. Harland's mind had lost balance. Be it the snakebites, vengeance, whatever ... he'd gone completely mad. With that said, and I'm somewhat afraid to admit this:

MARK WAYNE McGINNIS

this has been an excellent test. In the realm of things, only the very best, the most proficient and resourceful—those who are true survivors, are of any interest to me."

"Well, isn't that nice for you. But there's simply no fucking way I'd ever work for you," Pippa said, returning his smile.

"On the contrary, Agent Rosette, you already do. You both do."

"What are you talking about?" I chimed in. "I've been underground for over a year. Who even knows I'm still alive? And most importantly, I'm retired. Done."

Calloway looked amused. "There was never a moment when we didn't know where you were hiding out. You may be interested to learn that Mr. Skykora has worked for my organization for more than six years."

I observed his mind and he was telling the truth.

"There are very few people who are privy to the existence of this organization. The president of the United States is one of them. I do not work for him ... nor does he for me. But he supports what we are doing emphatically. As do select leaders throughout the world. Again, our directives go beyond the borders of any one nation."

"And are they ever at odds with the U.S.?" I asked.

"Not if one knows the reality of the situation. That's not always apparent to the general populace or even their political constituency. I provide full disclosure—transparency of our motivations. You may not always agree, but you'll have far more access to decision-making than you've had in the past."

Calloway turned his attention to Pippa. "Agent Rosette, you will contact your previous supervisor, Assistant Director Hayes at DHS. He will verbally confirm your reassignment. There will be no paperwork. Nothing that can be tracked or later used to tie you to SIFTR. Mr. Chandler, your situation was somewhat more complicated. Suffice it to say you have a choice to make. Right here and now. Work for me, for SIFTR, and be one hundred percent cleared of all charges."

"Or?" I asked.

Calloway looked bemused. "Continue to be sought, by multiple agencies, in multiple countries—living a life on the run."

He was, it seemed from what I could determine, telling me the truth. "That seems like a tall order," I said.

He casually shrugged, "With the exception of one foreign state, namely Russia, no one will be looking for you." Calloway stood and looked down at us. "Over time you will be brought up to speed on your long-term operational directives."

"And short term?" I asked.

"Keep your promise to Mr. Skykora."

CHAPTER 26

Escorted by several of his armed team, Calloway left in a hurry. Another man, also wearing a well-tailored suit, this one in dark gray, entered the hotel's former dining room. About forty, he had olive skin, was of medium height, and his black hair was trimmed short. He moved with confidence and efficiency. Like myself, he was an agent—a trained killer—I had little doubt of that. He had been waiting in the wings for Calloway to finish. He sat in Calloway's chair and laid a briefcase on his lap.

"My name is Curtis Baltimore. You can call me Curt, if you wish. I am your point of contact from this point on. All communications will transpire through me. You will not deal with Mr. Calloway directly, unless otherwise directed to do so." Baltimore opened the briefcase and brought out a thick manila envelope; closing the briefcase, he placed it on top. "There are several points that need to be discussed before we move forward."

"There's no way I'm working for you," Pippa said.

Baltimore looked over to me. "Same for you?"

I shrugged. "Speaking for myself, as I told Mr. Calloway, I'm out of the business. Retired."

Pippa looked at me without expression.

Baltimore looked relaxed, as if he'd had this same conversation many times. He turned to the soldier closest to him, who passed over what looked to be the latest generation satellite phone. Baltimore took the phone and entered a series of numbers. He held the phone to his ear and listened for several moments, then entered another, longer set of numbers. I was in his head, hearing the key tones. A voice broke into the line and said: *"Please hold for the president."*

There was silence and then another voice broke in. *"Baltimore, I need to make this quick. I have the Secretary of State waiting outside my office."*

"Yes, sir," Baltimore said. "They are both here. I'll put you on with Mr. Chandler first, then Ms. Rosette."

"Fine, let's move it along. Hand over the phone to him."

Listening through Baltimore's mind, I immediately recognized the voice of James C. Morrison, the president of the United States. There was no mistaking that it was him. I took the phone from Baltimore and put it up to my ear. "This is Chandler," I said.

"Hello, Mr. Chandler. May I call you Rob?"

"Yes, sir."

"Do you know who I am?"

"Yes, Mr. President. I do."

Pippa, who had been watching me, sat up straighter in her seat, looking surprised.

The president continued: "Do you trust me, Rob?"

"I do, sir."

"Then please take Mr. Calloway and Mr. Baltimore's request for continued service seriously. I want you to know that you will be working toward our country's best interests. I would not compromise the welfare of our country, Rob. There may come times when you'll doubt what you're doing is right. Trust me, it will be. I'm putting my faith in you and Ms. Rosette. Do you understand?"

"Yes, sir. I believe I do."

"Good. Both you and Ms. Rosette have a highly unique skill set. I've been told you are the best of the best at what you do. Perhaps most importantly, you've both been operating well beneath the radar for over a year. That alone is an advantage. There's a new mission in the works—one that's of the utmost importance. Within the week you'll both be deployed back to Europe. Understand, national security has never been in more jeopardy than it is right now. Foreign infiltration into our covert agencies is at an unprecedented high level. Double agents have become the issue at hand. So you will be joining the most covert of all black-ops organizations. I'm counting on you, Rob. If you don't have any quick questions, please put Ms. Rosette on the line," the president asked.

So much for my decision of getting out of the business, I thought.

Pippa took the phone and held it to her ear. Her brow furrowed; she looked nervous. While she was having what was probably a similar conversation with the president, I used the time to peer into Baltimore's mind.

There was nothing unsettling going on that I could read; no red flares, indicating he was being anything but truthful. What I did detect was fear. Whatever was happening in Europe, the reason for this new mission, he was not optimistic about it. Bringing Pippa and myself into the mix might very well be a last-ditch effort before something cataclysmic took place.

Pippa handed the phone back to Baltimore. Her expression was one of concern; she looked to be carrying the world's weight on her shoulders.

Baltimore leveled his eyes on me first, and then on Pippa. "Ms. Rosette, you will be leaving Arizona within two hours. You are booked on a direct flight to Dulles. You have a meeting in Washington, where you'll be debriefed."

"Mr. Chandler, please think about what resources you'll require to complete your assignment in Kingman. In a few days, as soon as you're done here, you'll meet Ms. Rosette at a still-undetermined location somewhere in Europe. I have some reading material for both of you to get up to speed on. You'll also find a burner phone, flight itineraries, your new identities, passports, and credit cards." Baltimore handed a packet to each of us. "I'll give you a few moments to say goodbye."

Baltimore was off his chair and heading out of the room before we knew it. The security team followed on his heels.

"What the hell was all that about?" Pippa asked me.

I shrugged. "All I can tell you is that both Calloway and Baltimore believe what they are doing is the right call. There's no apparent deception going on here," I replied.

"What's this mission we're being deployed into?"

"Baltimore has less faith in our abilities to succeed than Calloway. It's a dire situation, whatever it is. Neither of us is expected to survive, in any case."

"Now you tell me!" she exclaimed.

"Hey, the president of the United States just asked for our help. You going to tell him no?" I asked with a smile. I stood up.

Pippa got up and shook her head. "This is all happening too fast." She turned and looked at me. A long moment passed where neither of us spoke. She looked away first and headed off in the same direction the others had gone. Still walking, she looked back over her shoulder. "Don't forget to tap in once in a while, Rob ... see ya."

"See ya," I replied.

PART 3

MAD POWERS

CHAPTER 27

There were a few specialty items I needed from Curtis Baltimore and his SIFTR organization, in regard to me keeping my promise to Ladislav Skykora. It actually made no difference that Skykora was associated with SIFTR. What I was going to do for him was personal. If the story was true, Drako Cervenka had taken something profoundly precious from my friend—the life of his sister and her daughter.

According to the paperwork Baltimore had given me, I was booked into the Kingman Best Western, here in town. Although a step or two up from Motel 6, I stayed with Motel 6—and my already established access for tapping in. I spent the afternoon running errands. I needed new clothes, shoes, and a few specialty items for tonight. I'd driven by Drako's estate and surveyed the surrounding landscape. Literally built into the jagged cliffs, along the furthest outskirts of Kingman, Drako's estate was a formidable property. Access via the cliff behind it would be nearly impossible. At the top of the ridge-line, set back and out of view from the street level below, was an electrified, twelve-foot-tall fence. Multiple roving sentry/canine teams patrolled 24/7. At the single-entrance driveway was a metal gate and guard station. Armed guards could be seen patrolling on the grounds below as well. The house itself was a modern affair, with eight adjoining glass and concrete platforms jutting out from the cliffs at varying heights. An eight-car garage, testimony to Drako's love of cars, was the only ground-level structure.

It didn't surprise me that Drako had covered his bases, with ridiculously tight security perimeters, and very limited access to the property's interior. In the end, I wouldn't be sneaking into this fortress—I'd simply knock on his front door.

I'd rented a new car with my new I.D., credit card, and license, provided by Baltimore. I showered, dressed in my new clothes, and tapped in on my way out of Motel 6. By the time I arrived at the guardhouse at the end of Drako's long driveway, it was close to five in the afternoon.

I pulled up to the gate and smiled and waved in the direction of a camera mounted on a ten-foot-high pole. A stern-faced, all business guard came out of the small structure. He had a clipboard in his hand and was looking at it as he approached my driver's side window.

"Who are you?" he asked, bending down and looking first at me and then into my rental car.

"Name's Rob Chandler."

"What do you want? This is private property."

"I know it's private property. I'm here to see Drako."

"You're not on the list."

"That's correct."

"Turn your car around. Don't bother Mr. Cervenka again."

He rose up and stepped back, waiting for me to back up and leave. I stayed where I was. Irritated, he came closer and bent over again. "Did you not hear me? Get out of here."

"You need to go back in that little house of yours and call the boss. Tell him his good friend from the park is here to teach him again how to play chess."

"You're a friend?"

"Yes."

The guard stared at me for several long seconds, looking indecisive. I imagine Drako had few, if any friends who dropped by uninvited. This was uncharted territory for the guard and he didn't want to make the wrong move.

"Let me make this easier for you," I said. "Give me the phone and I'll talk to him myself. That way you don't have to man-up and talk to your own boss."

Anger flashed over the guard's face. He moved closer and peered down at me. "Stay here."

He went back into the guard shack. He was on the phone less than thirty seconds before he hung up and was standing back in front of me. "Drive forward until you are signaled to stop. Park where directed. You will be searched and checked for transmitting devices. Your phone will be temporarily held by security. Is that understood?"

"Uh huh. Just open the gate as your boss instructed you to do," I said, looking straight ahead.

I drove up a long, tree-lined avenue that must have cost a fortune in water bills to keep so lush and green beneath the hot desert sun. Up ahead was a circular turn-about. As the gatehouse guard had implied, there was another guard waiting there for me. Using hand motions, he directed me to park near the garage structure. I collected a small black satchel from the passenger seat and got out of the car. The guard walked toward me.

"Please stay where you are," he said.

I did as told. This guard was the spitting image of the other one. "Weren't you just down at the guard shack?" I asked.

"No, that wasn't me," he replied.

"I bet you get that a lot, huh?"

He gave a half-hearted shrug and brought up a long metal wand. "I need to check you for transmitting devices. Please hand me your phone."

I did as he asked and placed my phone in his outstretched palm, and he pocketed it.

"Please turn around and hold out your arms," he instructed.

I felt the wand brush against my arms, down my torso, and then up the insides of my legs. "Easy there, partner," I said. "Not without dinner and a movie first."

He took my leather satchel and unzipped it—looked inside—then passed it back to me.

Content with his search, he nodded and gestured toward the front door. "Mr. Cervenka is waiting for you inside. You don't need to knock, just go right in."

Two wide, ten-foot-high wooden doors stood atop a three-foot rise. Standing on the stoop, I noticed both doors were intricately carved, depicting some battle scene—a story—Chinese, or perhaps Mongolian. There were horses and men holding spears and swords. A warlord, larger than anything else, was carved into the center of the two closed doors.

"I said just go on in!" came the irritated voice of the guard still standing on the driveway.

I gave him a perfunctory salute, grabbed one of the wrought-iron door latches and pushed open the door on the right. I entered into a wide vestibule. A massive glass staircase rose in the distance, flanked by sheets of thick glass and water cascading into two identical-looking koi ponds.

A woman stood at the base of the stairway. She was black and dressed in a tan business suit and a dark brown tie. Her black hair was trimmed close to her scalp. She smiled, showing perfect white teeth between glossy red lips. "Please. This way, Mr. Chandler."

I followed her up the glass stairway. She turned and spoke to me over her shoulder. "My name is Cassie; please let me know if there is anything I can get for you while you're here. Mr. Cervenka is by the pool."

The stairs led up to what I guessed was the main formal living room. Plush leather furniture sat before an immense rock fireplace. Light streamed in through fifteen-foot-high plate-glass windows that stretched the width of the fifty-foot-wide room. The view of the desert below was extraordinary. A cantilevered ceiling thirty feet above had several thick wooden beams that continued on outside, through the front glass windows.

Cassie led me to another set of glass doors; these were opposite to the front of the house. As we stepped through the doors I realized I was looking at the far side of the rock cliff. We had walked through a tunneled-out opening and onto another massive concrete platform—one that was, somehow, cantilevered high above the desert floor below. A royal blue Grecian pool was flanked by eight thick marble pillars, which jutted into the air at varying heights. On the right was a gazebo, also made of marble, and there sat Drako, on a lounge chair. He waved for me to join him.

Cassie continued on in the opposite direction as I walked toward the right side of the pool. I approached Drako and stood before him. He was wearing dark blue swim trunks, a T-shirt with a design of different colored surfboards across its front, and Ray Bans. A MacBook Pro sat open on his lap.

"You surprise me once again, Rob."

"You did say you wanted a rematch," I said, holding up the leather satchel in my hand.

He smiled broadly and gestured me to take the lounge chair next to his.

Chapter 28

Cassie was back, holding a tray with a pitcher of iced tea and two ice-filled glasses. "Would you like a lemon slice, Mr. Chandler?"

"Lemon would be great, thanks."

Cassie deposited the drinks and hurried off. I unzipped my satchel, removed the folded up chessboard and, laying it out flat on my lounge chair, I positioned all the pieces.

"You know, Rob, I returned several times to the park, hoping to find you there."

"Haven't been back," I said.

"I take it your memory has returned?" It was more of a statement than a question.

I smiled. "Came back all at once. Pretty amazing, actually. Feels good knowing who I am again."

Drako nodded slowly. I was well aware he knew exactly who and what I was. Equipped with my full name, he would have had his people checking all national and international databases. By the time it took me to walk through his house and be poolside, he was up to speed.

"This is quite a spread you have here, Drako."

He turned to face me and scooted down on his chair where he could reach the chessboard. "Spoils of business, my friend. I conduct business similar to how I play this game ... always several moves ahead of my opponent. You, of course, may be the exception, Rob."

"Go ahead, Drako. I've put the white pieces on your side."

We opened with a standard Sicilian move: his white pawn to e4 followed by my black pawn to c5. This led to white pawn d2 to d4.

Drako glanced up and smiled. "Don't expect me to be as easy on you as I was before, Rob. Friends or not, I play to win."

"I'd expect nothing less from you, Drako."

"Would you like to add a little spice to the game?" he asked.

"What do you have in mind?"

Drako removed his Ray Bans. The smile on his mouth had not reached his eyes. He seemed to ponder the question and then said, "I have more money, riches, than I could spend in ten lifetimes. You, though, have little I would consider to be of any value. No offense, Rob."

"None taken."

"Information has value. Would you not agree?"

I nodded. "Sure. The right information most certainly has value. It's relative, though."

"Exactly! The information that would be of interest to me would be worth many millions." Drako leaned back, his arms outstretched. He looked off toward the back entrance of the house and then at the pool. "This house has an estimated dollar value of forty-three million."

"No shit?" I replied, then whistled.

"It's yours. If you win."

I let that sink in for several seconds. "The taxes alone on this place would bankrupt me."

"Part of the deal. House paid for, plus all taxes, all up-keep; everything paid up in advance, for thirty more years."

"And what's the other side, Drako? What on earth could I possibly tell you that would be worth such a grand offer?"

"I already told you. Information. The right information is priceless to me."

"Sure. Why not? What do you want to know?"

"You're not taking this seriously, Rob. That disappoints me. That means you're discounting me and our friendship."

"You're serious?"

"Quite."

I saw Cassie and another man heading towards us. He was carrying a briefcase.

"That's my lawyer. I hate lawyers. Hey, you know what an apple and a lawyer have in common?" Drako asked.

I shook my head.

"They both look great hanging from a tree." Drako laughed at his own joke as the man holding the briefcase joined us. Cassie smiled, waved, and walked off on her own.

"This is Mr. Chapleau," Drako said, without looking up at the lawyer. He was a stocky man with gray hair; his shirt displayed dark perspiration stains under his arms. He looked around for a place to set down his briefcase and set-tled, instead, on the concrete at his feet. With two jerks of his thumbs, latches snapped open and he raised the briefcase lid. Chapleau handed Drako two packets of papers the same size.

"Stay here and notarize our signatures."

"Yes, Mr. Cervenka."

I looked from Chapleau back to Drako. "You're serious about this? How could you possibly have all this prepared ... in what, the fifteen minutes I've been here?"

"Who said anything about fifteen minutes?" Drako replied, still looking over the paperwork. He gave a curt nod and held out an open hand to Chapleau. The lawyer gave him a pen and Drako signed his name on several pages, then repeated the process on the duplicate set. Satisfied, he looked up at me. "Your turn." He handed me the pen and both sets of documents.

"What is all this?" I asked, perplexed.

"Simple. It's all laid out in the documents in your hands. Winner takes all. Three matches played right here, right now. You win, the house, everything is yours. I win, I keep my house and you provide the specific and thorough information that I require. This is a legal and binding document."

I was listening to Drako talk as I read through the pages. It was a binding contract. Sure enough, he was handing over the property if, in fact, I won two out of three matches. I read down to the section relating specifically to the information he required. There were several questions I would need to answer truthfully:

1) Which government organization or agency did you meet with this morning?

2) Who is currently the person in charge of this agency? Specifically, who, at this organization or agency, do you report to?

3) To what higher power within the U.S. government does this organization or agency report?

4) As an agent of this organization or agency, what is your current specific objective, and or mission?

5) Specifically, where is the headquarters of this organi-

zation or agency located?

6) Provide a list of names of all the known people working at this organization or agency.

I looked up at Drako. "This is quite a list. How long have you known who I was?"

"I'm going to be one hundred percent honest with you, Rob. Understand, I expect the same honesty in return. I have friends within the Kingman PD. Your DNA and photograph were all I needed to access your CIA docs. Over a year ago you went to ground within Russia. I still do not know how you accomplished that. Impressive. This morning you were spotted talking to a Mr. Curt Baltimore in the back parking lot of the Beale Hotel. I am familiar with the man. There are only a few black-ops organizations that I do not know about, or work with, on a regular bases. Baltimore and the people he works for are involved in something new. This new organization has already caused me, as well as my associates, far too much trouble."

"Maybe we should forget the match. Call it a day." I said. All of a sudden, I doubted my own convictions. When I'd played against Drako before, he was distracted and playing multiple games at a time. His mind was amazingly quick and he was, beyond doubt, the superior player. By losing, I'd be providing classified information to a known criminal and, not to forget, I'd be a traitor to my country.

"I'm sorry, Rob. That's not an option. I pride myself on living by certain rules. Structure. Life is so much more challenging if a game has parameters. Neither of us can opt out of this one. There's one more caveat not mentioned in the contract on your lap."

"And what's that?"

"Cassie will put a neat round hole in the head of whoever leaves before the three matches are completed."

In the distance I saw a reflection. A gun sight was pointed in our direction.

"I'm supposed to just take your word on that? That she'll shoot her own employer?"

"Her employer will be determined by the signed contract—she comes with the house."

Drako lived for the game. Any game. He was telling the truth and had every intention of following through with all aspects of the contract. He also was a far more dangerous man than I had suspected. His reach into the U.S. government was profound. Numerous senators and congressman were in his pocket. I saw no specifics since his attention wasn't focused there. Also, he, or his associates, had countless active moles hidden within the various covert agencies. True to what he said, information was worth far more than money to Drako. He traded information. That was his business.

"How will you know if I'm telling the truth?"

Drako glanced up at the lawyer, who then withdrew from his briefcase a small square device with several long leads hanging from its end. "This is a lie detector. Incredibly accurate—light-years ahead in a technology that is more advanced than anything you might be familiar with."

"Looks like you've thought of everything. One problem. I know only a few answers, maybe three, to your six questions."

The lawyer stepped in closer and placed one of the adhesive leads on my neck—on my carotid artery. He placed another one on my temple. He turned the unit on and handed it to Drako.

"Which questions do you not have answers to?" Drako asked, keeping his eyes on the device.

"I know the answer to number one. Number two, I'll tell

you who the highest-level person I know about is; number three, yes, I do know the answer to that one, but I don't know the answer to numbers four or five; and number six, I could count the number of people I know about on one hand."

Drako looked up. "You're telling the truth." He reached over and took the documents off my lap. He took back the pen from the lawyer and crossed out several lines of text and initialed where he'd made changes. He passed them to the lawyer who reviewed them and also initialized the changes. The lawyer passed both contract packets back to me.

I signed the documents, but I had no intention of telling Drako anything more than I already had. I couldn't care less about owning this monstrosity of a house. In the end, if it meant taking a bullet, then so be it. For now, I'd play some chess.

"I believe it's your turn, Rob."

CHAPTER 29

We played chess. The lawyer stayed—he pulled up a chair and watched us; apparently familiar enough with the game that his expression changed when one of us did something warranting a reaction.

The last time we played we had multiple games going at once. Now, it was only one game at a time and Drako was impressing the hell out of me. He was the better player in every way. Every way except one—I could read his mind and observe his calculations and his typical five-to-six-moves-ahead strategies in real time. In some ways, this made things more difficult. I was being forced to track these multiple play-scenarios right along with him. Often, his choices, new directions of play, were made split seconds before he repositioned his pieces.

Halfway into game one, Drako was instigating a double attack, where two or more pieces are attacked in a single move. It was gutsy, and only the best of players could carry it off. What amazed me most about Drako's playing was its deceptive nature. He would lure me on with what appeared to be a simple misplay on his part, and only by stepping back, sensing the intended trap, a trap set for several moves ahead, was I able to not only anticipate, but also foil, his strategy.

Game one was almost finished. We both had a mere handful of pieces on the board. There was a sheen of perspiration above Drako's upper lip. His mind was still moving incredibly fast, but his frustration at my ability to anticipate his moves, his strategies, was evoking inner rage. He suspected I was somehow cheating but saw no possible way that I could be. I wasn't a hundred percent sure I could beat him—even with my ability to read his thoughts.

I'd come here for a reason, and it was time to bring Drako down. Before I did that, I needed to personally verify that he, in fact, was responsible for the death of Skykora's family and all the others who died in that sealed shipping container.

"I don't know many Slovakians," I said, "but there is one, who's also a master chess player. Perhaps you've met him—Ladislav Skykora?"

Drako's eyes stayed on the board and I knew he had actually heard. Finally, he said, "I know this man. He is not a friend, but we have done business together."

Drako was indeed telling the truth. His mind had flashed quickly to a sea freighter—to a metal container stacked full of women and children. He felt no remorse. His mind only calculated the loss of revenue upon discovering all had died. That image was all I needed: confirmation that he was indeed involved, not only in that sordid business, but directly tied, also, in the killing of Skykora's sister and her young daughter.

I found his mind was somewhat distracted from that point on—nowhere near his typical level of chess play.

I finished game one by cornering his king with my knight. It was check and checkmate.

"Excellent play. I believe, though, I have finally figured out how to beat you," Drako said. He stood and stretched.

I repositioned the pieces on the board and spun it around. What I discovered in his mind was startling. He knew, beyond little doubt, that I was reading his thoughts. He had been testing my thought-invasion prowess over the second half of our game. *How had I missed it?*

I moved first with a pawn to d4. He surprised me with knight to f6—Indian Defense. I did not perceive it first. He was now playing by sheer instinct—his mental strategies weren't coming across; all his cognitive thoughts were kept at bay. This level of mental control was a huge hindrance for him, but at his level of play, he could very well still beat me. I moved another pawn out to c4. He followed with a pawn to e6. I moved my knight out to f3, and he followed with his bishop to b4: Entering the Bongo. I had a sinking feeling in my chest. This second game was not boding well for me.

His plays were much faster now; the game would be over in minutes. After the next four moves each, I was quickly getting creamed.

"Checkmate," he said.

I hadn't realized his other knight was where it was. I'd been distracted by his over-active queen. I looked over the chessboard at the paltry four pieces I had remaining to his nine. He'd schooled me, and both of us knew how he'd done it.

"All tied up," Drako said. Now it was him resetting the board. His expression was passive; a slight smile lingered on his lips. "One more game. I can't tell you how enjoyable this has been for me, Rob. There is nothing more satisfying than beating a worthy opponent."

I simply nodded and tried to mentally prepare myself for our final game. Drako sat down and we commenced playing. Both of us brought out pawns to e4 and e5. Then both our knights went to f3 and c6. Drako's mind was quiet; I saw no imagery, no emotions ... he was a robot.

As with the second game, Drako was making fast work of me. My chess pieces were collecting at the side of the board twice the rate of his. I was going to lose the game. I had just about resigned myself to that when I tried something new. Since Drako was playing purely by the seat of his pants, with no real thinking going on, I wondered if he would accept my mental suggestions as his own. Looking at the board, my only chance at this point would be for him to move his queen to f3. From there I'd nail him with my bishop. His thoughts were in chess nomenclature mode, so I simply placed the thought of Bf3 into his mind. He moved his bishop to f3 and I quickly took it down. From that point on, evening up the score was only a matter of time. Emotions crept back into his mind: desperation, anger, and finally hopelessness, became self-consuming.

"Checkmate," I said, sitting back and watching Drako continue to look at the board.

I looked out toward the horizon where the last semblance of sunlight reflected off the scope of what was probably a high-powered rifle. I reached out with my mind to the tiny figure stationed there, lying flat on the rocky surface. It was indeed Cassie. She had been watching the match. She knew the rules—and what must transpire, depending on which man was the victor of two of the three games. In her mind, she no longer worked for Drako—she worked for me.

Looking through her eyes in real time, I saw the crosshairs of her rifle trained at a point between Drako's eyebrows.

I carefully collected my chess pieces, being extra-mindful not to touch the top of the white bishop. That chess piece was covered with Batrachotoxin poison. Thanks to SIFTR resources, a poison I had acquired earlier in the day and meticulously applied to that sole chess piece. A lethal dose to humans of this alkaloid is estimated to be 1 to 2 μg/kg. I'd used this poison before and I didn't want the effects to occur too rapidly. A very fast-acting lethal dose for a 160-pound man about Drako's size would be approximately one hundred micrograms, equivalent to the weight of two grains of ordinary table salt. I had adjusted the dose to half that. My guesstimate was Drako had less than two hours to live. There would be no antidote. At least nothing Drako would have access to in the limited time he had remaining on this planet. Soon, Drako's motor skills would start to falter. Neurons would cease to fire. Most likely, his heart would fail first. Unless this poison was specifically sought during the autopsy, Drako would be pronounced dead from cardiac arrest.

I stood and walked over to the pool; I then knelt down and dipped my hands in the water. The chlorine would neutralize any effects of the toxin still left on my coated fingers.

Drako stood. His anger was all consuming. He had never considered any possibility of losing the match. Right now he was looking for a way to countermand the contract. A way to still win. His mind was reeling. Drako's eyes leveled on the two stacks of paper still lying atop the lawyer's briefcase. He lunged for them. The sound of a high-velocity bullet ricocheting off a close-by marble pillar, followed by a distant gunfire report, stopped Drako in his tracks. Unsteady on his feet, he sat back down.

"Chapleau, do you work for my interests in this, as well?" I asked.

"Yes, I do."

"And all this is legal? Binding?"

"Absolutely. Here, take my card."

I pocketed the card. "Good. Have Mr. Cervenka's personal items cleared out of here within the next few days."

"Will do."

Drako leaned back on his lounge chair. He seemed to be having some trouble breathing.

I sat down on the chair opposite him, leaned in, and spoke in a low tone. "I want you to know Ladislav Skykora sends you his special regards. Your actions have caught up with you, Drako. Human trafficking and murder, to name a few. You'll be dead within ten minutes."

Drako tried to move his hands, tried to move his lips. Attempts that failed.

"No need to speak, Drako. Yes, I can most definitely read your mind."

Go to hell, Rob.

You first, Drako, I answered right back, directly into his mind.

I stood and turned to face the far off, rocky horizon and gave a quick wave to Cassie. I headed for the exit.

CHAPTER 30

Pippa was en route to Dulles on Calloway's Gulfstream G550. Although the luxury jet sat sixteen comfortably, there were only a handful of people on board. Pippa sat directly across from Calloway and found him an interesting, and highly intelligent man. Fastidiously dressed in sharply creased suit pants and polished wingtips, he looked just as fresh as he had five hours earlier, in the Beale Hotel. What surprised her most was how much he already knew about her—her life as a child, growing up in Westchester County, New York; her years in college; as well as her time at the CIA—and, most recently, at DHS. Her mind flashed back to the cellar of Hotel Beale and Calloway, standing above them, firing a bullet into Harland's head. He'd done it with an air of indifference, as if he were buying frozen peas from a supermarket. Pippa needed to remember just how ruthless, how dangerous, and possibly, untrustworthy, this man truly was.

"Do you own this plane?" Pippa asked.

"God, no. Charter service. We have a special arrangement," Calloway answered.

Pippa, feeling his eyes on her, felt somewhat uncomfortable by his always *on* intensity. Baltimore moved forward from the back of the cabin and took the seat next to his boss. He leaned in and said something into Calloway's ear. The older man nodded several times and then raised his eyebrows, as if surprised or impressed by the last thing Baltimore said. Baltimore sat back in his seat and looked out the window.

"Seems Mr. Chandler has accomplished his directive in Kingman. Remind me to never underestimate that man." With that, Calloway glanced over to Baltimore and the two exchanged a quick smile.

Pippa was uncertain what they were referring to but guessed it had something to do with those crazy-mad powers of Chandler's. If she hadn't experienced them herself, she wouldn't have believed such things were possible. Sitting here, on this fifty million dollar jet at thirty thousand feet, conversing with one of the most powerful men on the planet, she was reminded how important it was for Rob's secret to remain just that—a secret, and one that could never be revealed to men like Calloway.

"Can you tell me more about the mission we're being brought in for?" she asked.

"Sure," Calloway replied. "You and Chandler will be posing as Pam and David Craft, a recently-married American couple, visiting your relatives in Germany—primarily, your great aunt, Ingrid Krueger."

Baltimore passed Pippa a thick file folder.

"Where in Germany?" she asked. She'd spent several years working out of the U. S. embassy in Berlin and knew a number of locals there. She would be easily recognized.

Calloway smiled, as if reading her mind. "Not Berlin. You will primarily be working out of Baden-Baden. Are you familiar with that area?"

Pippa's eyes widened and she expelled a breath of air. "Europe's richest of the rich live there. I take it Great Aunt Ingrid is well-heeled?"

"Yes, quite wealthy."

"What's our directive?"

"As a visiting couple, you'll need to quickly merge into local high-society. Specifically, you will become friends with Mr. and Mrs. Goertz. Leon Goertz is one of the wealthiest men in Germany. Only recently have we uncovered his ties to a fanatical neo-Nazi group called the WZZ. They have one purpose: to bring Germany back to its former glory at the height of World War Two—and to become today's dominant superpower. The group is dedicated to the destruction of both the United States and Russia."

"What do they honestly think their group can accomplish?" Pippa asked.

"Militarily? Not much. But in the financial realm, Leon is a modern-day Caesar. He yields an immense amount of power within Europe's financial and securities markets. With his early prowess as a savvy investor, and later, as the founding partner of the venture capital group Wolfgang-Klein-Atkins, he now yields powerful influence into Europe's political and financial infrastructure. Whereas the 1930-40s Nazi regime's power lay in its military, and in strategically positioning its troops and artillery throughout Western Europe, the WZZ's modern-day-war machine is invested in targeting financial markets. They've already toppled several small Eastern-bloc corporations. We view these takeovers as running real-world experiments—testing their capabilities, first on a small scale," Calloway explained.

"They went after other countries' companies?" Pippa asked.

"Yes. In essence, that's what financial markets are comprised of ... powered by—successful, dominant, corporations. They'll use any number of methodologies, either to take control of, or outright dismantle, any non-German foreign business. If they succeed, one corporation at a time, the WZZ will become the premier financial player on Earth."

"To be honest, this sounds like a much bigger assignment than two lone agents will be able to handle. What specifically are we tasked to accomplish?"

"We've discovered that Leon Goertz's success over the years is more than having a great financial mind. Something he's kept secret is that his success is actually attributable to a propriety software program—a complex and highly versatile code, with algorithms designed to analyze financial systems like nothing else before. The software program, called Spatz, was originally designed by a German postgrad student named Horris Spatz. Apparently, the code was the basis of his doctoral project. Not only did Leon acquire the code before Horris was able to publish his thesis, Horris went missing over ten years ago. We need to find the single source of this Spatz program within the WZZ ... and we need to destroy it."

"If we're American, why would he befriend us? Wouldn't we be the enemy?"

"Definitely. But Rob's cover as an entrepreneur, in the early stages of taking his highly successful company public, will be enticing to Goertz. Rest assured, he will instigate the contact and friendship. He'll discover Rob's company is already a major supplier of a new, lightning-fast server system to companies such as Google, Microsoft and Apple, to name a few. He'll see that as a way to make inroads into the largest of the U.S. corporations. He'll want Rob's company for himself."

"What's my part in all of this?" Pippa asked.

"In some ways, bigger than Rob's. Heidi Goertz, Leon's wife, is a formidable, upper-class socialite. She has money of her own ... family money. We've already determined that Leon keeps the code for the Spatz program away from his office. We're guessing it's kept under tight security at their Baden-Baden estate. More like a palace. You'll need to get yourselves invited to their upcoming celebration—a birthday party for Heidi."

"I guess we should brush up on our German?"

"You're Americans. Don't want to come across as too prepared. Look, you and Rob will have some local support. We have a Baden-Baden contact within the Verfassungsschutz, Germany's homeland security department," Calloway explained.

Calloway, hesitating, looked over to Baltimore, then continued: "Agent Rosette, the Goertz's, in addition to their connection to the WZZ, are fanatical in wanting to bring Germany back to its former state of glory; regaining, anew, the power and presence it held in the early nineteen forties. Here things get murky; details are limited, at best. They are ruthless, and undoubtedly, murderers in their own right. And with their cult-like following, you'll be walking into an extremely dangerous situation.

Terrific, Pippa thought. She was wishing she'd never met Calloway. She had their mission file open on her lap. She had been skimming through the material as Calloway spoke. She read that her appearance profile was fairly specific: short black hair, blue eyes, curvy, and a small tattoo of a ladybug on her upper right buttock. She looked up at Calloway. "Tattoo?"

Curt Baltimore interjected: "Both covers, yours and Rob's, have been derived from actual people. Years in the making, and an extremely expensive proposition, we prefer you match their physical attributes as closely as possible. Temporary henna tattoos can fade ... never really look real."

"Who's going to be looking at my ass?"

"You'll be on a mission. Whatever impromptu situation might arise you'll be expected to deliver," Baltimore replied. Calloway didn't add anything to this and stayed expressionless.

Pippa thought about it. *Seriously? I'm to get a tattoo on my ass?*

Baltimore leaned forward, rifled through the file on her lap, and came up with an 8x10 color photograph. "Look for yourself. This is a picture of the actual Pam Craft."

Pippa looked at the photo and saw some resemblance to herself. The woman had similar features, similar bone structure. But where her own hair was long and platinum blonde, Pam's hair was black, cut above her shoulders, and she had a sassy, fun style Pippa actually liked. But the real Pam's body was quite different. Not as tall as she was, Pam also had the addition of several cup-sizes on her chest.

Pippa looked over to Baltimore with a furrowed brow. "That ain't happening."

Baltimore smiled and said, "We'd prefer you to be surgically augmented, but I understand there are a series of injections that will suffice instead ... temporary, but they will be suitable for the duration of the mission."

Pippa just shook her head, not really knowing what else to say.

"You and Rob will also have your facial bone structure somewhat altered via a series of strategically placed silicone injections."

"What will happen to the real Pam and David during this time?" Pippa asked.

"They've agreed to go to ground for no more than seven days," Calloway said.

Baltimore began rifling through the file on her lap again, eventually coming up with another photo. Smiling, he looked at it, then flipped it around to face Pippa. David Craft was approximately Rob's height and build. He also had red hair. Fire-engine red. Pippa giggled. Soon all three of them were laughing out loud.

CHAPTER 31

I spent the night again at Motel 6, and after tapping in early the next morning I made my way to the Kingman Regional Airport where I was greeted by Curt Baltimore. I followed him out to the runway where our ride sat, her engines winding up. I pointed to the G550. "That one for us?"

"Yep, she's been pretty much flown non-stop since yesterday afternoon," Baltimore answered.

"You too, I'm betting?"

"It's not a problem." He shrugged it off.

With the exception of a crew of three, plus Baltimore and myself, the plane was empty. I plopped down mid-cabin in one of the wide, stark-white leather seats. Baltimore sat directly across from me. Twenty-five minutes after takeoff, dual breakfasts of eggs Benedict and fruit plates were delivered by an attractive, thirty-something, flight attendant. With a quick look into her thoughts, I saw she was also an SIFTR agent.

Baltimore brought up a bulky briefcase and placed it on his lap. "We have a lot to go over in the next few hours." He handed me a fat file folder. "Why don't you go through this on your own first, then we can go over the particulars and any questions you may have afterward."

I dug into the file and later had a lot of questions for Baltimore. We were still at it when the plane set down at Dulles airport, three and a half hours later. I wondered how Pippa was coping with the changes in her life over the last few days ... new job, being taken prisoner by a psychotic maniac, dealing with me and my unique circumstances— not to mention the unresolved aspects of our past relationship. Maybe our relationship was just that: meant to stay in the past. I had kept my promise—had stayed out of her head. So I wasn't sure where things stood between us.

* * *

There were at least twenty covert agencies, in or around Washington, D.C., that I could think of off the top of my head. The more secret, mostly those associated with the Department of Defense such as NSA and DIA, the less restrictions there were. To get necessary funding, each agency was supposed to be under some sort of congressional oversight review board, but I knew this wasn't always the case. SIFTR was privately funded, according to what Baltimore told me on the plane, by an international committee. Even though it was a very small organization, its resources were staggering—in the billions, if necessary.

There was a black SUV waiting for us at Dulles. Baltimore got behind the wheel and we drove directly to Georgetown. We pulled to a stop in front of a three-story brownstone on North Street.

"You'll be staying here for the next few days," Baltimore said. I opened the car door and moved to climb out. "Be ready by 6:00 a.m.," Baltimore added. I shut the door and the SUV accelerated away.

Ten stair steps up, a large red door opened and a silver-haired man, casually dressed in slacks and a blue cardigan sweater, smiled down at me. "Good evening, Mr. Chandler." He held the door open and beckoned me to come on up. "My name is Tony; welcome to Riley House."

I stepped past Tony into a large foyer. He closed the door and entered a pass-code on a panel by the side of the door. I heard the sound of electronic actuators and some serious hardware lock into place.

"This way, sir," Tony said, walking forward past a large winding staircase to another set of doors, decorated with ornate brass hardware. I followed him into a large sitting room area that once was, perhaps in an earlier time period, a parlor. At the back of the room was another doorway, which led us into a large kitchen. "I'll leave you here with Ms. Rosette. Feel free to grab a snack. She'll get you situated in your room ... good evening."

"Thanks."

Tony strode back the way we'd come and I turned to see a long table that could easily seat twelve. Obscured by three cereal boxes and a jug of milk, I spotted a glimpse of blonde hair.

"Hungry?" Pippa asked, with a full mouth of Captain Crunch.

I sat across from her, separating two of the boxes so I could see her face.

"I was starving. Want me to get you a bowl?" she asked.

"No, thanks, I'm good. How long have you been here?"

"I don't know, maybe five hours?" she replied, shoveling in another mouthful. "You've been briefed?"

I nodded.

"I didn't expect you to show up. You made it pretty clear that you were out. Retired, I think you put it."

I shrugged. "Maybe after this job."

She seemed disinterested and her focus returned to the printed back on one of the cereal boxes. "So what is this place?" I asked.

"An old historic federal townhouse. Actually, all four townhomes on this side of the street are interconnected. More SIFTR assets. We'll be staying here while they prep us for the mission."

I looked around the kitchen and large dining area. "Had a chance to look around?"

Her eyes stayed on the box. She continued to crunch away. "Um, not really. Why?"

So this was how it was going to be. The cold treatment: more fallout for not finding some way to contact her over the past year. Truth was, I couldn't really blame her, and perhaps I should have done more ... somehow gotten a message to her.

"Basement."

"Basement?" I repeated.

"Utility room's down there. Passcode is 5612." Pippa got up, grabbing the boxes of cereal, and carried them into the kitchen; she disappeared into a pantry. I put the milk away in the refrigerator and deposited her bowl and spoon in the sink.

"How'd you get the code?" I asked.

"I'm not going to tell you all my secrets," she said, leaning against the counter with her arms crossed over her chest. Our eyes met for the first time and she continued,

"And remember, what goes on in here, is none of your damn business." She pointed with her thumb at her own forehead.

I nodded. "Promise."

"Good. I'll show you to your room—come on."

We left the kitchen through a different set of doors and passed through a game room with a sectional couch and large screen TV at this end and a pool table at the other. The back stairway was positioned at the rear of the house and I followed Pippa up the narrow staircase. I had to make a conscious effort to keep my eyes averted from her all-too-perfect backside, three steps in front of me. At the third level, Pippa pointed to a series of doors down an adjacent hallway. "You're there, on the right, second doorway. We have a meeting with Baltimore at 6:00 a.m."

"Yeah, he mentioned that to me."

"You'll find that your room has been stocked. Clothes, toiletries, everything you'll need." She continued on without looking back. When she got to what must be her bedroom, she entered, and without looking back, shut the door. I heard the sound of a deadbolt clicking into place.

Sure enough, there were clothes in the closet and toiletries in the bathroom. I peeled off my clothes and got the shower going. While I waited for the water to get hot I thought about what Pippa had said. Why had I agreed to work with SIFTR? There were a number of options available to me now, given my new talents. Did I really need to put my life on the line for an organization I knew little about? And even less about what their true motives were? I stepped under the hot water and brought my thoughts back to Pippa. She was the reason. She'd changed over the past year: more confident—self-sufficient. A year or more ago, she was prepared to leave the agency, give up her career so we could make a go of our relationship. Now, she was all business. A career agent.

I toweled off and found a pair of running shorts and a T-shirt in a chest of drawers in the bedroom. Everything fit, including a pair of new Nike tennis shoes I found on the floor of the closet. According to the clock on the bedside table, it was just after midnight. I slipped out of my room and headed for the stairs. I made my way down the three levels I'd traversed earlier and continued down another far less formal set of stairs that ended up in the basement. Sure enough, a metal door marked Utility was off to the left. I entered 5612 into the keypad next to the door and heard it unlatch. The room was brightly lit from overhead fluorescents. Two large, cylindrical elevator-drive motors, with flywheel assemblies, were stationary across from me. Thick metal cables were looped into each one and disappeared into the ceiling above, into what must be the elevator shaft. The power panels were to my right. Like so many electrical panels I'd come into contact with over the last week, I knew where to go—where to find the incoming high-voltage lines. It had become routine, like other bodily regimens, such as eating or going to the bathroom. I gave it little thought, other than always taking the necessary precaution to avoid getting myself electrocuted.

Four minutes into it, with my head resting against the cool steel pipe, something changed. The familiar connection, the song that routinely filled my consciousness, was now accompanied by something else—something far less abstract than I was used to.

Hello, Rob. Welcome back.

The voice was as familiar to me as hearing my own. Not since I'd sat within the crumpled confines of my crashed rental car on that Kingman highway had I felt this level of connection—the oneness.

Who are you? ... What are you? I asked, feeling my consciousness expanding—accelerating—pulled farther out, into the vastness of pure energy itself. Limitless, yet confined to a single trajectory, toward something or someone.

I've been searching for a thousand lifetimes, Rob. Will you help me?

I was getting closer, approaching a destination that seemed familiar, yet entirely new, too ...undefined edges of nothingness, the formless beginning to taking shape. I, myself, was taking shape.

You're almost here, Rob.

A loud clank and the sound of the elevator motors whirling to life jarred me back to reality. My connection gone, I heard the elevator settle to a stop one floor above me.

CHAPTER 32

I cleared out of the utility room, entered the passcode to relock it, and took the stairs back up to the first floor two at a time. I sprinted into the kitchen and heard footsteps in the game room. They were coming closer.

Tony entered the kitchen holding a Sig Sauer 9 mm at waist level. I came out of the pantry holding Pippa's same three boxes of cereal. Startled, Tony raised his weapon toward my head.

"Mr. Chandler, I didn't realize you were up and about."

"Stomach was grumbling. Must be a time zone thing. Sorry, Tony, did I disturb you?"

"It's quite all right, we're used to late-night fridge raiding here," Tony replied, while looking around the kitchen to see if I was alone. He walked to a door that led to the backyard. Checking that it was indeed locked, he lowered his gun and his casual smile returned. "I'll leave you to it; enjoy your snack."

I nodded and while he turned back the way he'd come, I read his mind:

Late night snack my ass ...

He was suspicious. He knew I'd been down in the basement, but he wasn't overly worried about it. I put the cereal back on the shelf and made my way back to my room.

Had I imagined the voice, that presence, pulling me toward something: Will you help me, Rob? I felt an uneasiness deep within myself. I'd heard and felt its desperation. One thing I knew for certain: I wasn't alone out there; wherever that was when I tapped in. I knew now that I needed to find out who, or what, needed my help. How the hell would I do that?

* * *

Tony, dressed in a different cardigan, this one rust-colored, offered me a hot cup of coffee as I entered the kitchen.

"Thanks."

Pippa was seated at the table in the same chair she'd been sitting in the previous night.

"Morning," Pippa said, not looking up from the NY Post held up in front of her. "Nice suit."

Before I had a chance to sit down, Baltimore strode into the kitchen. "Good morning, Tony. Ms. Rosette, Mr. Chandler, we have fifteen minutes to get across town."

Baltimore did an about face and hurried out. Pippa tossed her paper on the table, took another quick sip of coffee and followed. I took another sip, placed my half-empty cup in the sink, and scurried after them.

Pippa was already sitting shotgun in Baltimore's black SUV when I got to the curb. I climbed into the back seat.

The SUV lurched forward and we merged into the morning traffic. Pippa lowered the sun visor and slid open the little panel to access the vanity mirror. I saw her appraise herself, turning her head one side to the other—then her eyes momentarily flicked toward me. I smiled. She closed the panel and slapped the visor back into place.

"Where we off to?" I asked.

"First, we'll be meeting with Mr. Calloway and others on the team. The timeframe for getting you both into Germany has been accelerated. We have a lot to accomplish today."

Twelve minutes later, Baltimore pulled over to a red curb beneath a No Parking sign. He tossed a government-issued plastic tag onto the dashboard and we all got out. We were at the National Mall. Baltimore headed in the direction of the Lincoln Memorial. Pippa stayed to his left side, while I walked on his right.

"You two okay?" Baltimore asked, looking at Pippa and then over toward me.

We both replied at the same time.

"Great," I replied

"Terrific," Pippa said.

We hit the marble steps at the same time and climbed up toward the imposing statue of Abraham Lincoln, seated high above us. We passed through two marble pillars and looked up at the immortalized face of the sixteenth U.S. president. Baltimore veered off to his left and we followed closely behind, through another set of high-reaching marble pillars, until we were at the farthest south wall. There, waiting for us, stood a Washington D.C. policeman next to a plain wooden door. Baltimore nodded at the officer who opened the door, holding it wide enough for Pippa and myself to enter behind Baltimore. Two men in suits, unmistakably secret-service agents, were standing sentry at the top of a metal stairway. The agent on the right murmured something into his left sleeve.

Descending the winding stairway, the three of us were enclosed within the very foundation of the monument. One hundred years of moisture deposits dripped from small, white stalactites high above us. Six additional secret-service agents were stationed in a semi-circle at the northwest quadrant of the room. On that wall was a massive, rusted, iron door. Upon our arrival it started slowly to slide sideways. Metal wheels complained as they rolled on steel rails mounted to the floor. The first man through the door was James C. Morrison, president of the United States. Dressed in a smart navy blue suit, blue and red striped tie, and a small U.S. flag lapel pin, he moved with hurried purpose. Calloway, dressed in a dark gray suit, followed closely behind. In the distance, beyond the open metal door, I heard the unmistakable sound of a train or subway. I'd heard that there was a subterranean rail system for senators and congressmen to move about Washington in secret, when necessary. Perhaps the president himself had his own private means of subterranean travel around town.

Morrison moved directly toward the three of us and held out his hand, first shaking Pippa's, then mine. "Pippa, Rob, thank you again for committing to invaluable service to your country. By now you have both reviewed the mission dossier. The assignment objectives are straightforward: acquire the Spatz software code; destroy WZZ's capacity to utilize this code, and stop Leon Goertz from taking control of key financial markets. My presence here alone should convey to you how important I believe this assignment to be. The WZZ has infiltrated virtually every covert agency around the world. Bringing down Goertz is imperative."

Morrison looked over to Calloway. Appearing to weigh something in his head, he continued: "But I want more. I want the WZZ completely decimated. Now, Mr. Calloway does not believe the parameters of your mission should be expected to get all that accomplished."

Pippa replied first, "I assure you, Mr. President, we will do everything we can to accomplish what you've asked us to do."

I'd wasted no time before peering into President Morrison's mind. The stakes were just too high not to. There was something he wasn't telling us. Not so much a lie as an omission. And then there it was: he was feeling guilt. Pippa and I were to be sanctioned off at the conclusion of the mission. Success or fail, we were to be silently, and properly, disposed of.

Smiling, Calloway moved forward and, taking the president by the elbow, ushered him back toward the direction they'd come. The meeting was over.

I held up a hand, gesturing that I wanted to add something else. The smile quickly left Calloway's face, but the president, turning his attention back toward us, looked honestly interested.

"I would request that you reconsider one aspect of this mission."

Morrison looked confused.

"Termination of assets in the field, namely us, when the assignment is over."

Morrison's thoughts were written all over his face ... *how on earth could you possibly know that?*

I continued, "Agreeing to serve my country is one thing. Embarking on a suicide mission is quite another. Especially when the plan to terminate us has been conveniently left out of both Rosette's and my dossiers."

"You're out of line, Chandler," Calloway spat. "Have you forgotten who you're talking to?"

Pippa looked at me and then turned toward the president. "Is that true? Is what Chandler is saying part of your plan?" she asked.

Morrison kept his eyes locked on mine. When he finally answered, his voice was barely audible. "That determination was only recently arrived at. I apologize. These decisions are not made lightly. National security takes precedence over—"

I cut him off mid-sentence. I was very angry. Perhaps it was a year confined to a seven hundred-square-foot flat in Russia, or being set tup to plow headlong into a telephone pole on the outskirts of Kingman, or the fact that I could read the president's mind. It didn't matter. I wasn't the same person I was one year ago and I wasn't willing to play the spy game anymore. Not under these conditions. "Find yourself another agent. I'm not interested. I'm officially retired."

"Then you'll find yourself officially taken into custody. You won't be the first, or the last, agent to go to prison for insubordination," Calloway seethed.

I smiled at the tan, gray-haired man. He was a man who had his own secrets—things he certainly wouldn't want the president to be made aware of. I looked deep into his mind and knew in an instant that even the president was not beyond Calloway's reach. There were certain contingencies already in place—one such, called *Meridian*, was a course of action that would take care of a president who no longer went along with the philosophical dictums of the SIFTR organization.

I felt Pippa's hand on my wrist. Ever so slightly, she was shaking her head. She was telling me, with her eyes, not to go there—not to reveal things that I couldn't possibly have a way of knowing.

"No, Rob's right," Morrison said to Calloway. "Rob, Pippa, I give you my word. Succeed or fail, there'll be no repercussions—no action taken against either of you, other than to say thank you and welcome you back home. Please accept my apology—we need you for this mission ... both of you."

CHAPTER 33

I told the president I would complete the mission. I also said this would conclude my involvement with SIFTR and, thereafter, I would no longer work as an undercover agent for the U.S. government. I would officially retire and I fully expected, at that point, to be left alone. Calloway said something about us needing to talk further about that aspect, but he quickly left with the president.

The rest of the day was all about prepping for the mission ahead. We split up. Pippa had a doctor's appointment and then would be off to familiarize herself with every aspect of Pam Craft's life, as well as the essentials of Baden-Baden high society.

I was taken to SIFTR headquarters, twenty-five miles northeast of Washington, D.C. in Baltimore, Maryland—on the outskirts of Fort Meade. Unlike the massive National Security Agency headquarters building three miles away, the SIFTR building was nondescript and unless someone was specifically looking for the site, it would pretty much go unnoticed. It was a one-story concrete affair, and Baltimore and I entered through the building's front door into a wide lobby that looked as if it hadn't been updated since the 1960s. Even the security guard, sitting at an oak desk, looked to be wearing a policeman's costume from an era long gone.

We walked past the guard who barely acknowledged our presence. "Impressive," I said, joining Baltimore at an ancient-looking, paint-chipped elevator door. "This building ever make the transition from telegraph to telephone service?"

Baltimore, with a bemused expression, gestured for me to move ahead when the car arrived. The elevator had 1960s-style wood paneling on the walls and tired, worn linoleum flooring. From the exterior, it looked to be a one-story building so there was only one direction the car could go—downward. Five seconds into our descent, a projected, red-glowing virtual panel appeared to the right of the older, original panel. While the old panel showed three floors, the newer panel listed eighteen. Baltimore pressed his thumb against a small square area and brought his face closer to what I surmised was a retina scanner. The virtual panel changed to a pleasing blue color and Baltimore tapped at the number twelve. In seconds, the car came to a stop and the doors slid open.

We stepped into a bustling corridor where men and women hurriedly moved here and there. Gone was the archaic 1960s decor. Glass and brushed metal was the dominant theme and rich gray carpeting lay beneath our feet.

"First, we need to see how out of shape you are. Then, we'll determine what your skill-level is in close combat fighting, as well as your proficiency in handling weapons,"

Baltimore said. He held open a glass door simply labeled *Training.*

Baltimore led me into a locker room and showed me where I could find the necessary workout clothes I'd need. Five minutes later we were in an area of a gym covered with thick vinyl matts. Both of us wore protective face gear and padded gloves.

Baltimore was in decent shape. We did several minutes of stretching and it was then I realized how out of shape I really was. Baltimore was looking forward to smacking me around a bit. He was mystified why I'd been selected for the upcoming mission, when he, in his mind, was the far better choice.

As of late, I was finding it less and less an ethics-issue to read people's minds. Of course there would be exceptions, such as Pippa, but I could no more ignore my new sixth sense than I could any of the other five I was accustomed to using since birth. Right now, Baltimore was reviewing in his head how he was going to humiliate me with a combination of punches, kicks, and maneuvers that would pin me to the floor.

Baltimore was going to start with a backspin to his right and deliver a back kick into my solar plexus. I moved in preemptively with a front kick to his stomach, followed by a one-two, left-right series of uppercuts to his chin. Baltimore went down on his rear end.

He got to his feet and came at me like an angry bull. His mind was now working on autopilot and any advantage I'd had reading his thoughts was greatly reduced. He finished his attack with a spinning crescent kick to my chin and I went sprawling to the mat. For the next forty-five minutes neither of us could get the upper hand on the other. By the time Baltimore held up his hand saying we were done, we were drenched in sweat and heaving to catch our breaths.

"Shower, then the range. Perhaps you'll do better with a gun in your hand," Baltimore said, with a smile.

* * *

Baltimore was already there and shooting when I arrived at the range. The back counter held a wide assortment of handguns, and both semi- and automatic assault weapons.

"Let's start with handguns. Grab that Sig Sauer P226R, the .357."

I found the one he was referring to and ejected and checked its mag. Standing beside Baltimore, I racked the slide and chambered a round.

"Don't forget these," Baltimore said, handing over a set of ear muffs.

The man-sized target was set fifteen yards out. I moved up to the small counter, positioned my feet as I'd done a thousand times before, aimed the SIG, and rapidly fired off twelve rounds, emptying the high-capacity magazine.

Baltimore toggled a switch to retrieve the target. Two tight groupings: heart and head. Two rounds had landed a half-inch away from the others. "Not bad. Could be better," Baltimore said. He attached a new target and sent it back.

He was right. I was out of practice. I was irritated that my firing skills had slipped the past year.

Baltimore brought back a Glock 32, .357 from the back counter. He chambered a round and quickly fired toward the target. Upon a close review of his target, it was evident Baltimore was well practiced. Two groupings, like mine, but tighter and none had wandered.

"Nice shooting," I said.

We stayed there for two more hours. By the time we left, I was back in form, shooting as well as, if not better than, Baltimore.

We ate lunch in the commissary. The food was surprisingly good and the portions were generous. "What's next on the agenda for today?" I asked.

"Conference room. Dive back into the mission particulars—much more detailed." Baltimore smiled. "Later, you have an appointment with our quartermaster—our own version of Q."

But first, Baltimore, myself, and two SIFTR agents, Ben and Sylvia, went through the entire mission, from stem to stern. Digitized overheads were used and displayed images of all the players on a ginormous 70" screen monitor. Much attention was given to the Goertz's Baden-Baden castle and its sprawling countryside grounds. There were several snapshots of Leon's office and an adjoining small service room. I paid extra attention to where city power lines entered the estate, along with the multiple methods I might use to access that area.

We also reviewed the key players of the WZZ organization. All were male, German, and mega-millionaires in their own right. There was some discussion about meetings—where they actually assembled. To date, there were no pictures—not a hint how and where they met.

The last part of the meeting was dedicated to my cover: a multi-millionaire in my own right, I was MIT-educated, with a Ph.D. in Systems Architecture. At thirty I'd started my own company—providing proprietary cloud-based servers, with new, blazingly fast hard-drive technology that was years ahead of anything else on the market. Friendly photos, along with detailed correspondence—emails and legal contracts—had all been fabricated. Without too much digging, one could find pictures of me with Microsoft's Bill Gates, Google's Larry Page, and Apple's CEO, Tim Cook. I was high tech's new wonder boy of the hour.

By the time we'd left the conference room, I was starting to feel the effects of too many hours, both physically and mentally pushed well beyond what I was used to. A midday tapping-in session would help, but probably wouldn't be in the cards right now.

The SIFTR Lab was impressive. Two floors down from *Training*, it was departmentalized and occupied the entire floor. Beyond clean, beyond sterile, the lab looked right out of a sci-fi blockbuster. Baltimore ushered me down a long corridor flanked on both sides by floor to ceiling glass. Men and women in white lab coats worked at benches and conversed in cubicle offices. It was then I saw a familiar face. Sitting in what looked like a dentist or doctor's chair, her legs up and extended, was Pippa. A doctor, stethoscope hanging around his neck, was talking to her; his animated hands were describing something. Pippa caught my eye. She did not look happy.

"In here," Baltimore said, pushing a sliding glass door open wide enough for us both to enter.

"This is Bridgett Bigalow, SIFTR's quartermaster ... our version of Q," Baltimore said.

I was surprised to see not only a woman, but one who was quite young. I estimated her age to be mid-twenties to early thirties, max. She wore thick-lensed glasses, no make-up, and short dark hair pulled back into a tight ponytail. She reached up to my hair and with two fingers felt its texture. Her eyes looked enormous and distorted by her glasses. She pushed in even closer, totally invading my personal space. I'd met people like her before ... absolute geniuses, savants, but lacking even rudimentary social skills. With that not-ed, I instantly liked her. There was something refreshingly honest about her bare-bones practicality.

I watched her leave the room, then reenter a few moments later. She was holding something in her hand—a glass beaker, half-full of clear, water-like liquid. She set the beaker atop a workbench and put on latex gloves. She brought the beaker over to a small sink and poured some of the liquid over her hands. She turned to face me.

"Oops. You need to take off your clothes."

I looked over at Baltimore, who remained expressionless. I unbuttoned my shirt and slipped it off.

"Um ... Wait, go behind here," she said, pulling a plastic curtain around that hung from a curved rod affixed high on the ceiling. "Take off all your clothes."

I moved behind the curtain partition and took off the rest of my clothes.

I heard Bigalow rewetting her hands at the sink, and then she was back at my side, the two of us together behind the curtain. Her hands went to my chest, her small fingers wetting what little chest hair I had. She left, returning with wetter hands. Underarms, privates, and the hair on my head were doused with the clear, odorless liquid.

"Get dressed," she said, removing her gloves and throwing them into a small disposal bin attached to the wall. "You'll need to come back for the antidote."

"Antidote?" I asked, confused.

She'd apparently left, because I didn't get an answer. Baltimore was waiting for me when I came back around the curtain. "Where'd she go?" I asked.

"This way." Baltimore took me through several adjacent lab areas; we soon found Bigalow standing at a workbench where she was adjusting some kind of oscilloscope.

"Hold out your left hand," she said.

I did as I was told. Carefully, without disconnecting any of the electronic leads, she picked up a small gold band and slid in onto my ring finger. She looked up at me and smiled self-consciously. Apparently this was a more intimate procedure for her than putting that wet shit all over my body.

"These rings are amazing. The technology packed into these things is decades beyond anything available commercially. They're also expensive."

"How expensive?"

"Twenty million dollars. Each," she said.

The wedding band was average in every way except it had numerous leads extending out from the ring's inside edge. Bigalow was back at the oscilloscope and making some adjustments. She powered on another small electrical device, perhaps a frequency generator. I felt a small tingle around my finger.

"Okay, you're matched," she said.

"What does that mean?"

"It means this ring is configured specifically to your body's frequency wavelength. It won't operate unless it's on your finger. Or toe. I guess that would work, too."

She smiled at that and continued: "Watch carefully." She removed the tiny alligator clips from the leads at the edge of the ring. It was then I noticed the ring was actually octagon-shaped—with eight distinct sides. She touched two of its sides in her fingers and pressed them simultaneously. The small leads disappeared into the ring. Then she pressed three sides, using her thumb and two fingers. One of the sides turned black.

"Cool, look at that," I said.

"While in this mode, your ring becomes a highly sensitive data-transferring device. Simply by touching it to the surface of any USB connector, you can transfer and store substantial amounts of data."

"Can the electronics be detected? Picked up by a scanner?"

"No, only by pressing the three sides simultaneously will the device even activate. Any other time, it's totally inert. If the ring's removed from your finger, it cannot be activated at all."

I nodded my approval. Bigalow smiled, holding up both her palms. "Oh, that's not all it does ..."

CHAPTER 34

Baltimore picked me up at the townhouse in Georgetown at seven the next morning. Apparently, Pippa had remained in Maryland overnight and would meet us on the plane.

"So you'll be there too?" I asked him.

"Not far, the Armenian Consulate in Karlsruhe, in Baden Württemberg."

"Armenian?"

"They owe us a favor. As we covered, we also have an asset within the Verfassungsschutz. If things start to unravel, we'll have your six."

Baltimore took a folded newspaper from the center console and tossed it onto my lap. "Turn to the business section."

I paged through the paper until I found the business section and spread the pages out in front of me. I couldn't miss what he was referring to: it was the section's leading article.

Unprecedented Volatility with German Markets

The **Frankfurt Stock Exchange** (German: Frankfurter Wertpapierbörse, FWB) is the world's 10th largest stock exchange. Located in Frankfurt, Germany, the Frankfurt Stock Exchange is owned and operated by Deutsche Börse (**FWB**: DB1), which also owns the European futures exchange. This week, six behemoth-sized corporations, all German companies and previously traded publicly, have been purchased by a yet-undisclosed financial institution, or entity. News of the Frankfurt Stock Exchange volatility has had ripple effects across all international markets, including the NY Stock Exchange, which has seen its Dow Jones Index plummet three days straight ...

I closed the paper. "The WZZ?" I asked.

"Most definitely. This clearly shows their effect on not only German financial systems, but on international markets as well. The WZZ has started to flex their muscles. Undoubtedly, utilization of their Spatz software directed them toward which six companies to privatize—which companies would produce the most dramatic domestic, as well as international, financial repercussions. Imagine the WZZ playing the same buyout games in the U.S., causing the NY Stock Exchange to tumble. We could be catapulted into a depression that would make the crash of 1929 look like a summer picnic."

* * *

The same Gulfstream G550 was waiting for us on the tarmac. I was told not to bring anything. All my clothes, shoes, even toiletries, had been purchased beforehand and packed away. Everything was stowed in the jet's hold. Baltimore got out of the SUV and came around the front of the vehicle.

"Not coming with us?" I asked.

"No. From this point on, everything will be scrutinized—including who disembarks from the plane once it's on the ground in Germany. Even the charter registry of the plane needs to show David Craft as the principle, not SIFTR. I won't be far behind. On a commercial flight, later today."

We shook hands and I headed for the Gulfstream and the already lowered stairway.

The same SIFTR agent/flight attendant greeted me as I entered the cabin. Her eyebrows shot up in surprise. "Oh, Mr. Chandler! Welcome aboard." I nodded to her and kept walking.

At the rear of the cabin was Pippa. She was bundled up tight in a blanket and her seat was extended out for sleep. She was wearing a sweatshirt with the attached hood covering most of her face. She had a small roller-type suitcase positioned on the seat adjacent to hers. Obviously, she didn't want to be disturbed. Then her eyes opened and she saw me in the aisle, standing near the front of the cabin. It started out as a giggle. Both hands soon covered her mouth. Then I heard the flight attendant behind me; she too began laughing. I turned and scowled at her.

"Sorry," she said. "They said it would be red, but good golly, that's really red!"

I gave her a condescending smile and sat down, facing forward. The giggles continued from behind me so I flipped Pippa the bird without turning around.

I'd been just as surprised this morning when I went into the bathroom. To my amazement, all the hair on my head and body had turned fire engine red. Apparently, Bigalow's clear water-like formula was a slow-acting catalyst that changed the color properties of my hair. I now understood her reference to an antidote. I'd be stuck looking like this until I got myself back in that lab of hers.

I slept for the better part of the thirteen-hour flight. I looked out the window as we landed on the runway and taxied for several minutes. When the plane finally came to a stop, I stood and waited for Pippa. She was already coming down the aisle and I almost didn't recognize her. Her hair was short and very black. It bobbed and bounced as she walked. It looked fantastic! But it wasn't her hairstyle that held my attention. Normally tall and slim, with an athletic-type build, she was now anything but. Although trying to hide the fact beneath her oversized sweatshirt, she was obviously carrying some substantial boobage.

As she came closer, I smiled innocently at her.

"Don't say one fucking word," she said, not looking back at me.

* * *

A chauffeur-driven black Mercedes sedan took us to Baden Württemberg. It was already early morning in Germany when we approached Great Aunt Ingrid's home, Villa

Becksberg. The house itself was a nineteenth century red sandstone mansion, with a singular tall steeple along its dramatically angled roofline. Four storied, with an ivy-covered portico, it was an impressive estate. We pulled into a wide circular drive and stopped in front of the villa's double door entrance.

The chauffeur Manfred, slim and elderly, moved with slow deliberation to open Pippa's door. She stepped out and I scooted out right behind her. I nodded thanks to Manfred.

A scream emanated from behind us as a seventy-something woman with blonde hair rushed toward us.

"My little Pamela! Oh my ... oh my."

Pippa ran into the arms of her long lost Aunt Ingrid. For anyone watching, you'd think they were kindred souls, reuniting after years of separation. Truth be told, the two had never met.

Next, Ingrid's arms were opened wide, beckoning me in for a hug. She swallowed me up in her arms and rocked me back and forth. *Boy, she's really playing this up.*

She pulled away from me, holding my face in her hands. "Look at you ... well, that certainly is a ginger mop, isn't it?"

Pippa answered for me: "Well, it's something."

"Come, come, let's go inside and get you situated," Aunt Ingrid demanded.

I turned to see Manfred wrestling with one of Pippa's oversized suitcases. "Would you like some help with that?" I asked.

He furrowed his brow and mumbled something under his breath that sounded like *Verpiss dich.* I certainly knew enough German to know what that translated to.

"Okay, well good luck with that, then," I said, and followed after the women into the villa.

The wood-paneled foyer was empty but I heard murmurs coming from down the hallway. I found the two women in the kitchen, talking in low tones. The friendly smile was gone from Aunt Ingrid's face, and Pippa was nodding in agreement to something she'd said. Both turned toward me.

"You're late," Ingrid said in a guttural, heavily-accented German voice.

"We are? When were you expecting us?" I asked.

"Yesterday. Plans had been arranged for the two of you. I don't need to remind you of the jeopardy this operation puts me in, do I?"

I was tempted to let her remind me, but Pippa beat me to the punch. "We apologize. Of course, we know how important your involvement is. Now that we are here, what can we do to get everything back on track?"

"I need to get you introduced to Heidi and Leon Goertz. They have no idea yet who you are. I was supposed to introduce you at the theater last evening. Everything was in place; your seats were right next to theirs." Ingrid sized up Pippa: "You'll need a hat. A spectacular hat."

Pippa nodded in confusion. "What? Why do I need a hat?"

"The races, my dear. We're going to the horse races."

CHAPTER 35

Once Manfred extracted our luggage from the car, he carried it up into our room on the fourth floor. As a married couple, separate rooms definitely wouldn't do. Appropriate appearances needed to be kept up. On any given day, maids, cooks, even delivery personnel with loose lips could foil the mission.

Pippa was hanging up clothes in the closet. I sat on the bed and watched her.

"You're not looking so good, Rob."

"I'll be all right," I replied.

"You need to do that thing ... Tap in?"

"Yeah. It's about that time."

"Does the electricity in Germany work the same? Will there be a problem?"

"Nah. In fact, it's all 240 volts here; probably better, easier on me. But higher voltage would still be best."

"Are you able to read my mind?"

"Right now? No ... haven't had that capability for several hours. I'm just like everyone else."

Pippa nodded as she came over to the bed and, zipping her suitcase closed, put it away at the bottom of the closet. "How about I hang up your clothes for you?"

"I'd like that, thanks," I said. I stood and looked out the window. I'd been gazing at the view of distant hills and the Black Forest and missed what was literally right before my nose: two thick, black utility cables. I stepped to my right a bit to spot where they were connected. Sure enough, one of the lines was connected to a large transformer unit secured to the left side of the villa, and I estimated it to be about fifteen feet from where I currently stood. From what I could see, nothing was going on outside; no one was around. I opened the window and stuck my head out to get a better view of the transformer. I'd need to get across the roof. I spotted a room's window I'd have to cross in front of, but the biggest obstacle would be countering the pitch of the roof, which was pretty steep. I heard the mournful request over and over in my mind: *Can you help me Rob?* I'd have to risk it.

"What are you doing?"

"Transformer. I think I can get to it."

"Like right now, in the middle of the day? What if someone sees you?" Pippa came over to the window and looked out. Her shoulder was touching mine and I could smell the fragrance of her shampoo. She saw me looking at her and stepped back. "I guess there's no one around. You going to try it?"

I nodded.

"Maybe a different pair of shoes?" she asked.

I looked down at the loafers I had on.

"You'd slip right off that roof —might as well be wearing roller skates." She lifted my suitcase onto the bed and unzipped it. Within several moments she held out a pair of tennis shoes. "These would work better."

I changed shoes and took another look out the window—all clear. First, I hung one leg outside, then the other, and slowly clambered onto the roof. The slate shingles were big and slippery even with sneaks on. I had to sit on my ass and crabwalk to my left. Pippa stuck her head out the window and was watching my progress. When I came to the next window, I peeked around the corner into the room. Peering through sheer curtains, I could see enough of the room to determine it was empty. A large mahogany poster bed, covered in a frilly comforter, was across from a dresser displaying a flat-panel TV. The TV was on—some kind of German soap opera. A shadow crossed from farther back in the room, where the bathroom was. Then I saw her. It was Ingrid's bedroom. She was getting dressed for the day's events. When she disappeared back into the bathroom I quickly scooted across the window to the other side.

Even from three feet out I felt the familiar beckoning. The power line was connected to the far side of the transformer. I needed to get closer. Ideally, close enough to place my forehead right next to the high-voltage cable, but the only way I'd accomplish that would be to come at it from its far side. Unfortunately, over there, the roof slanted downward into a sheer drop. I maneuvered myself so one leg hung over the roof's edge, against the side of the house, while I precariously clung to the transformer itself. I leaned over and tapped in.

As if quenching a dire thirst, I drank in the power. My mind expanded into the grid, spreading across countless power networks, until I was one with it, a part of it.

Where have you been, Rob?

Tell me who you are?
I'm a captive. I'm in a dark place. Can you help me?
Help you what?
Get free.

The sound of Ingrid's window opening pulled me back. I saw fingers pushing curtains aside and her face leaning forward.

"Isn't it beautiful!"

Ingrid leaned farther out and turned to her right. It was Pippa who'd gotten her attention. I pulled my leg up and lay against the slate shingles. Ingrid and Pippa talked for several minutes before Ingrid leaned back in and closed her curtains, after the window was slid shut.

* * *

Both Ingrid and Pippa were wearing dresses and wide-brimmed hats. The color of Pippa's small pink purse matched her hat and the floral design on her dress. It fit her perfectly and accentuated her recently endowed bosom's cleavage both provocatively and tastefully. Ingrid's sea green floppy hat was becoming on her and complemented her green-patterned silk dress. Pippa, earlier, had selected my attire—white slacks, button-down shirt, ascot, and navy blue blazer. We were dressed for the races.

Manfred drove as Ingrid spoke to us about our destination:

"Now the Iffezheim Racecourse, with its magnificent views of the Black Forest, is home to the Grosser Preis von Baden race. The Iffezheim racetrack is about eight miles from the small village of Iffezheim. This course is truly one of my favorites; it's both prestigious and elegant."

"And what will we be seeing there today?" I asked.

"There are two heralded festivals held yearly at Iffe-zheim racetrack ... Spring Festival, and Grand Week, which is going on now, and started several days ago. The festival consists of six race days ... I believe there are nine races run per day, but don't quote me on that."

"What's the plan for getting us close to the Goertzes?" Pippa asked.

"My good friend, William Genz, has agreed to let us share his box seats. This is no small measure, I assure you. Genz has a thoroughbred running today. Genz's and Leon Goertz's horses will be racing against each other. Their rivalry, although kept friendly for the most part, goes back many years."

I thought about what Ingrid was telling us. "Can you get us back into the stalls, pre-race?"

Ingrid stared at me blank-faced for several seconds. "I suppose. Let me check."

She reached for the limousine's mobile phone, thought for moment, and said, "I think I know his number ..." She dialed and held the phone to her ear. "Willie?" She laughed at something he said and then spoke quickly, "Yes, you must be frantically busy and I'm so sorry to be a bother. Would it be possible to see *A Grand Dream*? Get into the stables?" Ingrid smiled and nodded several times while listening to whatever Genz was saying. "You are my prince in shining armor. Yes, you can think of something special as your reward." She immediately flushed, looking over at Pippa and me, and hung up the phone. "It is all set."

CHAPTER 36

This was no small affair. The traffic was backed up for several miles before we could enter the racetrack grounds. Manfred maneuvered the big diesel Mercedes past bright orange cones and was waved through by officials into a smaller lot at the back of the park.

Ingrid was in high spirits and took both Pippa's arm and mine as the three of us made our way to the stables.

Horses and trainers and owners and stable boys and members of the press, along with hundreds of others, moved about the intersecting cobblestone paths. The clip-clop of iron-forged horseshoes echoed off concrete walkways, as some racehorses were led from their freshly painted, white clapboard stable stalls. In contrast, the strikingly colorful silks worn by jockeys boosted up onto their mounts added to the already exciting and festive, parade-like atmosphere.

"Let's find William," Ingrid said above the noise. "He'll

want to show us around—be the consummate host. Ah, I think I see him!" Ingrid waved a white-gloved hand high in the air, shouting, "Willie! Willie!"

A robust-looking man in his early seventies—wavy salt and pepper hair, tan, and exuding a powerful presence—broke away from a small throng of people. He was dressed similarly to myself, though his blazer was dark green, and complemented Ingrid's green and white attire.

"Oh, Willie, you look so dashing!" Ingrid gushed to her friend in German.

"And you ... the most beautiful creature here," he said back, giving her a quick kiss on the lips.

She gave his upper lapel a little slap and smiled. "I want to introduce you to my beautiful niece, Pamela, and her husband, David."

William took Pippa's outstretched hand and held it between two of his own. "So nice to meet you," he said, in heavily accented English. "Should I call you Pam, my dear?"

"Yes, please do."

William turned to me and we shook hands. It was a powerful grip from a man that weighed other men by the temper of their shake. He stepped in and said, "David, very nice to meet you. Hopefully, we'll have a chance to talk more, later on."

"I'll look forward to it, sir," I replied.

William took my place between the two women and, arm in arm, directed them toward a top-half-open stall door. "This is *A Grand Dream*," William said proudly, presenting his open palms in the direction of the thoroughbred standing within the confines of the stall. Shiny, black, and muscular, the racehorse stood tall, as if posing for a photograph. His ears twitched and his head nervously rose into the air with a snort.

"Oh my God, he is magnificent!" Pippa exclaimed enthusiastically. She moved to the gate and, as if on cue, *A Grand Dream* came forward. Pippa rubbed his long nose and looked over to me. "Isn't he gorgeous?" she asked, waving me in closer.

I took her place in front of the horse and was instantly in his mind.

Do you mind if I talk to you?
I don't mind.
Can you win this race today?
I want to win.
What horse or horses stand in your way?
Obvious Choice, Bingham, and Charlie's Wish ...
Well, you go ahead, run your best race, and I'll see what I can do about those other three ...

The inner stable door clanked opened. William and the trainer were ready to bring *A Grand Dream* out of his stall.

* * *

Pippa and I broke away from Ingrid and William. I promised we'd find them, back at their box, soon. I wanted to place a bet and I also wanted to have some time alone with Pippa. I'd had a hard time keeping my eyes off her; watching her here, she was like a small child, bursting with excitement. This was the Pippa I remembered—the one I'd fallen in love with all those months ago.

She yelled above the crowds' noise, "Why do you need me to make a bet?" She looked mystified.

I smiled and continued to pull her along through the hordes of people, acting as if I hadn't heard her.

We passed one of the small, circular counters and I

grabbed up a little pencil and a betting form. I was familiar with horse racing and had been moderately successful picking winners while in college. I placed the betting form on the counter while Pippa and I looked at it. Not only was it worded in German the betting structure here was somewhat different. I needed a little time to think about it.

"What's the problem? Fill it out and let's get back!" Pippa said irritably.

"Give me a second," I said.

I saw the four horses listed that I was interested in: *Obvious Choice, Bingham, Charlie's Wish,* and *A Grand Dream.* Often, when betting on a horse race in the U.S., I'd go with what is called a Trifecta Part Wheel. I not only betted on a certain horse to come in first, I selected the horses to win second- and third-place as well. The odds paid out substantially well, and by making this kind of bet here, I'd be sure to get the attention of Leon Goertz.

"I'm going to make a Trifecta bet, and hopefully win in a way that will grab Leon's attention."

"How will your bet—"

She cut herself short and looked at me with brows furrowed. "You're going to cheat? You're going to use those mind powers of yours somehow to cheat."

I wasn't sure if she was scolding me or not. I did feel somewhat guilty about it. The fortunes and/or misfortunes that my actions might possibly instigate could be substantial. But we were on a mission. In the scheme of missions, where people often died as a result of my directives, this deception seemed almost inconsequential. Pippa must have come to the same conclusion, because she now wore a somewhat sly smile on her lips.

"You can really do that? I mean, make that happen?"

"I don't know; I need to hurry up. I still have to get pretty close to those other three horses."

"Go! Tell me the order the horses will finish in and I'll stand in line—make the bet."

"You sure?" I asked.

She nodded, not even attempting to hide her smile. I wrote down their order and gave her ten one hundred dollar bills from my wallet—then kissed her on the cheek. "Catch you later."

I heard bugles trumpeting up ahead. The jockey-mounted horses must be making their way to the starting gate. I edged through the crowd as people slowly moved toward the sidelines. I saw patches of brightly colored silks moving in the distance. I needed to get above the crowd and have a clear sightline to the horses, while they were still close enough. There was no way. Then I noticed a man above me on an upper level wearing gray overalls and sweeping trash into a long-handled metal dustpan. The section he was working on was closed off, but it had an excellent view of the track.

"Hey. Kann ich dort für ein paar Minuten. Auf der Suche nach jemandem."

I'd asked him if I could get up there for a few minutes. That I was looking for someone. I held up two crisp hundred dollar bills.

He looked at the bills, and then looked around to make sure nobody was watching. "Sie müssen runter, bevor das Rennen beginnt."

I'd need to get back down before the race started. I climbed up the wall and he helped me over the iron railing. He went about his business and I watched the horses on the track directly in front of me. I'd memorized the three horses' names in reference to the assigned starting position numbers worn by their jockeys. I'd start with number ten,

Obvious Choice.

> *Hello, Obvious Choice. I have some bad news for you.*
>
> *Who are you? Why are you talking to me?*
>
> *If you win this race today, you'll be gelded, first thing tomorrow morning. Right there in your little stall. Do you know what gelded means?*
>
> *I know what that means. Who are you?*
>
> *I am the one that sired you. I am your father.*
>
> *You are Triumph's Glory?*

Oh, yes, I am he. Now, listen to me. You will not come in first today—you will come in second. Not third, or any place else, just second. A gelded horse is a disappointment. Do you want to disappoint me?

I will come in second. I will not disappoint you, Father.

CHAPTER 37

By the time I arrived at William Genz's box, Pippa was already there. William and Ingrid welcomed me in and were all smiles. I noticed we were practically standing in front of the finish line. Pippa held up the betting ticket. She looked excited and pulled me in for what I thought was a quick kiss. Hugging me, instead, she whispered into my ear, "Did you do it—talk to the horses?"

I whispered back, "Yes. They seemed to understand me. Was only able to talk to the top four horses, so they'll have to stay ahead on their own. It's a risk. We'll just have to see what happens."

"How do you talk to them?"

"I don't know ... it's not like I'm talking to Mr. Ed, or anything. More like our thinking is synchronized— meshed."

Ingrid caught my eye and with the slightest nod of her head gestured to the box kitty-corner to ours. It was one of the larger reserved boxes, holding ten people. Leon and Heidi were instantly recognizable to me, since I had reviewed their dossiers extensively. Leon, in his early fifties, looked fit and trim and had a commanding air about him. I noticed William also watching Leon, and he looked as if he'd just tasted something unpleasant. I leaned over and asked William which horse belonged to Goertz.

"Number ten, *Obvious Choice*," he replied.

I nodded. "That horse will come in second, right behind yours," I said.

"You think?" he responded, chuckling. "He's quite the three-year-old. Amazing track record, actually."

Pippa repositioned herself, moving to the corner of our box, and was within several feet of Leon. She looked over to me and gestured for me to come join her. Leon had already noticed Pippa and was eying her cleavage. Although trying to be discreet, he was edging closer to the back corner of his box, nearer to where Pippa was standing.

As I joined Pippa, she pulled me closer. She held up the ticket and spoke loud enough for Leon to hear: "So *A Grand Dream* will come in first; second, will be *Obvious Choice*; and *Bingham* will take third, right?"

Leon's attention was fully on Pippa. "*Dreierwette?* You're betting a Trifecta—all three horses finish in that specific order?" he asked her with an exasperated expression on his face.

Pippa glanced back at her ticket and then up to Leon. "Yeah, I've got it on good authority that's exactly how the race will finish." Pippa smiled back at the older man with a flirty shrug.

"Sorry, dear Fraulein, you've wasted your money. *Obvi-*

ous Choice will win today. Hell, I'd be surprised if *A Grand Dream* finds his way out of the gate. Unfortunately, not the smartest horse ... questionable genetics, you know."

William heard this last remark and gave Leon a crooked smile. Leon winked back at William and then turned back toward the track. I could see Pippa was thinking of some way to reengage with Leon when the man suddenly turned toward us again.

"Leon Goertz," he said, holding out his hand.

Pippa took his hand in hers and said, "Pamela Craft. Nice to meet you, Leon. This is my husband, David."

He extended his hand to me. "Well, enjoy the race. I hope you didn't bet the farm with that ticket of yours."

"No. Actually, I wish I'd bet more."

Leon looked at me and shrugged. "I'd be willing to make a side bet," he offered.

"What kind of bet?" I asked. But I was already in his mind. Sure enough, he was certain his horse would win. He'd spent millions procuring *Obvious Choice*—as well as acquiring the best trainer in Germany, and, of course, the horse's lineage was superb. His horse simply couldn't lose.

He looked back down the track, where the horses were being prodded into their respective gate enclosures. "Not money, too pedestrian. How about a simple gentlemen's bet?"

"Sure, why not?" I said, and we shook hands again.

I looked over the heads of thousands of spectators and colorful hats. My eyes followed the grassy track into the distance. I tried to connect again with *A Grand Dream*, but without actually seeing him, I couldn't. Now, sensing the final preparation for the start of the race, my confidence level wasn't nearly as high as it had been earlier. Winning today, and in a very big way, was our only ticket to gaining the attention and respect of Leon Goertz. *What was I thinking? This isn't going to work.*

The crowd had quieted and the announcer was providing last-minute information before the starter bell. Leon glanced in my direction and gave me a nod.

The bell rang. "Und sie sind weg!" The horses were off and running.

European tracks were longer: a mile and a half, compared to the usual mile-long tracks in the U.S. Although I could see the horses running off into the distance, there was no way I could differentiate one from another. Pippa's eyes were wide and she held our ticket to her lips. I turned toward William and Ingrid, giving them a reassuring nod. The crowd had come alive and everyone was screaming for their favorite horse to run faster.

Heidi moved closer and now stood alongside her husband. Both were yelling toward the distant horses. Heidi was younger than her husband by at least fifteen years—somewhere between thirty-five and forty, I guessed. Her hair was blonde and was pulled back and braided; the braid, tied with three pink bows—one at the top, one in the middle, and one at the end—fell far down her back. She turned her head and quickly sized up Pippa and then me. Her eyes lingered on me for several beats before she looked toward the track again, yelling in German for their horse to move it along.

The jockey riding *A Grand Dream* was wearing bright red and black silks. I could just barely make him out, in the galloping chaos, three quarters of a mile away. He looked to be in third position, maybe fourth. Yellow and green silks held the first spot—Leon's horse, *Obvious Choice.*

A Grand Dream had fallen back to fifth. It was *Obvious Choice* in first, *Bingham* in second, *Charlie's Wish* in third and

Flapper Boy in fourth. *A Grand Dream* seemed to be struggling. I screamed along with everyone else, "Move your ass, you old nag!"

Pippa looked up at me and burst out laughing.

Two of Leon's friends, seated in his box, now joined him at his side. One had his hand on Leon's upper back. Leaning in, I heard him congratulate Leon, telling him the race was all but won.

At a half mile out, I could clearly see the horses. Funny, how this simple bet with Leon was eating away at me. Maybe it was the man's smug attitude. More than the mission, I wanted to beat him—humiliate him in front of his arrogant friends.

Finally! I was now able to connect with *A Grand Dream*. *What are you doing? You need to move your ass.*

I'm tired. Very tired.

Soon the other horses will slow. You can still win this, I promise.

I will try harder.

Next, I connected to *Bingham, Charlie's Wish* and *Flapper Boy*. The latter horse needed to be brought up to speed on what would happen to him if he continued running at his current fast pace. The others also needed reminding what would happen to them if they didn't place exactly where I had earlier directed them. With the exception of *Obvious Choice*, the horses immediately slowed—allowing *A Grand Dream* to move forward into second place.

William and Ingrid were ecstatic. Both jumped up and down as their voices screamed encouragement. Leon's face had turned red. He held a meaty fist in the air and yelled angrily for *Obvious Choice* to hold his lead.

All the horses galloped toward the finish line. They were close enough to hear their hoofs pounding on the grassy track, and jockeys yelling encouragement, as their crops whipped across sweaty, tired flanks. I jumped into *Obvious Choice*'s mind.

I know you want to win. You've gotten caught up in the race. I want to win. I always win.

That's fine. Gelding is not so bad. Although ... you'll be like a mare ... you'll be one big mare. A laughing stock.

That seemed to do it. As if hitting the brakes, *Obvious Choice* fell back and became even with *A Grand Dream*. Together, they ran side by side, neither giving an inch. At thirty yards out, there was no way to tell which horse was going to win. At ten yards out I had time for one more ... *You'll be a laughing stock.*

A Grand Dream won the race by a nose. *Obvious Choice* came in second, followed by *Bingham* third, and *Charlie's Wish* fourth.

Pippa held the ticket up and checked it, as if uncertain. "We won ... We won!" She jumped into my arms, screaming uproariously. Ingrid was enveloped in William's arms, also screaming. Looking over Pippa's shoulder, I watched as Leon stood staring at the track, as if wishing the last few minutes could be replayed and the race could have a different outcome. His face, still flushed red, turned in my direction. I read his thoughts. I wish I hadn't.

CHAPTER 38

The four of us, William, Ingrid, Pippa and myself, stopped for dinner at an intimate Baden-Baden restaurant. We ordered a bottle of fine wine, followed by a second one, and more food than any of us could possibly finish. I spotted Pippa surreptitiously peeking into her purse every so often, as if she needed to verify the cashier's check I'd handed her to hold on to was actually real.

Even though William was the big dollar winner at the table, it was unilaterally decided that I should be the one to pay the bill. I gladly did so. Ingrid and William said their goodbyes in the parking lot. He waved to us and climbed into the backseat of his limousine.

The ride back to the villa was jubilant. Tipsy, Pippa and Ingrid chattered away, recounting the race in ridiculous detail, and Leon's utter surprise at its final outcome. Ingrid imitated the expression on Goertz's face as the horses crossed the finish line. The two, laughing hard, had tears in their eyes.

I was less amused. Looking into his mind at the track, I saw images—unexpected things. I'd noticed that Leon was deeply preoccupied. With the race results announced and over, I'd had a better chance to look into his mind. What I saw was disturbing: incongruent fuzzy jumbles—mostly nonsensical. I saw a scene where it was dark, lit only by a nearby burning torch. Death, for someone, was eminent. Then, the scene was replayed, over and over again. Was it a sacrifice? An offering? Whatever it was, Leon couldn't stop mulling it over. The lost horse race was of lesser importance to him than the event he'd attended the night before.

As it turned out, once Leon gained control of himself and his shock at losing, he was overtly cordial and congratulated William and Ingrid on running a fine race, as well as Pippa and me on our dramatic winnings. With Heidi at his side, they invited the four of us to attend their German Reunification Party the next day—*dress casual—no, no need to bring anything* ... Leon then took another last look at the winning ticket I'd pulled from Pippa's fist.

"How much, David?" Leon asked.

"It was an exceptionally large pool today," I replied.

"Yeah ... so how much?" he asked again.

"Close to four hundred twenty thousand dollars, U.S., give or take a few grand."

Pippa's eyes opened to the size of small saucers, while Leon simply shook his head in disgust. One of the men consoling Leon had taken an interest in me. With a quick check, I saw he indeed did recognize my face, my red hair.

Good, I thought, *that's very good.*

* * *

By the time we rolled into the villa's drive, it was pushing midnight. Begrudgingly, Pippa agreed to let Ingrid keep our check in her safe. We climbed up the stairs to our bedroom. Several times Pippa glanced back and smiled at me over her shoulder. When she got to the door she didn't open it. She turned around, with her back to the door, and waited for me to come close.

"Just because we're sharing a room doesn't mean anything's changed."

"No, of course not," I replied.

"And although we had a good time today, not to mention making a boatload of money, we should remember why we're here, right?" Her eyes looked up at me, beckoning me closer.

"I couldn't agree more," I said, stepping closer, leaning against the closed door beside her. I felt her warmth, smelled the sweet wine on her breath. Her arms came up around my neck and she pulled me near. We kissed with eyes open—slow and soft.

"This complicates things," she said.

"I don't care," I said, kissing her again, now more passionately.

She gently pushed me away with a smile. "I want us to wait until all this is over—when we're back in the States." With her hands on my shoulders she looked into my eyes: "Perhaps you should take a cold shower." She giggled, turned, and opened the door.

I stood there for several moments. I had the feeling Pippa wasn't done tormenting me. I'd take my punishment, willingly. I smiled to myself and followed her into the bedroom.

* * *

We slept in the next morning and had a relaxing few hours doing nothing special at the villa. Around 11:00 a.m. I noticed I'd received a text from Baltimore—he wanted an update.

After breakfast, I showered and ventured off on my own, into a small forest of trees off the villa's backyard. I called Baltimore.

"Chandler. What's the status?"

"Good morning to you, too. Things are progressing. We've made contact with the Goertzes."

"What about getting into his house?"

"We're invited to their party, later this afternoon. Sounds like it will be quite a shindig."

"Good. Everything hinges on you finding and downloading that code."

"I'm aware of that. If it's there, I'll find it. Oh, something else ..."

"What's that?" Baltimore asked.

"I won a few bucks at the racetrack—I'll want those transferred into my own account. That doable?"

"Shouldn't be a problem. Let's take care of that when we get back to the States. Anything else?"

I thought about the scattered, worrisome images I'd seen in Leon's thoughts. How would I explain them to Baltimore without exposing my *capabilities*? "Just that Goertz is into something ... I don't know ... dark, I'd guess."

"Let's talk later. You may see me around."

Baltimore clicked off. I wasn't sure what he meant by that.

I returned to the villa's manicured backyard of sprawling lawns, hedges, and even topiaries, pruned into little wildlife shapes. A crew of three had arrived. One man was pushing an ancient-looking lawn mower. I turned and surveyed the property. They'd be here for hours, probably the rest of the day. My eyes drifted up to the transformer affixed to the top right-hand corner of the roofline. *Crap*.

I came in through the sliding back door. Pippa was in the kitchen with Ingrid. I'd eaten Pippa's cooking before, albeit well over a year ago. She was a dismal cook. Could never make the simplest of recipes into anything edible.

She looked up; there was a patch of flour on her nose and although she'd put on an apron, she was pretty much covered with the stuff. Ingrid, at her side, was flour-free. Eggs, milk, bowls and utensils covered the thick woodblock island.

"What do we have here?" I asked.

"Homemade pancakes. Hope you're hungry," Pippa said, ladling some batter into a hot pan atop the stove.

"Smells good. Need any help?"

"No, just sit back and relax; I have a plate ready for you." Pippa, an oven mitt on her right hand, opened the oven and retrieved a plate stacked high with pancakes. They were dark brown ... almost black. "Oh, fudge. Looks like some of these got a little crispy." She flopped the top two cakes into the trash and set the plate down on the kitchen table. She scurried away, avoiding eye contact with me. I looked to Ingrid, who was standing at the sink. She made a choking expression, with her tongue out.

Pippa turned in time to see me chuckle. She looked at Ingrid. "Did you just make a face?"

"No," Ingrid replied.

"I saw you. You made a face," Pippa said.

Ingrid didn't reply.

I interjected: "I talked to Baltimore ... brought him up to speed." I buttered my pancakes.

Pippa brought over a bottle of syrup and slapped it down on the table in front of me.

"Thanks!" I said.

I smothered the cakes with syrup and cut into the stack. The top pancake cracked and broke into several small chunks. Pippa turned when she heard the sound, first looking at the pancake and then at me to ensure I wasn't laughing. She watched me take a bite. I raised my eyebrows and made an encouraging face. "This is good. I mean it, really good."

Not buying my act, Pippa shook her head and threw her oven mitt into the sink. "Hope you choke on it," she said, storming out of the kitchen.

Ingrid was smiling and started to clean up. "Some people are not meant for the kitchen. I imagine she has other talents."

"She does. Hey, I was wondering ... how long does it usually take your yard crew to mow and manicure this beautiful property?"

"I don't know," she said. "It takes as long as it takes." She walked over to the sink and looked out the window. "They don't do the manicuring and mowing on the same day. They're almost done for today. Probably be back tomorrow." I heard the lawnmower cut out in the distance. Ingrid waved to someone and said, "And there they go. Bye bye, Gustof."

Chapter 39

We arrived at the Goertzes' party fashionably late. Located off the Oos River in Baden-Baden, the estate, more like a medium-sized castle, was partially surrounded at its back by the Black Forest, and was only visible from the river, or by air, or once you've cleared its mile-long private drive. Although discreetly hidden, the estate's three hundred-eighty acres were surrounded by fifteen-foot-high fencing, topped with concertina wire. Armed patrols, some with leashed German Shepherds at their sides, roamed the perimeter on a 24/7, purposely varied, schedule. I'd studied the estate's geography, as well as its most recent architectural drawings. The castle itself had a rich and colorful history. The original castle walls, surrounding grounds, and vapor baths were remnants of early Roman settlements, existing around 150 AD. Leon had meticulously had the structure rebuilt atop its original foundation, and the ancient nearby Roman spas were brought back to their original glory.

As we approached the castle we merged into a small traffic jam of Rolls-Royces, Bentleys and Mercedes. For vehicles that weren't chauffeur-driven, there was valet service. Either way, autos pulled up, dropped off their passengers and, seconds later, were driven to a large clearing, in the distant trees, and parked a half-mile back from the estate.

Although we were told the dress code was somewhat formal, Ingrid assured us that that really meant *very* formal—black tie for men, gowns and sparkles for women. I couldn't remember the last time I'd worn a white dinner jacket, a cummerbund, and a black bow tie ... the whole nine yards. Manfred, armed with my clothing sizes, had returned from town with everything I'd need. Shoes were a tad tight but, all in all, he did a good job. Both Ingrid and Pippa had spent hours preparing themselves. I'd worked it out with Pippa ahead of time: she was to knock on Ingrid's door and together they would disappear into her bathroom for help with Pippa's makeup. This gave me enough time for one more *tapping-in* session at the rooftop's transformer. Fortunately, it was uneventful: no desperate communications—no one asking for my help.

Ingrid and Pippa sat side by side in the back seat. I sat in the seat across from them, facing backwards, and found it hard to take my eyes off Pippa. She was wearing a long, cream-colored sequined dress that contoured to her body in a way I wouldn't have thought possible. Her short black hair contrasted perfectly with the simple diamond necklace nestling at the base of her exquisite long neck.

We waited for Manfred to make his way around the back of the limo and open the rear passenger-side door. He helped Ingrid, then Pippa, out of the car. I got out and took in the spectacle in front of me. The sun had recently set, and hidden floodlights illuminated the block stone walls. Jutting out from the castle walls were two tall towers, both with conical spires atop them, reaching one hundred feet into the air. Although not a drawbridge in the traditional sense, the dual massive front doors certainly gave that impression. Young men and women, dressed alike in unisex black tuxedos, greeted guests as they climbed the stairs leading to the front entrance.

"Ms. Krueger, Mr. and Mrs. Craft: Hello, my name is Melinda. I'd like to welcome you to Weilerbaden Castle. May I walk you inside?"

Ingrid spoke up for the three of us, "Yes, please do, young lady." We entered through the doors and it was evident that we hadn't entered into the castle itself, but into a fortified barbican—an outpost or gateway that preceded the main structure. Thick-planked wooden flooring and arrow-slit windows gave the area a traditional, medieval ambiance. Wax candles, supported on high ironwork, flickered all around us. The three of us, along with other guests and their hosts, crossed through the room and out onto an arched stone and wood bridge. A roaring river, a moat of sorts no less than thirty feet wide, rushed beneath us, twenty feet below.

Pippa, holding my hand, was also awestruck by the grandeur of everything around us. Another set of tall doors, identical to the others, was held wide open. I heard the sounds of distant music.

"Mr. and Mrs. Goertz request that I bring you directly to them, just as soon as you arrive," Melinda was saying to us. She'd briefly turned and walked backward so we could hear her voice above the increasing volume of music and the other guests' chatter. I recalled the room from the drawings. This was the main, or great, room. Much of the medieval atmosphere was now gone. Although some stone and wood accents remained, the room was a modern and tastefully appointed space. Indirect lighting illuminated tall ceilings—thick timber beams stretched up to an interconnecting apex, high above us.

I noticed the errant security personnel standing in the shadows, observing the guests. Each man had a little coiled wire hanging from his left ear. With a trained eye for such things, I could see the slight bulge of concealed weapons beneath suit jackets. I also noticed that more than anyone else they were watching my every movement.

We followed Melinda across the room, past numerous bejeweled women in long gowns, and men garbed in black or white jackets; past servers laden with trays of sparkling, bubbling champagne; and toward a wall of tall, sliding windows that had been pushed aside and recessed into walls, allowing access to the expansive cobblestone patio beyond.

We walked together into a courtyard, easily the size of two side-by-side football fields. Now fully dusk, I could just barely discern the castle's far wall, and, atop it, a parapet-walkway off in the distance. Both back corners of the castle had formidable cylindrical-shaped towers with conical spires.

Outside, where we now stood, the real party was taking place. A band was playing lively music on an elevated stage and people were dancing—most guests held drinks in their hands. Melinda walked us past a long bar where men waited to order a drink. It was then that I noticed the bartender scurrying around, a bead of sweat on his brow. I couldn't quite keep the smile from my face. Baltimore glanced at me with an expression that could only say one thing ... *Don't say one fucking word.*

I saw the Goertzes up ahead, surrounded by six or seven guests. A tabletop, now overflowing, had been set up to hold Heidi's birthday gifts. Pippa carried a large gift box from the three of us. I didn't want to touch the thing. Earlier, while still getting dressed, I heard a soft knock on the bedroom door. I opened it and nearly jumped out of my skin. A horrific face rushed directly toward me. As my brain tried to determine what fight or flight instinct to go with, Pippa was already laughing, holding up some kind of freak mask.

"What the hell is that thing?" I asked.

"Punic charm mask—very old: Roman. Expensive and our gift for Heidi."

"Seriously?"

"She collects masks ... has a whole room somewhere in her home dedicated solely to her mask collection."

"Just keep it away from me ..."

Leon saw us as we approached and smiled broadly. Heidi turned toward us and also smiled. She had on a sleek black gown and wore matching gold earrings and necklace.

Pippa gave Heidi her gift, which she placed on the growing mountain of brightly wrapped boxes beside her.

"You didn't need to do that," Heidi said. "There should be some kind of rule that new friends are excused from that kind of nonsense."

"Oh, no, it was our pleasure," Pippa said. "We hope you like it."

Leon shook my hand and held it. "Glad you could make it, David. I want to apologize to you for not recognizing you—you know, at the track."

"There's no reason why you should have," I replied. "I'm nobody important."

"Let's dispense with false modesty, David. You are among the elite when it comes to forging new, cutting-edge technology. What you're doing with media storage will change the face of business."

"Well, thank you. I'm optimistic."

Ingrid noticed William Genz over by the bar and excused herself to join him.

"Look, there are some people I'd like you to meet. Pamela, can I steal your husband away from you for a bit?" Goertz asked.

"Uh, please, keep him as long as you want," Pippa replied, bringing a laugh from Heidi.

"I like this girl," Heidi said. "Come on, I'm gong to introduce you to the stodgy women of Baden-Baden." The two women walked off, arm in arm.

Leon laid one hand on my shoulder and spoke to me as we walked toward the castle proper. "What do you say we get ourselves a drink?" We bellied up to the bar and Leon held up two fingers to Baltimore. "Scotch," he ordered, above the noise of the crowd. Baltimore poured the drinks and put them in front of us. He looked worried. I took a quick look through his thoughts. Something was cataclysmically wrong—he was barely holding it together.

I had a hard time tracking the rapid influx of thoughts and images coursing through his brain. If he'd just take a damn breath and calm down, I'd be able to catch what was happening. And then I put it together: a phone conversation from Calloway ... an alarming CNN report, discussing the potential financial implications of three U.S. goliath-sized companies taken off the market, becoming privately-held institutions ... Earlier today the NY Stock Exchange was forced to stop all trading as stock prices plummeted.

The man standing at my side was bringing the world's financial markets to their knees.

CHAPTER 40

Pippa walked alongside Heidi; every few paces they were stopped by a friend, or an associate, wishing her a happy birthday. Heidi was small and petite and Pippa felt she towered over the fair-haired German woman.

"There you are!" A robust woman, looking uncomfortable in very high heels, stepped toward Heidi for a hug and a mutual kiss on each cheek.

When introduced to Pippa/Pamela, the woman hugged and kissed her as well.

"Sorry," Heidi said, as they moved on toward the far side of the courtyard, "kissy crowd. That was the mayor. Never misses a party, or free booze, for that matter." The last comment was given without a trace of humor.

Heidi withdrew a small bottle of sanitizer from an almost-invisible pocket and squeezed a few dabs into the palm of one hand before vigorously rubbing both hands together. "Why can't women learn to just fist-bump, like men do?"

She held both palms in the air like she was signaling some-one to stop. "Sorry, I'm particular about who touches me."

"That's fine—perfectly understandable," Pippa said.

"Hey, how would you like to see the spas?" Heidi asked.

"You have spas here?"

"Do we have spas here? This is Baden-Baden! Our cas-tle was built on one of the original ancient spas found in the area. Come, come, I'll show you." Heidi grabbed Pippa's hand and pulled her along. *Well, okay ... I guess I rate higher than the mayor ...*

"This way, watch your step," Heidi said, as they entered through an unremarkable wooden doorway placed beneath a sign reading *Verjüngende Spas*.

Concrete steps led down to a platform that transitioned into age-worn stone blocks. "You're going to love this. It's why we built, actually rebuilt, the castle here in the first place."

They were descending into a cavern. The air smelled musky.

"The surviving foundation and subterranean spas of Weilerbaden Castle date back to the first century, A.D. This is original Romanesque construction." Arched stone-block doorways, some padlocked, led off to unseen corridors. Hei-di continued to talk as they descended. She'd removed her shoes and was carrying them by their straps in one hand. There was something innocently playful about the way she hopped barefoot from step to step.

"In the twelfth century the castle was repurposed to protect the area's surrounding silver mines. Later, in the late-seventeenth century, it was besieged, nearly totally de-stroyed by French soldiers during the Dutch War. The cas-tle wasn't rebuilt until we came along, five years ago."

They'd reached the pools. Four of them, in total, were

of different sizes and shapes. More worn stone steps led into each pool, at various locations. The air was hot and steam misted-off the water. Heidi dropped her shoes, the sound echoing off the cavern walls. Both hands were working the zipper at the back of her dress. In a fluid motion the zipper came down and she stepped out of the dress as it slid to the floor. Naked, she descended the largest of the pool's steps. Pippa watched as Heidi let the water envelop her. When the depth of the water reached beneath her small perky breasts she lowered herself, until the water level was right beneath her chin.

"Aren't you coming in?"

Pippa smiled, somewhat uncomfortable with Heidi's immodesty. "What about your guests? I don't know, I'm—"

"Oh, come on ... just for a minutes or two—you'll see—it's beyond wonderful."

Pippa shrugged and within several moments removed her own dress, bra and panties. She eased herself into the water and positioned herself close to Heidi.

"This is amazing," Pippa said, feeling her body sway in the pool's gentle currents.

"What's that a tattoo of?" Heidi asked.

Pippa had to think about that for a beat, then remembered: "Oh, that's a ladybug."

"That's cute. Stand up—let me see it," Heidi said, looking around Pippa's back.

Pippa hesitated, then stood and turned around so the tattoo was just above the waterline. She felt Heidi trace the contours of the ladybug with a finger and then let it linger on her upper butt cheek.

"Way too hot in here for me," Pippa said, "and my hair's getting frizzy." Pippa waded over to the steps and got out of the pool. To her surprise, there were now two large, folded, bath towels stacked by their clothes. She felt Heidi's gaze linger on her from the pool, taking in every inch of her body. She pulled one of the towels free and wrapped it around herself.

Heidi was out of the water and at her side. "I want you both to spend the weekend here with us."

"Oh, I don't know," Pippa said, still feeling somewhat uncomfortable. "David's in the middle of some business and—"

Heidi cut her off, her raised voice filling the cavern, "No! You'll stay here."

Pippa realized the woman was not used to being told no. After an awkward silence, Heidi eventually attempted a smile. "Come on. We'll have so much fun … get to know each other."

Pippa shook her head. "Sorry, if I'd known … But we didn't pack anything."

Heidi smiled. "I've already dispatched your driver; it's Manfred, isn't it? Anyway, he's bringing your clothes, everything, back here as we speak."

"Then I guess we're your house guests for the weekend," Pippa said.

"Let me," Heidi said, reaching up and zipping Pippa's dress the last few inches.

* * *

Curt Baltimore needed to meet with Chandler one-on-one, right now. Seeing him at the bar, there wasn't a chance to slip him a message. Unfortunately, talking on the phone or even texting was no longer a secure option. Their mission may be compromised. Baltimore had already suspected

Goertz was on to him, that his cover had somehow been blown. *But how?*

He told the barmaid he needed to take a piss—be right back. He made his way to a nearby restroom but wasn't sure if he was followed by any of Goertz's security goons. Once inside, he rinsed his face with cold water and tried to think straight. He watched as the handle of the bathroom door jiggled.

There was a knock. "Ist jemand da?" *Is anyone in there?*

He'd have to chance it. Baltimore brought out his phone but before he could text, the bathroom door slammed opened. Two security guys, one tall, with a passive, indifferent expression, and the other, who had a mole on his cheek and looked angry, was pointing a pistol at Baltimore's head. They rushed in and closed the door behind them. Baltimore's phone was grabbed away and pocketed.

"Come with us. Make any commotion, and you will be dealt with on the spot. Understood?"

Baltimore nodded.

The security goon with the gun stood behind him, while the tall one opened the door and looked out. "Okay, it's clear," he said.

Baltimore was shoved from behind to follow. The three moved deeper into the castle, away from the courtyard and the partying going on outside. They made a left and then a right and then started to descend a long, steep, staircase. Even with the layout memorized, Baltimore was becoming somewhat disoriented.

Baltimore slowed his pace, which brought the swift response of a gun muzzle jabbed into his lower back. He picked up his pace for several steps, only to slow again. This time Baltimore was ready. Anticipating another poke in the same spot, Baltimore spun, grabbed the guard's outstretched arm and pulled. The guard's center of gravity shifted forward. Baltimore moved out of the way as the guard toppled down the stairs and into the back of his partner's legs. They both continued in a tumbling squall of arms and legs. The guard dropped his gun and it came to rest ten steps below Baltimore. He leapt three steps at a time but mole-face was already recovering and moving to retrieve his weapon. Mole-face got to it first. As his fingers tightened around the gun's grip, Baltimore was in the air, leaping off with both feet. Baltimore drove his heels—heels assisted by two hundred-plus pounds of momentum and gravity—into mole-face, who took the brunt of the force on his nose, driving it straight back into his skull. Splintered cartilage and bone shot into his brain, killing him instantly.

Baltimore tucked and rolled, coming to rest at the bottom of the stairs, where the other guard still lay unconscious. Moving to get up, he realized he'd cracked at least one, maybe two of his own ribs. He retrieved the gun, still tightly gripped in the dead guard's hand.

He took in his surroundings. Dimly lit by a single light bulb further down the corridor, he determined he was standing on the landing where the stairway and two corridors intersected. He needed to get these bodies hidden. The taller, living, guard was coming around. Baltimore moved in behind him, crouched down and took his chin in one hand and the back of the man's head in the other. In a rapid, twisting motion, Baltimore snapped the guard's neck.

He searched the body and came up with a gun, which he placed in his jacket pocket, a wallet, a small flashlight, and some communication gear wired to the man's ear-comms. A quick check of the guard's wallet revealed nothing other than the man's name: Brian Gaertner, and he lived in Frankfurt. He retrieved his cell phone.

Baltimore used the flashlight to search behind the back left side of the staircase. Nothing. He moved around to the other side and found a door. Unlocked, he discovered it was a broom closet. Within two minutes, both guards were stacked at the back of the closet beneath a bundle of rags and several mop buckets. He needed to get back but wanted to take a quick look around first.

There was a door twenty paces down the main corridor that looked to be open. As he approached he saw a flickering light coming from inside. After the racket he'd made on the stairs, he doubted there was anyone close by. He peeked into the room. It was an assembly hall of some kind. Flags, draped from beams high above, were all the same—black swastikas, upon white circles, on backgrounds of vivid red. Three men sat in high-back chairs on a raised platform at the front of the room.

"Come in, Mr. Baltimore."

CHAPTER 41

The band had stopped playing and large circular tables and chairs had been brought in. Servers were carrying trays with platters of hot food.

I saw a hand waving in the air in the distance from a table close to the stage. Pippa was signaling me. She was seated next to Heidi. Another woman sat on her other side. Leon and I joined our respective wives.

"I hope you're not driving our guests crazy with too much business talk on my birthday," Heidi said, reprimanding Leon.

We sat down on the chairs across from our wives. Pippa was smiling but her eyes were serious. She also was casually tapping a finger to her temple. I was a bit slow on the uptake; she obviously wanted me to read her thoughts. Her mind was reeling.

I hope you're reading this: this woman knows Pamela. We're apparently friends and I have no idea who the hell she is. She's getting suspicious. Our cover is about to be blown!

As I began to answer her I saw her visibly relax.

Next to you is Rosie. She and her husband Carl are old friends of David and Pamela Craft. Hold on ... let me see what's on her mind.

Rosie was definitely suspicious. She was also hurt that *Pamela* was acting so distant. Okay, now I was getting more, as sentimental thoughts and images appeared. They had been best friends in college; Pamela was also maid of honor at Rosie and Carl's wedding. And something else ... Rosie was thinking about divorcing Carl. She'd confided this to Pamela recently in a letter and now wanted to talk about it.

I was back in Pippa's mind.

Lean over and whisper in Rosie's ear. Let her know you're going to have to get alone with her later to talk about her and Carl's marriage problems.

Pippa's eyes met mine. *Seriously?*

As our dinner plates were filled, casual table talk halted for a moment. I nodded in Pippa's direction. Pippa leaned over to Rosie. I lingered in the background of Rosie's consciousness and heard Pippa whisper to her while I observed Rosie's conscious reaction. I caught Pippa's eyes and smiled.

That worked. She's relieved—has no doubt that you are her old friend Pamela.

"David, I think you know this old dog here ..." Leon said.

A man returning from the bar came over and put his hand on my shoulder. "David! Good to see you, old buddy."

I watched as a montage of images flashed across his mind: *teenagers playing basketball—Chargers, written across their jerseys; a funeral in the snow—attendees wearing black coats, with collars turned up against the wind; David and this man racing together on a catamaran.*

I'd listened to audio of the real David Craft. Our voices were similar but uniquely different as well. Mine was somewhat deeper and had a subtle accent from my Chicago upbringing. I did my best to sound like the real David Craft. "Certainly didn't expect to find you here," I said, grasping for some indication of what his name was. I stood up as he came closer.

"Seems we have a mutual friend in Mr. Goertz. We were in Berlin on business when we got the call," the man said, pushing away my outstretched hand and giving me a bear hug instead. With two hands still on my shoulders, he pushed me away and looked at my face. "You look good ... Pamela must be taking good care of you." But there was concern in his eyes. Something seemed odd to him. He was looking for a scar. *A scar that should be on my right cheek below my eye.*

I touched my face where he'd been looking. I pictured his instant recall of a sail, suddenly caught in the wind, and an aluminum boom whipping into David Craft's cheek. There had been lots of blood and deep feelings of guilt from this man.

Rosie said, "Why don't you sit down, Carl? It's time for dinner."

Oh, so this is Rosie's husband, or soon to be ex-husband.

"I had it removed," I said. "One of those things I now wish I had just let be. You don't still feel responsible for that, do you, Carl?"

Carl shrugged. "Maybe a little bit."

Dinner was fairly uneventful. Much of my time was spent talking with the other men at the table, while periodically *helping* Pippa converse with Rosie and Heidi.

The mental multi-tasking was taking its toll. Then something Leon was saying grabbed my attention.

"This property is completely self-sufficient. Going off the grid here would not be a problem. We have our own water supply from natural springs, and the same hydro-thermal conditions that heat our underground spas also generate the necessary kilowatts to power Weilerbaden Castle's complex."

"Sounds like you put a lot of thought into this place," I commented. "So you have a power station on the premises?" This was news to me, since none of the architectural drawings I'd reviewed indicated one. From what I had gathered, the property got its power from the same municipal sources other Baden-Baden residences or businesses did.

Leon shoveled in a forkful and spoke with a mouth full of orange candied carrots before he answered me. "All underground. What you've seen is but a fraction of Weilerbaden Castle. If you play your cards right, I'll give you the complete tour tomorrow."

"Your wife's already had a bit of that tour, didn't you, Pamela?" Heidi asked, with more than a little *tease* in her voice.

Pippa smiled and nodded but said nothing.

The band was back and taking their places on stage. I saw Pippa eye the dance floor and then glance back toward me. She looked somewhat self-conscious; no doubt from the growing male scrutiny focused on her from around our table, and from tables beyond. It wasn't just her figure— her ample cleavage; she was strikingly beautiful tonight. As an active agent, Pippa had gone out of her way over the years to downplay her looks, often not wearing any makeup at all. But now, seated across from me, her gown shimmering in the soft lights from above, I was as captivated as the rest of the men.

The music started up and couples from around the courtyard moved toward the dance floor.

"Would you mind if I asked your wife to dance?" Carl asked.

"No, be my guest," I said.

Carl stood and walked around to where Pippa was seated. He held out his hand to her, but I couldn't hear his voice over the music. Pippa smiled, nodded, and got up. There it was again, a quick tapping gesture toward her head.

What am I supposed to do now? This guy knows Pamela. He's expecting me to chitchat with him.

Before I could reply, Heidi threw her napkin across the table at me. She looked at me, eyebrows raised. "What does a girl have to do to get asked to dance around here?"

I pointed to myself. "Me?"

"Yeah, you," she said.

"Well, come on then, let's show them how it's done, Heidi," I replied, getting to my feet. I looked over to Leon for his approval.

"Go right ahead ... have fun, kids." His eyes never left his plate; what was left of his half-devoured steak was being cut into small, cube-like pieces.

Heidi took my hand and led me to the dance floor. She moved gracefully and swung herself under my arm and then came in close. Small and compact, she moved seductively. She pressed in against me and looked up into my eyes. "I've been looking forward to this all evening."

I peered into her thoughts. She was excited to be dancing. She was curious about me—was attracted to me. There was a deep hunger in this woman ... for attention ... for sexual gratification. Now her thoughts were being pulled back to an earlier event. Almost identical to the thoughts I'd observed in Leon's mind at the racetrack, hers, too, were dark, incongruent, fuzzy jumbles—mostly nonsensical: there was darkness, lit only by a nearby burning torch ...death, involving a sacrifice for someone ... although in Heidi's mind the death had already occurred. She appeared naked, blood on her hands and face, and in a frenzied, disoriented state of mind. The expression on my face must have alerted her.

"What's going on in that mind of yours, David?" Heidi asked, her own expression now one of concern.

"Oh, sorry. I was just thinking of something I'd forgotten to do. There's someone I need to contact."

"Well, hopefully that can wait. Leon isn't much for dancing. I guess I'm fortunate he doesn't mind me dancing with others."

From the way she was pressing herself into me, she was more than a little accustomed to dancing with others. I foxtrotted us over to where Pippa and Carl were dancing and telepathically asked her how things were going.

Fine. I told him I just wanted to dance, save the chatting for later.

Carl looked to be enjoying himself. He spun Pippa around and glided smoothly beside her. She moved with him to the music as if they'd practiced their dance steps together for years. I certainly wasn't the dancer Carl was, but that didn't stop me from stepping it up a little with Heidi. We danced until the band announced they'd be taking another break.

Leon was up on stage and tapping the microphone. "This on?" His voice boomed from speakers on both sides of the stage. "I'd like to thank you all for coming tonight. You've made this a very special evening for both Heidi and myself. I'd like to take a moment to present my wife with a very special birthday present from me."

Heidi and I moved closer to the stage, along with Pippa and Carl. Others were getting to their feet and joining us. From somewhere high above, a spotlight turned on, instantly bathing Heidi in a swath of bright white light.

Behind Leon a large movie screen lowered. Nighttime shots, taken from above New York City, filled the screen. Sinatra's "New York New York" played softly in the background as camera footage zeroed-in on several Manhattan skyscrapers. Soon, only the Chrysler building, with its one-of-a-kind art deco architecture, remained. The video screen zoomed in—showing stainless steel ribbed cladding, next to large, triangular windows; it all came together in the building's dramatic sunburst pattern. One of my favorite buildings, not just in New York, but the world. I was somewhat perplexed why Leon was showing this to us.

"It wasn't that long ago when we were on our final approach to JFK, with the city's lights shining up from below. Do you remember telling me how much you loved that building?"

Smiling, Heidi nodded her head, still looking as confused as the rest of us.

"As of three o'clock yesterday afternoon, the building now belongs to you," Leon Goertz told his wife. "Happy birthday, sweetie, I hope you like it."

Heidi screamed with excitement, jumping up and down on the dance floor. Applause erupted from the guests as a wheeled cart was rolled over to where she stood. Easily six feet tall, her birthday cake was a detailed replica of the Chrysler building.

I looked toward the stage and saw Leon staring at me. The message was clear: before long, nothing in this world would be beyond his reach.

Chapter 42

Pippa and I sat on the edge of the stage and ate our cake. We watched Heidi continue to hand out plates of cake—piece by piece, small sections of the Chrysler building were slowly being cut away. In the distance, the bar was still somewhat crowded with partygoers getting drinks, but I saw no sign of Baltimore.

Leon joined us at the stage. "That was quite a gift, Leon," Pippa said.

"It will be a nice project for her. We've been talking about getting a place in New York," Leon replied. "Pamela, I'm going to steal David away one more time ... show him my offices, introduce him to some business associates of mine. Word got out that David would be here in Baden-Baden. He's something of a celebrity, you know. I promise to return him in several minutes."

"No problem," Pippa said, jumping off the stage. "It looks like your wife could use some help."

Together, Leon, Carl and I walked into the main building. "Let's take the elevator," Leon said, gesturing toward a stone wall. It was only when I stood right in front of it that I realized the wall was actually an elevator door. The wall separated and revealed a car waiting for us. The doors shut. Leon was prompted to provide an optical scan.

"Confirmed," said a woman's voice.

Carl and I exchanged a quick glance.

Leon pressed the button for the third floor and the car started to ascend.

"That's quite a bit of security for a private residence. Impressive," I said.

"I do far more business here than in my offices downtown. Perhaps it may seem like excess, but there are organizations around the world hell-bent on acquiring our technology. In fact, we discovered a covert intruder earlier tonight. One that I will deal with personally, later on," he replied.

That could explain Baltimore's disappearance from the bar. Was this mission in the process of unraveling? I tried to keep my expression neutral, while considering the implications.

I'd been monitoring Leon's thoughts since we'd left the courtyard. His heart rate was elevated. He was making his move into international markets. By early next week he would control enough of the world's most influential corporations to be virtually unstoppable. What I was not prepared for were the tumultuous emotions brewing inside him: love of country, zealous dedication to the memory of his parents and grandparents, and continuing on their legacy. The phrase *Blut und Ehre*, blood and honor, was like a silent mantra Leon repeated over and over again in his mind. I'd also seen he was questioning my authenticity. Preliminary investigations had not been one hundred percent conclusive. Both Pippa and myself were to be further vetted this evening: me by Leon, Pippa by Heidi. He was prepared to do something he'd only done twice before: bring non-German nationals into his organization. Simply put, he needed high-profile American executives to join his ranks. The days of separatism were over. A one-world economy was not only inevitable, it was close at hand.

The elevator came to a halt and with a soft *ding*, the doors opened. Two men smoking cigars and drinking from cut-crystal tumblers looked up. We had arrived in Leon's office suite.

I turned and took in the space. Surrounded by windows on three sides, the office looked out on the courtyard and the Black Forest Mountains beyond the fortified walls of the castle. Music from the band below was filtering up into the room. Behind me, behind a glass wall, was another section of the office. Cast in a soft blue light, I could see row upon row of black server racks.

"David Craft, Carl Braden, this is Thomas Numen and Derek Rogers," Leon said to those in the room.

The others stood and we exchanged handshakes. With a quick look into their minds, it was evident the three men were disheartened, beaten. Leon gestured for us all to sit as he took a seat at the head of the table.

"David, Carl … I'm sorry to interrupt the party, but what I'm about to say cannot wait." Leon glanced around the table and one of the men nodded for him to continue. "The world as we know it has changed. As of Monday morning, when the U.S. markets, Wall Street, resume trading, a new financial order will have begun."

"Does this have to do with the FCC halting trading on the NY Stock Exchange?"

"It does, David. I'm going to say some things here that might come across as grandiose—perhaps come up against your patriotic loyalties."

"Go on, I said."

"Things must change for this world to survive. Corporate greed will lead us to destruction. Climate change, starvation, sickness, petty wars, terrorism ... hell, the threat of total nuclear annihilation ... the list goes on and on. The world's misdirection simply cannot continue on its present trajectory."

"The world is a messy place," I said, "but there's nothing new about that."

"I'd like to talk to you about the WZZ. Think of it as the new *Economic United Nations*. A group of like-minded individuals joined together—united, above an allegiance or patriotism toward country; above any corporate interests of loyalty; above all self-serving predications ... I'm sure you know the top one percent of the world's wealth is controlled by a very few individuals. So imagine what will be accomplished when all the financial resources of the world are no longer competing, at odds with one another."

"That does sound somewhat grandiose, Leon," I said. It also sounded utopian, and more than a little crazy, but I kept that to myself.

"On the contrary, David, not so grandiose at all ... Remove from mankind his inclination to invade neighboring territories—going to war for perceived slights, or wanting to control other factions, which often deprive the weakest of the barest necessities ... and life on this planet has a good chance of surviving."

"What makes you think others will go along with your ... ideals?"

"That's the beauty of it, David. At this point, a chain of

events, which will alter civilization forever, has already been triggered."

I fought to keep an expression of interest. In reality, I was finding his comments ridiculous.

"It's all legal—I assure you," Leon said

With the tap of a few keys on the laptop before him, the glass wall turned white and totally opaque. A moving graphic took shape. Thousands upon thousands of colorful particles shimmered and moved. Groupings, like tiny schools of fish or flocks of birds, darted together one way and then another. Spirals of movement broke off, forming their own clusters, then rejoined the mass of particles again. Whatever we were looking at seemed to be alive, have a consciousness.

"In the span of a nano-second, thousands upon thousands of shares are sold across multiple markets. About ten years ago, a man named Spatz, someone a lot smarter than me, and evidently smarter than anyone else, discovered something called *micro-tides.*" Leon gestured toward the moving tides of particles on the glass wall. "Only by observing massive amounts of economic data, with the help of tethered supercomputers, can these economic *micro-tides* not only be tracked, but manipulated. Shares are sold or bought in waves—bulk transactions that manipulate pricing, and values change ownership in a flash. What you're looking at, these moving clusters, are the world's largest corporations. Shares of publicly held companies, like Google, Microsoft, Exxon Mobil, can be acquired in vast amounts before they know what is happening. *Micro-tides* are quantifiable mathematical algorithms. With this tool, the WZZ now yields the most powerful financial advantage ever devised. David, this proprietary program, one we call Spatz, is changing world economics even as we sit here."

I was speechless. I looked over at Carl and he had an expression of resignation. He had known for weeks about the WZZ, their pursuit of monetary control, and the devastation they'd bring worldwide to all financial markets' status quo. And like so many other CEOs, executives, across the globe today, it was either join the WZZ or watch your own personal wealth disappear.

"This is most impressive, Leon. Your WZZ has found a way to influence the purchase of public corporations—to buy up any and all available shares, and, if necessary, maybe even go after majority shareholders to take control. So what is it you want from me, Leon? My company is privately held—not really something the WZZ would take notice of."

"Rest assured, our intentions are not to go after your company in a hostile manner. No, I'm not looking to ravage your company. On the contrary, I'm looking to bolster your company's business by a factor of ten. By partnering, becoming a member of the WZZ, the rewards will be staggering. Simply put, David, capitalistic ideals of the past are no longer viable. Join us, as Carl has, and hundreds of others, and together we'll make history."

I looked around the table. Carl and the other two men appeared mentally and emotionally exhausted, defeated—prepared to do anything to hold onto a lifestyle they'd worked for, invested in, grown accustomed to.

"You've provided some interesting, dynamic concepts here, Leon. I hope you're not expecting an answer right this minute. A lot to think about," I said. I smiled approvingly at him but the truth was, I was angry with what Leon and his WZZ were doing, not only to the men in this room, but others like them, worldwide.

Leon smiled sympathetically. He got to his feet; apparently our impromptu meeting was over. "I certainly didn't expect a definitive answer here and now. But I have the whole weekend to work on you, right? Please don't let our little discussion derail the party going on downstairs and our plans for the weekend."

I looked at him quizzically, as the rest of us rose.

"Oh, Heidi hasn't told you yet? You and Pamela, as well as some others, are staying as our guests for the weekend. Heidi has big plans for us to get to know each other better by spending some quality time together."

Chapter 43

As soon as Baltimore entered the assembly hall he was greeted by two of the largest men he'd ever seen. Blond and blue eyed, thick and strong looking, they could have been brothers. They both held pistols pointed toward his heart.

Baltimore was relieved of the handgun he'd taken from the guard on the stairs. His wrists were pulled behind his back and secured with plasticuffs.

He was shoved down onto a chair. "Nicht bewegen und ruhig lagern," *Do not move and keep quiet,* one of the guards said.

Baltimore sat for close to an hour before Goertz entered the hall. He moved to a raised dais at the front of the room and sat down.

"As you undoubtedly know, my name is Leon Goertz. These are my employees, Heimi and Lance."

Baltimore didn't respond.

"Who are you?" Leon asked.

"I'm the bartender."

Leon smiled and studied Baltimore for several moments, then nodded toward Heimi. Heimi moved from Baltimore's side to his front. He punched Baltimore in the face with enough force to knock him out of his chair. Heimi and Lance each grabbed an arm and repositioned him back onto his seat.

"One more time, who are you? Who do you work for?" Leon asked.

Baltimore tasted blood at the corner of his mouth. He shrugged and smiled back at Leon. With his hands still bound behind his back, he also took this time to administer a combination of depressions onto his own multi-sided wedding band. He'd just transmitted that his cover was blown—he'd been apprehended.

Baltimore looked up at Goertz and spoke very quietly. "I'm going to plant my forehead into the middle of your nose."

Not hearing and not understanding, Leon leaned in closer, while keeping his distance. "Don't you fuck with me, Mister. What did you just say?"

Baltimore looked to be on the verge of unconsciousness, and mumbled again: "I said, I'm going to plant my forehead into the middle of your nose."

Leon's temper was already boiling over. "He gestured for the two giant-sized guards to hold him, while he moved in somewhat closer.

Baltimore saw the split-second opening and made his move. He sprang, pulling the chair right along with him. As promised, Baltimore drove his forehead into Leon Goertz's face—but missed his nose. He landed a solid blow squarely onto Leon's left cheekbone. Skin tore and blood sprayed into the air as Leon staggered awkwardly backward.

"Sie dreckig ficken!" *You dirty fuck!* Goertz bellowed.

Lance and Heimi nervously manhandled Baltimore back onto his chair.

Fists hammered Baltimore's face, taking him to the verge of losing consciousness.

Leon stood, wiping at his cheek with a bloodied handkerchief. "Take him to the chamber. Strip him and prepare him for tonight's ritual."

Heimi and Lance brought Baltimore to his feet and half-walked, half-dragged him toward the door. Leon turned and said, "We have many years of practice in the ways of procuring information. Rest assured, we won't be waterboarding you here, Mr. Bartender. Heimi and Lance enjoy their work. They take pleasure in a job well done. Unfortunately for you, that will entail a substantial amount of disfigurement. You need to prepare yourself for that, young man." Leon exited the room through a different door than the one Heimi, Lance, and Baltimore used.

Back in the corridor, Baltimore was ushered down another long flight of stairs, a hundred feet below the castle grounds. Everything here was ancient stonework; ornate pillars and archways led in multiple directions. Like the catacombs of ancient Rome, the place was immense and more than a little creepy. Flames in gas lanterns flickered but provided little real light. *It would be easy to get lost down here,* Baltimore thought.

It was the smell that alerted him first. This must be what Leon had referred to as the chamber. Rank body odor, feces, and a smell Baltimore was well acquainted with— decomposing flesh. It was a circular chamber, with fifty or more prison-type jail cells around the outer perimeter. In the center of the room stood a massive wooden table, along with a stone fireplace, where red-hot embers glowed brightly, adding to an already hellish atmosphere. The heat emitted from the fireplace felt like a blast furnace.

An elderly man, with long white hair and wearing nothing more than rags, turned to see Baltimore and the guards approach. He stoked the fire with a couple of quick jabs from an iron rod, then gestured toward one of the cells.

Heimi and Lance dropped Baltimore onto a cobblestone floor within the empty cell. Approximately ten by ten, there wasn't much to it: a wooden frame with a blanket on it in one corner, strewn hay lay on the floor and a metal bucket that clearly hadn't been emptied since its previous occupant.

"Isolieren Sie ihn nach unten," *Strip him down,* Heimi said to the old man.

Both Heimi and Lance pointed their guns at Baltimore while the old man methodically removed Baltimore's shoes, socks, pants, shirt and underwear. The old man eyed Baltimore's ring, spat something unintelligible, then smiled a toothless grin. With one more glance the old man scurried out.

Lance followed him out and walked over to the fireplace. Several moments later, Lance was back and holding the red-hot iron poker. Baltimore backed away as Lance came nearer. With his back against the wall, Baltimore looked for something, anything, he could use as a weapon. Both Lance and Heimi were smiling, clearly enjoying themselves. The still-glowing point of the poker drew ever closer, now less than a foot from Baltimore's face.

"Wer arbeiten Sie?" *Who do you work for?* Heimi said in a calm, almost friendly voice.

Baltimore had his hands up, ready to grab the metal rod as soon as it got any closer. In a quick movement, Lance lowered the rod and drove it deep into Baltimore's upper thigh, inches from his private parts.

"Sie verpasst haben, Lance," *You missed, Lance,* Heimi said, with an abrupt laugh.

Baltimore fell to his knees, holding his damaged leg. The smell of burnt flesh and hair brought bile to the back of Baltimore's throat. Gasping through the pain, Baltimore readied himself for the next strike—for more pain. But Lance and Heimi were already out of the cell, locking it behind them. Lance tossed the metal poker back into the fire.

"We see you soon," Heimi said in broken English. Together the two giant men left.

Baltimore continued to sit on the floor, his hand gently resting on his upper thigh.

"What did they do to you?" came a soft voice from across the chamber.

Baltimore moved his head so he could see around the legs of the wooden table in the center of the room. In the cell directly across from his own, stood a small, bald-headed man of Indian descent. He wore wire-rimmed glasses with one lens cracked.

"They jabbed me with that hot poker," Baltimore answered.

"I'm sorry," the man said.

"Not your fault."

"Sorry just the same. My name is Horris."

"You can call me Curt," Baltimore said. "How long have you been here?"

"I don't know, maybe a year."

Baltimore let that sink in for a moment. The thought of being incarcerated here, along with Heimi and Lance, was sobering.

"Why are you here? What do they want from you?"

"They want my mind. I'm a programmer."

Then it hit Baltimore. Of course, he's Horris ... Horris Spatz.

CHAPTER 44

A t least we knew Baltimore was still alive. Pippa and I received the same momentary flutter of two, and then three distinct vibrations emanating from our wedding bands. Just one more capability our SIFTR rings possessed. There were a variety of the rings' Morse code-like signals we'd memorized before arriving in Germany.

I watched Pippa as she sat on the bed appraising the room. The party had wound down about an hour earlier and we were shown to our room by the same hostess, Melinda, whom we'd met earlier. More like a luxury suite, the accommodations included a bedroom, sitting room with television, small kitchenette, and opulent his and hers bathrooms.

I opened a set of French doors and walked out onto a small balcony. The last of the tables and chairs were being trucked away from the courtyard, four stories below.

Pippa joined me at the concrete railing. "With Baltimore taken prisoner, our mission has gotten much more difficult," she said.

"Our orders are specific in that regard. We're to complete our primary objective first, before anything else, including any rescue attempts," I reminded her.

Pippa used my shoulder for balance as she leaned backwards to study the other windows facing out along our side of the building. "Okay, there's Leon's office," she said, pointing to a set of windows to the left, one floor below. "If you can't gain entry via the elevator, you could try jumping from balcony to balcony. Or I could do it," she said, making a face ... "At least I could have, before I got these puppies added to my anatomy." Pippa pointed toward her ample chest. "God, I'll be happy when these things get back to normal size."

"Yeah, me too," I said, but I was only half listening to her. Pippa was right; maybe balcony jumping was the best means to enter Leon's office.

She punched my arm. "You didn't have to agree with me." Brow furrowed, she continued, "There's a good eight feet between balconies, Rob. You've been out of circulation for over a year, are you sure—"

"Yes, I'm sure I can manage," I said. "The problem isn't so much getting down there, but getting his patio door open."

Pippa stepped over to the room's French doors and examined the latch and locking mechanism. "Shouldn't be a problem. Like all doors in the castle, they're electro-mechanical. Once initiated, your ring will generate the necessary code string."

I'd forgotten about the ring's capability to unlock electronically controlled door latches. She was right; I had been out of commission for a long time. Perhaps too long?

"I'm going after Baltimore while you're playing Batman."

I wanted to argue with her, tell her to wait until I had secured the Spatz code. But once I entered Leon's office I was fairly sure alarms would sound ... we'd have only a few minutes to find a way out of the compound.

We needed to wait another two hours before people went to sleep. We changed into jeans, dark T-shirts, and tennis shoes. Periodically, I looked over the banister and, eventually, one by one, room lights turned off. Everyone had retired.

"I'll give you a few minutes head start," I said.

Pippa nodded and said, "Thanks. Don't kill yourself hopping around out there."

"I'll try not to."

She stepped in close and kissed me hard on the lips. We held each other tight for several moments—neither wanting to break the connection. Eventually, she turned away and headed for the door. She looked back over her shoulder, smiled, and opened the door to our suite, making sure the hallway was clear before stepping out and closing the door again.

I waited fifteen minutes before climbing onto the foot-wide ledge of the railing. I'd need to cross over three balconies, and then lower myself down one level to gain access to the balcony off Leon's office. I'd also have to accomplish this standing up. There was no way I'd be able to leap across the eight-foot expanse without getting a running start.

Standing upon the ledge, I let my eyes drift down to the cobblestone courtyard, seventy-five feet below. My balance wavered. Dumb idea. I moved back several steps, took a deep breath, ran and leapt high in the air. I landed two inches in on the opposite ledge and reached for something to hold on to. There was nothing there to grab but air. I felt my momentum pulling me forward, over the side, and only by lowering myself to my knees was I able to regain my balance in time. I held myself there, perched on the narrow ledge, for what seemed like minutes. The noise of my shoes hitting the concrete railing seemed deafeningly loud. *How could someone not have heard that?*

Slowly, I rose to my feet and positioned myself for another leap. I'd barely cleared the last ledge so I decided to add an extra step to get some momentum going. Again, I took a deep breath, ran, and leapt high in the air. This time I'd cleared the ledge with more than enough room. But halfway into my airy leap to the next balcony, lights came on— the balcony was flooded in light.

I came down on the ledge, knees bent, on the balls of my toes, absorbing the weight of my landing somewhat more quietly than before. I stuck my landing like an Olympic gymnast. Sheer curtains allowed just enough visibility to see a woman moving around inside. I was fully illuminated and perched there like a statue in a museum. *Can she see me?*

Then I remembered to do the obvious. My eyes locked on her, standing behind the curtains. I reached into her mind. She was hungry. Hungry and mad. *They couldn't save even one piece of cake for the fucking mayor?*

I remembered seeing a fully stocked minibar in our own suite at the back of the kitchenette. I projected a suggestion into her mind.

Check the minibar. Lots of goodies in there …

The mayor quickly padded off toward the kitchenette. I heard the sound of the minibar opening. She'd likely be there a while, but I wasn't going to take any chances. I ran and leapt again. Another perfect landing. I held there for several moments to ensure I hadn't been heard.

Getting down to the balcony below was going to be a challenge, to say the least. I knelt down and looked over the railing's ledge. It was close to twelve feet down. I slid down on my stomach and let my legs hang down over the banister. First with one hand, and then the other, I grabbed at concrete-pillar balustrades. Thick and rounded, they were difficult to get a grip on. I felt my fingers slipping. I let go and grabbed the bottom edge of the balcony. My body was now hanging in the air. I kicked my feet backward, and then foreword, creating a pendulum-like effect. Another deep breath and I let go.

In my mind's eye I had totally missed the balcony below and was falling to my death. Then I felt my feet touch down and I was able to breathe again. I'd landed on the balcony itself, versus the railing's ledge. I moved to the French doors. They looked identical to those on our own suite. Inside, I could see soft-blue illumination coming from the server room. I needed to unlock the door. I held up my hand and looked at my ring. My mind went blank. *Had Bigalow shown me how to use this feature?* Then I remembered. I positioned my fingers and pressed down on three sides—three times consecutively. I felt a quick flutter. The mode had been initiated. I reached for the metal door handle and waited. A moment later there were two more rapid flutters. I turned the handle and the door opened.

Except for the server room, the office was dark. I knew I had to move fast. Security—hell, Leon himself—could be here in minutes. In the conference room, Leon had accessed the graphical representation of the Spatz program from the laptop. I'd start there. The laptop was still open just as Leon had left it. The graphical program was still running.

My ring finger fluttered. It was repeating the same damn message as before. *Yes, I know Baltimore has been cap-*

tured. Then I realized the fluttering message was not in regard to Baltimore. It was now Pippa who had been captured.

CHAPTER 45

I wanted to forget the mission and go and find Pippa. I'd just have to hurry up and find what I'd come here for. I spent several minutes looking through the files on the laptop. As I'd expected, the graphical representation Leon had shown us was merely that: a simple graphical representation, not the actual Spatz program. I got up and moved over to the server room. The glass door was locked and required a cardkey to gain entry. I didn't think my ring would work opening cardkey devices, but to be honest, I wasn't even remotely sure.

Again, I positioned my ring finger and pressed down on three sides—three times consecutively. I felt the quick flutter that told me the mode had been initiated. I placed my ring atop the small card reader and was surprised when a little LED flashed green and the door unlatched. When I got back, if I got back, I'd have to give Bigalow a big kiss.

The room was cool and the noise from all the whirling CPU fans was distractingly loud. I'd been wrong; these weren't simply servers, they were Cray XK7 super computers. Each one was the size of a large refrigerator, and there were at least ten of the beasts chugging along in the room.

There was a workstation terminal with a keyboard off to my left. There was also a metal pipe affixed to the desk along with a set of handcuffs hanging from it. I sat down and moved the mouse. The screensaver disappeared and I saw the Linux Operating System desktop screen. Not an expert programmer by any means, I wasn't a total slouch either. I clicked on the icon to bring up the Terminal window. There are two methods for searching for files with Linux—*find* and *locate*. *Find* is a better, more extensive way to search a directory structure; *locate* is faster—and that's what I chose. Unlike Windows, where applications would typically have a .exe extension, Linux works quite differently. I ensured I was at the root directory and typed in *locate* and the word *spatz*.

The screen scrolled with thousands of listings. I'd hit pay dirt. I noticed that all associated files were in a subdirectory, called *spatz prog*. Next, I located the I/O ports at the back of the terminal. At the screen prompt I typed in the command function to initiate a total file transfer to the specified USB port. I then configured my ring as Bigalow had directed me. The ring fluttered and was ready. I placed the ring atop the port and used my other hand to hit the Enter key. The file transfer process started immediately.

After three minutes only 8% of the files had transferred. That's when the lights came on in the outer office. I ducked my head down and watched two men enter; both were carrying handguns and both were freakishly tall. One at a time, I peered into the thoughts of both men. Having witnessed others who were sociopaths, such as Harland, I was surprised at the ruthlessness these two were capable of: inflicting pain and prolonged torture were what these two got off on. And it was definitely them who'd captured Baltimore and Pippa. All I could discern from their thoughts were quick images ... flashes of events ... Baltimore being jabbed with a red-hot poker. *Had they done something similar to Pippa?*

With my face inches from the workstation screen I watched as the transfer continued at an excruciatingly slow pace. 12% turned to 13%. They'd searched the office and were heading back in the direction of the server room. They still hadn't noticed me, crouched down at the far side of the room. I picked up their names were Heimi and Lance. Heimi, the goon with thicker, more pronounced lips, tried the door and found it locked. Neither had an access card to get inside. Lance turned, confident no one was there. Heimi turned away as well—then jerked his head back in my direction. We made eye contact. I smiled up at him. His eyes bore into me as he talked into the comm unit at his sleeve. *Leon was on his way.*

The file transfer had jumped all the way to 76%. Encouraging, but I needed to do something—anything—fast. I popped back and forth between Heimi's and Lance's minds and finally settled on Heimi, who had spotted me first. He seemed the denser, more simple-witted of the two.

I have complete control of your mind.

Heimi pulled his hand up and touched his ear, as if he'd heard my voice over his comms.

I am in your mind, Heimi, and you will do as I instruct you to do.

He was now looking at Lance. "Did you say something to me?" he asked, perplexed.

"What the fuck you talking about? I've been talking to

you all day."

"No. I mean just now?"

"No," said Lance.

If you want to live, you'll point your gun at Lance and shoot him in the head.

Heimi shook his head and looked around.

"What are you doing? Stop that!" Lance said.

I put all my concentration on giving Heimi a headache, something I hadn't thought of trying in the past. I picked a location right behind his eyes and envisioned a drill bit, spinning and churning out bits and pieces of his brain. The effect was instantaneous. Heimi dropped his gun and was down on all fours, his head buried in his hands. Lance was startled and looked around. He wasn't sure if Heimi had been shot or what was happening. He looked in my direction, then back at Heimi.

Heimi. Do you want the pain to stop?

I heard his scream through the glass door. *YES! Stop the pain.*

Pick up the gun, point it at Lance's head, and pull the trigger. Do it now.

Keeping one hand on his head, Heimi searched the floor for his gun.

It's to your right, Heimi.

Heimi's hand brushed against his gun. He picked it up while rising up off the floor. His eyes were clenched shut in agony. He was shrieking and saying things that were pretty much unintelligible.

I'm waiting, Heimi.

Heimi pulled the trigger and kept pulling the trigger until he'd emptied the clip. Lance had taken two rounds to his head and the rest went wild into the office walls. I glanced at the terminal. 100% file transfer complete. I had one more thing to do. At the prompt I entered the command, **rm −rf/**. Everything, on all hard drives and all attached media, began erasing—nothing of the Spatz program or anything else for that matter would be left.

It was then that I realized my mental powers were gone and I was totally spent. Heimi was sitting back on his haunches, staring at his dead partner. I swung open the server door with all my remaining strength. The metal handle hit Heimi between the eyes and catapulted him backwards into the office. His dead body lay even with Lance's. Both had their eyes open as if they were stargazing together.

I scooped Lance's gun off the floor and shoved it into the back of my pants. I heard running feet and voices coming from the hallway. The thought of jumping between balconies again made me consider just shooting it out, here and now. But then I thought of Pippa and I knew I had to do whatever was necessary to rescue her.

By the time I was halfway over the balcony, the office door opened and men with guns were piling inside.

CHAPTER 46

With a gag tied tightly around her mouth, Pippa sat on the floor, her arms securely fastened around her back to a wooden post.

Earlier, she'd retraced the steps she and Heidi had taken to the underground spas. At that time she'd noticed the locked doors and numerous other corridors. She could pick a lock with the best of them but as she explored the castle's honeycombed underground, it was only a matter of minutes before she became hopelessly lost—one corridor looking nearly identical to another. It was by mere chance she saw several people, dressed in what looked like costumes, excitedly heading in one particular direction.

Soon, other partygoers were joining them and she struggled to keep out of sight. Whatever it was that was drawing them into the bowels of the underground, they were all keyed up. Pippa recognized several people who had attended Heidi's birthday party. Having to duck behind an ancient archway, she watched four more costumed people pass her by. They were speaking German and she could only hear bits and pieces of their conversation. She was certain she'd heard Vaterland, Wiederauftauchen, and United Reich ... It was then Pippa realized those weren't costumes; no, they were uniforms. Like those distinctly worn by the Nazis, in World War II.

Somewhere behind Pippa came the distant sounds of moaning. She was tempted to follow the Nazi group but felt more compelled to find Baltimore. She started down one passageway only to discover the moans weren't emanating from that direction. She rushed back the way she'd come and tried a different corridor. The sounds of moaning grew louder. She dreaded what she'd find—who she'd find.

She felt heated air coming from up ahead ... waves of heat and bad odors. Instinctively, Pippa swiped at her nose and began breathing through her mouth. She slowed her pace and kept close to the wall. The moaning persisted and coincided with other sounds—metallic clanging sounds. Around the next bend, Pippa saw the corridor had opened into a large, circular chamber. A rock fireplace dominated the center of the room. A scraggily old man, with white hair, was scurrying around, placing what looked like tools onto a table.

Jail-like cells surrounded the outer perimeter of the room. Some were occupied; others seemed to be empty. Suddenly loud screams filled the chamber—Pippa gasped and the hairs on her neck stood straight up. Then Pippa noticed someone lying atop the table. The air, dark and smoky, made visibility from her distance difficult. She squinted her eyes and took a tentative step closer. It wasn't Baltimore ... no, a smaller man, with a bald head.

The old man started to talk to himself. Now, while he

was holding up one of his sharp metal tools as if inspecting it, Pippa was on the move. With three long strides she was abreast of the table. Not knowing, or caring, what it was she grabbed for, she drove one of the old man's sharp, heavy, spiked tools down, onto the back of his skull. He dropped like a bag of rocks.

"What took you so long?" came a voice from the outer rim of the chamber.

"Baltimore?" she called out.

"The one and only," Baltimore replied.

Pippa looked at the bald-headed man lying on the table. He was dressed in rags and was gazing up at her with surprise in his eyes. "I'm going to get you off of there. Hold on, okay?" Pippa found that the small man had been bound to the table by his wrists and ankles that were tightly secured by leather straps. She used one of the dead man's knives to cut through the straps and helped the bald-headed man off the table.

"What is your name?"

"Horris."

"Why was he doing this to you?"

"It's how they get me to work for them. I've tried to hold out many times, but I'm weak and cannot handle the pain."

"Can you walk?" Pippa asked.

"Walk? No ... hobble, maybe," he replied.

It was then Pippa noticed that his skin was deeply scarred and he was missing most of his toes.

"Hang tight there, Horris, while I release my friend."

A large metal ring, holding several dozen long keys, hung from a peg on the side of the chimney. Pippa flipped through the keys and noticed she'd have to try each one of them ...

"They're numbered, Pippa. You just have to look closely at the keys themselves," Baltimore said, standing at the bars of the cell directly in front of her.

"Oh, I see." There was a large number 23 carved into the stone above Baltimore's jail cell. She found the corresponding 23 key and used it to open the metal gate.

"Where are your clothes?" Pippa asked, eyeing Baltimore wrapped only in a shredded, bloodied blanket draped loosely around his hips.

"Who knows? It's the least of our worries. What's going on with getting the code? Was Chandler successful?"

"I haven't heard a peep from him," she said.

When she looked up at Baltimore she saw he was no longer looking in her direction. Neither was Horris.

A crowd had formed at the passageway into the chamber. At the front of the group stood Leon Goertz—hands on hips, chin raised in defiance. A small bandage covered his left cheek. He was dressed in a black Nazi uniform. A red band, emblazoned with a black swastika, was worn on his upper left arm.

"You have disgraced yourself, young lady. I'm terribly disappointed in you," Leon said. He waved his hand and four similarly dressed soldiers hurried forward, their guns raised. "Bring the two of them here. Put Horris back in his cell. And find David Craft, or whatever his name is."

Pippa, now gagged, tied up, sat with her back against a roughly hewn wooden post. Baltimore was close by and also secured to a post. No less than fifty armed Neo-Nazi soldiers stood guard around the room's perimeter.

If their situation wasn't so dire it would have seemed ludicrous. Pippa was well aware that Neo-Nazi cults, in the main, had been eradicated in Germany. The truth, sadly, was one was far more likely to find fringe, crackpot groups like this one back in the U.S. But here they were—men and women parading around in 1940s-era military garb and saying Heil Hitler, left and right, like actors in a crappy World War II B-movie.

The assembly hall was large enough to accommodate several hundred people and on this night it was filled to capacity. The raised dais platform held four high-back chairs, two on each side of a podium.

Pippa felt the lingering stares of the onlookers. If her hands hadn't been tied behind her back, she would have flipped each and every one of them the bird.

Leon Goertz with three followers walked onto the platform and the audience stood, cheered, and clapped their hands. The big Nazi flags hanging from above, on each of the hall's walls, gently swayed in the ongoing commotion. Leon stood behind the podium and held up his hands, signaling everyone to settle down.

"Thank you. Everyone, please sit … we need to get started." As the audience settled back into their seats, Leon looked around the hall and smiled. He turned back and looked at Pippa and Baltimore with an expression of disdain.

"Soon, I'll introduce our esteemed leader. But first, I would like to thank you, all of you, for your continued faith in our cause. It is only through your support we have accomplished so much. We have bided our time. We have been patient for sixty-five years and withstood ongoing worldwide condemnation and humiliation. Soon, very soon, the fatherland will rise again—take its place as the world's dominant power."

The audience cheered and applauded and continually sang out *Blut und Ehre! Blut und Ehre! Blut und Ehre!* until Leon gestured for them to quiet down.

"We've struck, not with guns or missiles or tanks, but where civilization is most vulnerable … its financial infrastructure. With nary a shot fired, we have invaded into the very core of our enemy and soon we will control every aspect of the world's economy."

Blut und Ehre! Blut und Ehre! Blut und Ehre!

"Now … there are these here—sent to destroy us … to keep from us what is so rightfully ours."

Leon turned and looked at Pippa and Baltimore.

Blut und Ehre! Blut und Ehre! Blut und Ehre!

"We must send out a decisive message that we will not tolerate interference. With the execution of these covert operatives, we will convey a clear message to the United States and other nations, that Germany, our new and rejuvenated *fatherland*, will not be disempowered ever again. With that, I present you our esteemed Frau Fuhrer!"

The audience was back on their feet and clapping feverishly. *Frau Fuhrer! Frau Fuhrer! Frau Fuhrer!* Heidi Goertz walked onto the raised dais dressed in a black military jacket and skirt. She wore the same red, white, and black swastika band on her upper arm as her husband. Her blonde hair, as she typically wore it, was pulled back into a long braid that fell down her back. Perched atop her head was a German officer's cap.

"*Danke.* Thank you. *Danke.* Thank you all. *Blut und Ehre!*"

The audience cheered, tears filling many an eye. *Blut und Ehre!*

Heidi looked at her watch and smiled. "Today is Sunday. Tomorrow, Monday morning, when the world's markets reopen for trading, the WZZ, and all of Germany, will begin its final charge. As one goliath company after another falls, becomes the property of the WZZ, a new world order will emerge. Our job is still not complete. We must pound our adversaries into the ground. We must punish them. We must drink the very blood of our enemy! Let the ritual begin ..."

Frau Fuhrer! Frau Fuhrer! Frau Fuhrer! Frau Fuhrer!

The audience stood and the room became quiet. Several men removed the four chairs and podium from the raised dais. A long wooden table, with two metal vats, was carried in and positioned in front of Pippa and Baltimore. Two men roughly grabbed Baltimore's arms and he was pulled up on his feet. Two other men did the same to Pippa. A leather collar was fitted around her neck and fastened to the post.

Next she felt a prick on her forearm. Pippa's mind was racing. She tried to resist, to pull away from the post and the hands holding her. She felt the sting as an IV needle was inserted into her arm. She screamed into the thick material covering her mouth. A long polyurethane tube hung from Pippa's arm and drooped down into one of the metal vats. Pippa watched as the tube filled and turned red, blood freely flowing from her arm, down the tube, and into the awaiting vat. Pippa heard Baltimore yelling behind his gag. He, too, was filling a vat with blood.

Pippa watched as Heidi approached her. She'd removed her hat and military jacket, revealing a crisp white dress shirt. Inches from her face, Heidi spoke with a soft voice.

"I so wish this could have turned out differently. I had such hopes for us. Truth be told, I don't have many close friends. So, so, disappointing." Heidi leaned in and kissed Pippa on the cheek, and then touched her cheek with the back of her palm.

Heidi stood back and looked to the audience behind her. Jackets had been removed. Hats and caps removed. Everyone stood quietly and waited. Heidi moved to the far side of the table, and stood before the first metal vat—Pippa's vat.

The bottom of the container was now completely covered in thick red blood. Pippa knew the average woman held a little over three liters of blood. *How much blood can I lose before I die?*

The audience was moving, forming a line behind their leader, *Frau Fuhrer.* Heidi took one more look in Pippa's direction and then leaned over the vat. Using hands cupped together, as one would when getting a drink from a stream, she dipped them into the warm red liquid and brought them up to her lips. She sipped and swallowed. She wiped the blood onto her face and down across her crisp white shirt. *Blut und Ehre!* Heidi moved on down the table and repeated the same movements with Baltimore's blood. *Blut und Ehre!* Leon's turn followed, and then other high-ranking Neo-Nazi officers. Eventually, the first ones from the audience stepped onto the platform and stood at the table.

Feeling light-headed, Pippa looked out at the hundreds of guests quietly waiting their turn. She wondered if there would be enough blood to go around. She realized that if she turned her body ever so slightly and she raised her head against her bindings, she was just able to peer into the metal vat. *Already so much blood.*

The movement had had another effect, as well. It pulled and put tension on the long polyurethane tube. Pippa felt the pain in her arm as the I.V. needle pulled against her skin this way and that. Was it loosening? Could she pull the needle free before she bled out?

She then thought of Rob; she hadn't told him—she needed to tell him—how much she loved him.

CHAPTER 47

By the time I jumped down to the next balcony below, I was finding it difficult to stand—and, unfortunately, I was still two floors up. My mental interactions with Heimi had been so intense and focused, well beyond anything I'd attempted before. That steely concentration depleted all my vitality, strength, and natural recuperative ability—something I'd have to keep in mind for the future. The problem at hand was worsening too: withdrawal symptoms. There simply was no way I could jump down to the next balcony. I'd have to break into the room next to me.

I used my ring to unlock the French doors and shuffled into the suite. Empty. It was another office space, smaller and less appointed than Leon's. I staggered across the office to the other entrance. I opened the door several inches and peered out. The hallway was clear—no one around. Out in the hallway, I pushed myself forward. My arms and legs had begun to spasm, something new added to my deteriorating condition. I found a stairway and, one slow step at a time, descended to the ground floor.

I knew where I was. This was the great room, where we'd first entered into the castle. I slowly stepped around a corner and came face to face with a guard dressed in a Nazi uniform. Looking as surprised as I was, he started to raise his AK47. But he was a fraction of a second too slow. I already had Lance's pistol in my hand and pointed at his face. "Lass die Waffe fallen," *Drop the gun,* I said.

He let the gun fall to the floor. "Sie sollten sich selbst aufgeben. Jeder ist für Sie suchen."

He told me to give myself up—everyone was looking for me.

Shakily, I brought the pistol up to his nose, "Das wird nicht passieren. Wo ist die Frau, die ich mit angekommen?" *That's not going to happen. Where is the woman I arrived with?*

He stared into the muzzle of Lance's gun for several more seconds, then said, "Die Montagehalle." *The assembly hall.*

I told him to take a step backwards and turn around. I retrieved his AK47. "Gehen. Zeigen Sie mir." *Walk. Show me.*

We both hesitated when loud alarms blared from every direction. Then came the sound of multiple helicopters, hovering above the courtyard outside. It seemed the cavalry had arrived.

"Bleiben Sie in Bewegung!" *Keep moving,* I needed to get to Pippa—not stop for anyone, even the good guys.

It took every bit of my quickly fading energy to walk forward and continue holding up what had become an excruciatingly heavy weapon. It took five minutes to descend more stairs and reach the assembly hall. I was now dragging my left leg behind me in a pathetic attempt to keep moving.

Upon first look, with the exception of hundreds of chairs, the assembly hall appeared empty. Then I saw them, strapped to posts at the front of the room.

I screamed at the guard, "Bindet sie los!" *Untie them!*

As I came closer I saw Baltimore was alive, his eyes tracking me. In little more than a whisper, he asked, "Get the code? Destroy the server?"

"Yes." But all my attention was on Pippa. Her skin was blue-gray and she wasn't moving. The Neo-Nazi guard released her bindings and lowered her to the floor. I yelled at him to help Baltimore.

I saw a trickle of blood on her forearm and a now-disconnected IV needle, hanging loosely down to the floor. I sat close to her and placed her head gently on my lap. Her skin was cold and lifeless. Her chest was still and unmoving. She was dead.

My vision blurred as tears filled my eyes. I felt anger rising in me like a cyclone. None of this was worth her life. Nothing, ever, would be worth losing her.

"Six presses," came a soft voice.

I turned to see Baltimore trying to make his way over to me. "Press one side of her ring six times. Quickly!"

I looked at him, uncomprehending. Baltimore crawled over to me and Pippa. He reached for her hand and found her ring. He pressed on one of its octagonal sides six times in rapid succession. There was a loud clap as a jolt of electricity coursed through Pippa's body. She went rigid, then gasped for air. Her eyes opened.

EPILOGUE

I was done working for the U.S. government. Officially retired, I took a long sip of my iced tea, leaned back, and felt the pool's cool water lapping against my legs.

After the events in Baden-Baden the previous month, I returned to Drako's estate, now legally mine, in the rocky cliffs outside of Kingman, Arizona.

Cassie cheerfully greeted me as I walked through the front door as naturally as if I'd lived there for years. Truth be told, I had no idea what I was going to do with the place—or with my life, for that matter.

In the end it had been the ring's heart-defibrillating capability that not only saved Pippa's life—but my own. Both Pippa and Baltimore had found a way to pull their I.V. needles from their arms—though both had bled out to dangerous, near fatal, levels.

Baltimore never understood why anyone, namely me, supposedly of a sound mind, would purposely go and shock themselves with seven hundred volts. But he didn't need to know. I hadn't tapped in during that fraction of a second jolt, per se, but it gained me another few minutes of life. As the three of us waited in that Neo-Nazi assembly hall—each of us knocking at death's door, it was none other than Pippa's Great Aunt Ingrid's boyfriend, William Genz, who'd found us. He was our *inside man*, within the German Verfassungsschutz.

Even now, as I float in the pool, working on my tan, I wonder: was it worth it? Sure, we'd stopped the Spatz program and acquired the code. But Heidi and Leon Goertz were in the wind, somewhere. Once the alarms started blaring, mere minutes before I had come upon Pippa and Baltimore, the whole kit and caboodle of them fled through subterranean tunnels and escaped.

The German Verfassungsschutz forces had been alerted, I suspect, by Baltimore ... Maybe, once he was certain I'd accomplished what we'd come there to do, he used his ring ... I'm not really sure. When they stormed the castle they found it pretty much emptied—with the exception of Pippa, Baltimore, and me, and a few badly mistreated prisoners ... and oh, yes, the guy dressed up as a Nazi soldier. Horris, under U.S. government provided protection and medical assistance, along with Baltimore, was escorted back to Washington, D.C.

The truth was, I'd only accomplished half my mission. The WZZ, albeit significantly disrupted, was still out there—somewhere. I had a score to settle with Leon and Heidi Goertz, but that wasn't going to happen today, or tomorrow, and probably not the day after that, either. But happen it would.

I watched the heat rise in distorted blurry waves off the desert floor in the distance. A lone hawk circled above, then dove out of sight below a rocky ridgeline. I thought about Pippa and how I'd almost lost her. I wasn't going to let that happen again. I closed my eyes and recalled those last moments when I was certain she was dead.

I felt her vinyl float lazily bump into mine. She was lying on her tummy with her bikini top untied. She turned her face toward me and smiled. "Yikes, you might want to turn over—looking a bit pink there," she said, splashing me and then pushing her float away from mine.

"Mr. Chandler," Cassie interrupted.

I looked over to the edge of the pool. "Yes, Cassie?"

She held up a wireless phone. "Phone call."

"Take a message."

Cassie continued to hold out the phone. I knew what she was going to say before she said it. "You may want to take it; it's the White House."

*Thank you for reading **Mad Powers**. To be notified of my next book's release in this series, entitled **Deadly Powers**, email me at: markwaynemcginnis@gmail.com. Subject Line: **Deadly Powers**.*

If you enjoyed this novel and would like to see this series continue, please leave a review on Amazon.com. It's very much appreciated.

Acknowledgments

First of all I'd like to thank my wonderful wife, Kim, and my mother (again) for the support and encouragement to write these books. Out of all the books I've written, this is the most thoroughly edited, so thank you to my amazing editors, Lura Lee Genz , Rachel Weaver, Marta Tan and Mia Manns—the many hours invested are so very much appreciated. Thank you Mia for all the research and going above and beyond the call of duty. Much appreciation goes to Brad Leppla for his technical firearms review. Thank you L.J. Ganser for your audiobook support on past and future books (and friendship). Thank you Erin Arik for your amazing cover art with two of my books. Thank you to Lura and James Fischer for your continued support, it really means a lot to me. Thank you to Chris Derrick for the help with formatting the print version and making everything look so professional. I'd also like to thank the many subject matter experts and others who supported, contributed, and reviewed this book, I'd also like to thank the fans who enjoyed the initial novella, Tapped In, and pushed me to finish the complete book, Mad Powers. I read every one of your emails and enjoy your comments.

Books by Mark Wayne McGinnis:

Scrapyard Ship (Scrapyard Ship series, Book 1)

HAB 12 (Scrapyard Ship series, Book 2)

Space Vengeance (Scrapyard Ship series, Book 3)

Realms of Time (Scrapyard Ship series, Book 4)

Mad Powers (A Tapped In Novel, Parts 1, 2, 3)

39254505R00172

Made in the USA
Lexington, KY
15 February 2015